CW01425597

# MURDER IN AIX

# Susan Kiernan-Lewis

*Book 5*

*The Maggie Newberry Mystery Series*

Susan Kiernan-Lewis

San Marco Press
Copyright 2013

# Acknowledgements

I'd like to thank the members of my writing group, Cheri Roman, Mark Vance, Cynthia L. Enuton, Tracie Roberts and Rae Yates, who helped me sort out the storyline for this book and suggested many twists and turns that I ended up using.

I also want to thank my editor Elizabeth White for catching and correcting all the technical errors and so giving me the courage to publish it with confidence, and to my friend Raphaelle Simmons Tellier, who vetted the French for me in order to reduce the inevitable number of letters I'll receive from mystery-loving-Francophiles who found something I didn't intend.

Finally, as usual, endless thanks go to my husband, Del Kiernan-Lewis, who spent hours listening to plot changes and external antagonists' motivations with interest and loving support.

Susan Kiernan-Lewis

# Chapter 1

The moment Julia asked for the wine list, Maggie knew it was going to be *that* kind of lunch. Not that Maggie had anything against wine. Her husband was a vintner, for heaven's sake. They practically drank the stuff for breakfast. No, it was the fact that her friend felt the need for a bottle instead of just a glass or two. A bottle she knew wouldn't be shared because Maggie was eight months pregnant. *A bottle of wine at lunch in the middle of the workweek did not bode well.*

"You won't have any, Maggie?" Julia asked, still squinting at the wine list and not bothering to look at her. They'd gone through this a few million times before. Julia already knew the answer.

"Nope. Not today," Maggie said, smoothing a hand over the fabric of the sundress that was stretched tightly across her stomach. "Hopefully, by this time next month."

The restaurant was situated just north of the main boulevard, *Cours Mirabeau*, in a tangle of streets known as *Vieil Aix*. This was the old section of Aix-en-Provence, and the part of France that Maggie found most charming. It had been worth the traffic and the lengthy walk past all the food markets to get to the little bistro. As usual, Julia had chosen well.

Julia ordered the wine and handed the list to the hovering waiter. Now that Maggie knew something was up—*and something was definitely up*—she watched her friend closely. When Julia called the day before to suggest lunch in Aix, she had sounded casual and unstressed. *Had she been drinking then, too?* While it was true they hadn't seen each other in a couple of weeks, they'd stayed connected by texts and by phone. Maggie felt she was very much up-to-date with Julia and her current project, an exhaustively comprehensive cookbook on culinary mushrooms.

Maggie had asked Julia to choose the restaurant since she was the one who lived in Aix and knew all the great ones. This one featured a wide, uncrowded terrace with an unobstructed view of *Place Jeanne d'Arc*. Maggie could see the tiny leaves from the ubiquitous plane trees littering the cobblestones of the terrace as prettily as if they'd been hand-placed. She sipped her *l'eau gaseuse* and tried to determine what was going on with her friend. "How're the 'shrooms coming?"

"It's transcendent, Maggie," Julia said, her eyes glassy with joy at the thought of her cookbook. "I am immersed totally and completely. I do not remember ever feeling this way about anything. Ever."

"We're still talking mushrooms?"

"I created this one dish and the aroma from the sautéed mushrooms—they were wild morels—was transformative. I literally left my body."

"No way."

"I kid you not. If only you would let me cook them for you," Julia said, nodding at the waiter as he poured her wine and retreated. "I didn't think people still had pregnancy food issues this far along. I thought that was first trimester stuff."

"Who knew? I won't even let Laurent burn toast in the house. I go into a hormone-induced rage."

"That is not believable," Julia said, sipping her wine. Maggie noticed she closed her eyes to savor it as it slid down her throat. "Laurent would *never* burn the toast."

"Well, I guess we're both being hyperbolic today. Laurent will *definitely* burn the toast the day *you* leave your body over a skillet full of fried mushrooms. Unless, of course, they're a different *kind* of mushroom."

"Oh, funny girl," Julia said, her English accent still sharply evident even after ten years in France. Her eyes crinkled as she smiled at Maggie. Her short blonde hair was a tousle of curls that belied her age. She was a good twenty years Maggie's senior but her youthful air and athletic build, coupled with a smile she was rarely without, had her often mistaken for her contemporary.

"You're really not sick of mushrooms yet?"

"I am not. And trust me, they are all I eat. My next door neighbor jokes with me that I put them on my morning cereal instead of berries."

"And you don't?"

"What can I say? I happen to think obsession is good for the soul."

"How very French of you."

"It is, isn't it? Oh! Did I tell you about the snake I stepped on yesterday?"

"Is this a metaphor?"

"I was doing my thing, foraging in the lower threshold of a vineyard just north of the city."

Maggie knew Julia spent at least half her day tramping about in the forests and meadows surrounding Aix looking for edible mushroom specimens. Julia was a big believer in foraging as the only true way to gather wild mushrooms, which she believed had the deepest flavor.

The server came with their meals and Julia stopped to produce a moment of praise at the presentation of the two large dishes of duck baked in a crust of salt and herbs on top of risotto with eggplant and tomatoes. Maggie, too, allowed a gasp of delight to escape as her plate was set in front of her. With the waiter mollified —Maggie had noticed he was becoming annoyed at the fact the two non-French women were spending more time talking and less time anticipating the main reason they were there—to eat—Julia leaned back into her story.

"I went straight to the base of this really ancient olive tree, covered in moss. Honestly, Maggie, you must come out with me sometime. The colors are so vivid and rich. Anyway, I must have stood there for a full ten minutes, staring deep into the depths of the moss until I saw it."

"The snake?"

"No, silly. Why would I step on the snake if I saw it first? No, I saw—almost completely hidden—the *trompette des morts.*"

"Oooh. *Death trumpets.* Yummy." Maggie spooned into her risotto.

"Well, the name may not be appealing," Julia admitted, "but the mushrooms themselves are to die for. Especially when sautéed with a large knob of butter and a simple seasoning of rosemary."

"You've got to try this, Julia. It is amazing," Maggie said as she enjoyed her first taste. "So when did you step on the snake?"

Julia shrugged and picked up her fork. "Oh, on the way out. At that point I wasn't looking down any more. My basket was full."

"Non poisonous, I assume?"

Julia looked up with a start. "What?"

"The snake. It wasn't poisonous?"

"Oh. No, I don't think so."

"Is everything okay, Julia?"

Julia sighed and reached for her wine. "Well, yes and no."

Maggie took a bite of her duck and waited. Julia would talk when she was ready.

"Jacques called," she said, shrugging.

Maggie frowned. "What did he want?"

"To meet."

"What did you tell him?"

"You really don't want me to see him, do you?"

"It's what *you* want that matters."

Julia sighed again and shrugged. "I told him okay."

Maggie knew Julia had been receiving the occasional note from Jacques asking if he could come by. It appeared he was getting impatient.

"Look, Maggie, I'm not getting back together with him if that's what you're afraid of. I just need some closure so I can move on."

Maggie gave her a skeptical look, but as Julia had probably figured, there was little she could say in response to that.

"He's been ill," Julia said. "I actually feel sorry for him. Things don't seem to be going well for him these days."

"When are you going to see him?"

"Tonight."

*"Tonight?* As in *after dark?* At *your* place? Tell me you're not meeting him alone at your place."

"I'm making him dinner."

Maggie shook her head.

"We have a few things to say to each other," Julia said. "*Private* things."

"He wants to get back together with you," Maggie said.

"Yes, but that will not happen."

"Are you sure?"

"So very sure, dearest. Not to worry on that score."

Maggie wedged her bulk behind the steering wheel of her Renault and took a moment to catch her breath. She hadn't been able to park very close to the restaurant, but the walk had been good for her. Still, her legs ached and there was a spasm in her back she couldn't seem to ease. She rolled down the window and let the cool breeze that had been whipping up the dried leaves and flower petals on the Cours Mirabeau caress her face. She placed a hand on her belly and smiled at the answering kick into the palm of her hand. Whoever was in there had *not* enjoyed the overdose of garlic at lunch.

"Settle down, *ma petite*," Maggie said. As she spoke, a cloud sifted across the sky and darkened the interior of the car a shade. Maggie frowned, her hand resting on the stick shift, and thought of Julia's excitement over her cookbook project. It was so like her to get so completely immersed in the recipe book. She was like that about everything—totally passionate to the point where she nearly lost all sense or perspective. Her relationship with Jacques Tatois was a good example of that, Maggie thought. Handsome in a wolfish sort of way, with penetrating blue eyes that seemed to see only one woman. Unfortunately for Julia, that hadn't necessarily meant one woman at a time.

She and Julia had connected a little under a year ago. Both ex-pats, they had found plenty to bond over when they met at a wine tasting hosted by Laurent's co-op in Avignon. Julia had attended on the arm of her then boyfriend, Jacques Tatois, an acquaintance of Laurent's from Paris. Julia and Maggie hit it off immediately. Grace Van Sant, Maggie's best friend, had recently moved back to the States, leaving Maggie feeling abandoned and lonely. Julia stepped neatly into the void and the two never looked back. In many ways, Maggie mused as she adjusted the car's rear view window and prepared to merge into traffic, Julia was actually closer in temperament and shared interests than Grace had been. Julia was creative, like Maggie. She was ruled by her passions and was spontaneous, like Maggie. And unlike Grace, she cared not a fig for fashion or status, appearances or money. Like Maggie.

Maggie drove carefully out of the city, mindful of the late afternoon traffic. She wasn't late getting back but she knew Laurent would be looking for her. As her pregnancy had advanced, he had become more and more attentive. She smiled at the thought.

Yes, meeting Julia last year had been the saving of Maggie in many ways. And while she still missed Grace—would *always* miss Grace—she had effectively replaced her friendship with someone who, just possibly, was a little more like her in the ways that mattered.

*Which is why it was so frustrating to see her even considering opening herself back up to Jacques!*

Maggie's cellphone chimed from inside her purse on the passenger's seat, alerting her of the receipt of a text message. Knowing she shouldn't but unable to help herself, she fished the phone out and glanced at the screen. It was from Grace: *Hoping the weather is warm this week, darling. I could use the change!*

Maggie dropped the phone back into her purse and, frowning, refocused her attention on the road.

*Now what in the world did that mean?*

\* \* \* \*

Laurent pulled the *gratin* from the oven and set it on the zinc-topped table in the kitchen. He glanced at the hand-painted clock face next to the kitchen window and felt a small prick of worry. She's not late, he told himself. The light from the window was still enough to flood the kitchen without need for electric light. He wished she had allowed him to drive her to Aix—he could've gone to the *patisserie* and the *charcuterie* while she visited with Julia—but he understood she was feeling a little restrained lately. It was harder to give her the space she wanted but he was determined to do it—*up to a point.*

The kitchen was simple and spare, with terra cotta–tiled floors and the large, zinc-topped table at its center. The sloping and spacious salon had a double set of ten-foot French doors that opened out onto a graveled courtyard. Their one hundred-year-old *mas* was a solidly constructed stone building made to withstand the powerful *Mistral.* The surrounding grounds included Laurent's vineyard—twenty-five hectares of local grape and lovingly pruned and tended vines—and another 15 hectares of sprawling lawns punctuated with olive, plum, fig, and cypress trees.

To Maggie's never-ending delight, lavender and rosemary bushes grew all over their property. On the slate terrace, she had set pots of lemon trees and bougainvillea once she finally gave up on her beloved azaleas and Georgia gardenias, which she planted every spring and watched die every fall. Laurent's herb garden was tucked neatly into a side corner of the terrace nearest the kitchen, an endless source of thyme, basil, lemon verbena, and several different kinds of rosemary. In the middle of the terrace, underneath a canopy of the tall plane trees, sat a large stone dining table.

Most summer evenings, while it was still pleasant—not too hot by day and yet not too cold in the evening—Laurent and Maggie ate outside, carrying the dishes and cutlery to the table in shallow wicker baskets. The last tomatoes of summer were served fresh-cut and drizzled with olive oil from the region, vinegar, and chopped fresh herbs from Laurent's *potager.*

This afternoon, Maggie had surprised him by bringing home lamb chops from the *charcuterie* in Aix. He shelved the makings for the *pissaladier* he had planned and got the outdoor grill going instead. When they finally settled down across from each other at the large stone outdoor table, steaming plates of grilled chops with rosemary, thyme and garlic redolent in the early evening air, Maggie found herself absolutely relaxed—even without the customary glass of *vin-du-Domaine St-Buvard*. Laurent served up a hefty spoonful of potato gratin with buttered gnocchi and Gruyere cheese on her plate. As usual, she had left all the kitchen work to him and gone straight upstairs to bathe and change clothes.

"You had a good lunch in town?" he asked.

"I did. But Julia is planning on seeing her ex-boyfriend, Jacques, tonight."

"Ahhh." Laurent served himself and then took a sip of his wine. It was one of theirs from the local co-op. "Where did you eat?"

Maggie stopped with her forkful to her mouth and grinned at him. "Because that is the most important part of my lunch," she said. "It was *Le Poivre*. Do you know it?"

Laurent shrugged, which could mean yes or no. Maggie was never sure which.

"Was it good?"

"Yes, it was wonderful. I had the duck. Mouthwatering. Not to worry, French national pride is safe from yet another innocuous luncheon by two unknowing foreigners."

"If you are unknowing, why would it matter?"

"Anyway, the other thing about the lunch, *besides* how the bistro managed to keep its one-star rating—"

"It was rated?"

"I'm teasing, Laurent. Not rated. Still really good. May I continue?"

He nodded and broke a piece off the baguette on the table and handed it to her.

"She is making dinner tonight for her ex-boyfriend,

Jacques. You remember him, right?"

"*Le bâtard*," Laurent said on cue.

"Yes, that's right. The total *bâtard*. He wants to get back together with her."

Laurent looked up when Maggie stopped speaking, his expression blank.

"Well, don't you see? Julia is very vulnerable right now. She might well do it and that would be disastrous."

Laurent poured himself another glass of wine. "Surely a half glass could not hurt *le bébé*," he said. He reached for a small pitcher of water.

"Sure, okay," she said, holding out her glass. "Did I not ever tell you the story of how they broke up?"

"He hit her?"

"Okay, so I did tell you. Yes! He hit her during a drunken row."

"And for that she broke up with him?"

"Well, not that that isn't enough, but there was plenty of other stuff too. It was the icing on her cake, him slapping her."

"So a slap, not a hit?"

"You think there's a difference between slapping and hitting a woman?"

Laurent took a bite of his meal. "Of course."

Maggie frowned at him and took a sip from her wine glass. "Okay," she said. "One is bad. And the other is very, very bad."

"Are you worried, *chérie*?" Laurent asked, a smile tugging at the corner of his lips.

"Don't be silly."

"Because if ever I was tempted to beat *ma femme*, it would have been last year when you went to Paris and yet here you sit —intact and unharmed."

"Very amusing. In any case, I happen to know that Julia was beaten by her father."

"*C'est terrible.*"

14

"Yeah, so Jacques taking a whack at her was all the worse for that."

"The chops are *parfait*, Maggie. *Superbe*."

"They are, aren't they? Well, you prepared them."

"But you thought to get them. And after an upsetting lunch, too."

"Well, I don't like to see Julia doing something I know she's going to regret."

"It is annoying when our friends must constantly ruin their lives when if they would just listen to what we tell them. No?"

"I see what you're doing, Laurent, and you're wrong. I am not interfering. I'm being a friend. I'm *helping*."

"Did she ask for your help?"

"The request was implied as soon as she told me Jacques was coming to dinner."

"And is she still having him to dinner?"

"Okay, fine. But as a friend, I reserve the right to tell my friends when they're about to make a horrible mistake."

"No wonder you have so many friends."

"I have just enough, thank you. And besides, it's an American thing. It doesn't translate over here and Julia isn't French so it works just fine for us."

"*Si tu le dit,*" he said with a teasing smile. *If you say so.*

After dinner, Laurent stacked the plates and the two sat in the oversize lounge chair on the terrace. Laurent draped a thick cotton throw across Maggie's lap. When he sat down next to her, she snuggled comfortably into his lap and was rewarded by the feel of his warm, strong arms enveloping her. It had been a long day, and she tired easily lately.

At one point Laurent laid a large hand on her belly, as if to feel the baby's movement.

"He just kicked!" Maggie said. "Did you feel that?"

"*Oui.*"

"Is our child going to speak both French and English?" she

mused idly.

"Of course."

"That'll be nice." They were both silent for a moment, looking up at the night sky and watching the stars. "Does it ever scare you at all?" Maggie asked. "All the changes that are coming?"

"*Non.*"

"Really? And you swear you've never done this before?"

"Not before you," he said.

"What if it makes us different? What if we disagree about major stuff in raising him? What if he looks nothing like you?"

Laurent laughed and kissed Maggie on the cheek. "I am secure," he said. "As long as he looks nothing like *Detective Inspecteur* Roger Bedard, I don't care."

Maggie turned to look at her husband in the semi-dark. "You don't really think that's possible, do you?"

"Not as long as what you told me is true, *non.*"

A few years ago, Roger Bedard and Maggie had worked to solve a series of murders in Arles at a time when Maggie was struggling with her first year of marriage. Roger had made it very clear he would like nothing better than for Maggie to struggle right into his open arms.

"Change is good," Laurent said. "Without change, we stay the same and nothing grows." He patted her stomach.

"Yes, but we *just* figured out the happy marriage thing," Maggie said. "And it took us forever to do it. What if *this* change pushes us into a whole other realm of problems?"

"It probably will."

"Well, that's not good, Laurent!"

"Have faith, *chérie*. We will master all problems that come to us—even a demanding baby who wants to push *le papa* out of bed and keep *la maman* all for himself! Now *that* is a concern."

"You don't even know if it's a boy," Maggie said, turning

back around and nestling closer to him, feeling and enjoying the heat from his body as an icy breeze wafted through the terrace.

"I know I will love you no matter what comes."

Maggie sighed with pleasure and relaxed deeper into his embrace. She could smell the scent of orange blossoms—gone many months ago—lofting down to her on the cold autumn breeze.

Susan Kiernan-Lewis

# Chapter Two

Jacques narrowed his eyes and watched the group pick their way across the parking lot toward the café. His eye was caught by a young woman who dropped her shoulder purse at her feet, followed by her cellphone, which skidded and bounced on the irregular stones. He could hear her moan of dismay and watched as her friends gathered around to help her pick up the pieces.

The girl was wearing dark leggings with a form-fitting tunic pulled over the top. She had an athletic build and a fine, shapely bottom. Jacques licked his lips and found himself hoping she would look up—even in her crisis, even in the crowd—and see him. But the drama was quickly resolved and the group—and his new love—moved on and out of sight.

He sighed, but felt happy for having enjoyed the little scene—even to have almost been a part of it. *If only she had looked up, even just for a second.* This was proof to him that he didn't need to sleep with a woman to enjoy her. If he never saw that girl again, he had enjoyed her immensely just sitting at his table at the café while he waited for his cousin to appear.

*Where was that connard?* Jacques flicked his eyes to the screen of his cellphone to confirm that the *trou du cul* was indeed late. *How can you be late for a rendez-vous at your own bar?* he thought, the pleasure of the girl quickly receding and replaced by the annoyance of being kept waiting. True, Florrie's people knew not to hand him a bill. And they were as attentive to him as they were to any of their paying-customers.

That is to say, not very. But it didn't matter. *Florian's Café*, if you could call it that sat one street off the main highway. If you didn't know it was there, you would never find it. So far from Aix, there was no annoying stream of students or tourists that one was forced to endure. How Florrie made a living on the place, though, was a mystery.

*Still.* Free drinks or not, nobody likes to be kept waiting. Jacques caught the eye of the sole waiter and gave a nearly imperceptible nod. The man disappeared inside.

"*Allô, mon cousin.* You are waiting long?" Florrie appeared as if from thin air, rubbing his hands together but remaining standing in obvious anticipation of the embrace he expected from Jacques. Grumbling, Jacques lurched out of his chair and held his arms out to receive the hug and cheek kissing Florrie was clearly determined to bestow upon him.

"I am waiting only however long past the time you said you would be here," Jacques said, reseating himself at the table.

"Forgive me, cousin," Florrie said, heaving his heavy frame into the wicker chair at Jacques's table. "I had to take a call. Aunt Lily called to confirm that we would be by on Sunday for lunch. Now more than ever."

"Good God, the woman is relentless," Jacques said as he reached for his cigarette packet. The waiter appeared with a pitcher of water, and two more glasses of *pastis*. "Aren't we *always* there for Sunday lunch?"

"Well, one of us is, at least," Florrie said pointedly, pouring his drink and holding it up to watch the liquid instantly cloud into ribbons of milky yellow.

"Well, *one of us* may have to do for this Sunday as well. It appears that Julia and I are getting back together."

"Are you serious? That's wonderful, Jacques!" Florrie leaned over and squeezed his cousin's arm. Jacques had to admit the man looked genuinely pleased for him.

"When did this happen?" Florrie asked.

"Well, it hasn't exactly happened yet," Jacques said, lighting up his cigarette and blowing a large cloud of smoke into the air around his head. "I am seeing her tonight for dinner."

"She is cooking?"

"Yes, of course she is cooking. She loves to cook for me. You know that."

"I hope you like mushrooms. I hear that's all that's on the menu these days."

"Trust me, that is *not* all that's on the menu tonight." Jacques's eyes glinted with double meaning.

"Well, I'm glad for both of you. I always liked Julia. I was sorry to see you two break up. Just be careful, eh?"

"*Careful*? What the hell does that mean?"

"I just mean perhaps you should take it slow. She was very angry with you when you broke up. She said some things."

Jacques waved away Florrie's words as if they were no more than the choppy blue smoke floating between them. "We both said some things. People do when they are upset. *Ma belle* Julia is very passionate, eh? I would expect nothing less from her—in or out of bed."

"Just take it slow, Jacques," Florrie said.

Jacques put a hand to his midsection and winced. The pains were coming more and more frequently and he was nearly at the point of admitting he needed to see his doctor.

"Are you alright?" Florrie asked, worry stark in his dark brown eyes.

Jacques waved a hand dismissively at his cousin. "Yes, yes. Just a little gas. I'm fine."

"Well, you look like a groaning bag of shit if you want to know."

The woman who spoke the words stood behind Florrie, and because Jacques had his eyes closed as she approached he wasn't absolutely sure she hadn't just materialized amidst a cloud of black smoke and brimstone.

Florrie stood up immediately and faced her. She was petite, dark-haired and had obviously been very pretty at one time. That time was many years past, and now all that was left was the vestige of frustrated insistence and despair at not meriting the reaction from men she once took for granted.

"Annette," Florrie said. Jacques noticed his cousin neither greeted his ex-wife or offered her a chair. He just stood as if totally at a loss as to what to do. As Jacques's discomfiture receded, he found a prick of pleasure in his cousin's loyalty to him. Annette was formidable at any age and any stage. Even now, he could see heads turning to her from all over the café. And yet poor Florrie could only stand between the two ex-spouses, impotent and unsure.

Annette took a step closer to the café table and pointed a long polished finger at Jacques. At this range, he could see she had recently had some work done and he felt a moment's stirring for her—of sympathy, of understanding, of desire.

"You have failed yet again to pay the money that is owed to me, you bastard!"

Jacques took a long drag off his cigarette and motioned for Florrie to sit back down, but he didn't. "What money is that?"

"You know *what money*. The money necessary for your daughter to continue with her education. You know very well *what money*."

"I am not legally obligated to continue to pay that, as *you* know well, Annette. I have had this discussion with Michelle—"

"Well, *I* cannot pay it! I have no money!"

Jacques thought about suggesting she go to the same well that obviously paid for the expensive facelift she was parading about, but he didn't feel altogether well and was certainly not up for a public showdown on issues they had fought over endlessly already.

"Perhaps the poor child might find employment of some kind? I have a friend whose son did that—got a job. It was immensely appreciated by both parents, I'm told."

"You are despicable to let your only child wander the streets like a common panhandler to pay for her education."

"Well, that's certainly one way to do it, and I would applaud the child's initiative if that's what she chose to do."

"I hope you die of the gout," Annette snarled at him. "I hope your heart seizes up and strangles you in your bed—alone and desolate. I hope you die from all your sins at once."

"Thank you, Annette. Now please piss off. You're frightening the patrons."

"Your own daughter detests you!" Annette whirled around to face the more curious café diners. "She hates her own father and wishes he were dead."

"I'm sorry about this, Florrie," Jacques said as Annette pushed her way out of the café terrace and disappeared into the parking lot. Florrie vaguely shook his head as if to say *no problem,* but instead looked more like a man confused and undone by the situation. He sat down heavily and ran a hand across his face. Jacques thought about the changes to come— the money to come—and he smiled to himself. He drank down the last of his *pastis*, feeling the burn of the liquid as it edged its way down his throat. And he felt better.

*Wash the death trumpets gingerly with a paper towel or other kitchen towel. Linen is good if you are wealthy enough to throw away a perfectly good linen towel cleaning the dirt off a mushroom.*

Julia smiled to herself as she piled the newly cleaned mushrooms onto her chopping board. She would have to edit that entry later—or her editor would. Still, it amused her. She picked up one of the largest of the mushrooms and held it to her nose, inhaling deeply. Instantly, the moment that morning in the glade north of the city came back to her.

Even the feel of the early morning air, a brisk breeze holding all the promise of winter, came into her mind and seemed to flit across her bare arms. She placed the mushroom down and picked up her chef's knife.

She wasn't sure the time she spent each day foraging into the meadows and forest outside Aix weren't the best part of creating her mushroom book. She roughly chopped the mushrooms and set them aside before deseeding the green pepper she had purchased from the *Place Richelme* market that morning.

That was silly, of course. The search was just one more wonderful component to this her most amazing life project. Would she ever have imagined in her wildest dreams that one day she would become the recognized expert on culinary mushrooms? Was it possible to have imagined that even six months ago? Of course, she cooked. French or not, one could hardly escape *cooking* while living in France. But her impassioned industry, some might say driven fanaticism, to unlock the secrets of the simple mushroom—in all its glorious forms, in all its magical capacities—*that* had not manifested itself until after Jacques left her.

She nicked the tip of her finger with the sharp knife and dropped the utensil immediately in surprise. She couldn't remember the last time she had cut herself in the kitchen. She twisted a piece of paper towel around the stinging cut. The sensation, combined with the thought of Jacques, was enough to make her reach for a handful of the Death Trumpets once more and bring them to her nostrils.

She inhaled deeply and felt her heartbeat slow, her pulse steady, the tension in her shoulders relax. It was appropriate, she decided as she dropped a large knob of butter into a hot skillet on her stove, that one achieved these life-altering fungi by groping—no, groveling—around on one's hands and knees —in the dirt and the muck no less.

She watched the butter bubble and foam as it skidded its way around the perimeter of the pan, then she dropped in the Death Trumpets, the little bowl of crushed garlic and the diced pepper. She gave the handle of the pan a firm shake to redistribute the contents.

She could hear noises coming from the hall of her apartment building, and a quick glance at the kitchen clock confirmed it was time for the office workers to trudge up the stairs to their little sanctuaries within. What she had said to Maggie notwithstanding, she didn't know very many of her neighbors. They were happy to keep to themselves, as she was. She had chosen this apartment—deep in the heart of Old Town —during her first week in Aix. She was visiting a boyfriend who had moved here for business, and had long since moved on, and had fallen in love with the town. A small inheritance from her mother had allowed her to pack up her rented London flat and make the transition. She knew she left nobody behind in England. She often found herself wondering why that didn't bother her more.

She took the pan off the heat, setting it on a back burner, and walked to her front window, which overlooked the Rue Constantin. She opened the window to let the cold late afternoon air suffuse the little living room in her apartment. She spent so much time in the kitchen it often wasn't until she was nearly ready to suffocate from the heat and the smells of grilled, fried or baked mushrooms that she remembered to seek out a restoring breath of fresh air. She stood for a moment in the window, staring down into the street and watching the students, shoppers and workers, even a few tourists this late in the season, as they moved up and down the street below her.

And then she saw him. It was a wonder she hadn't seen him first. Unlike the constantly moving humanity, he stood silent and immobile, leaning against the single lamppost and smoking. And looking up at her window. Fighting the urge to retreat back inside, Julia forced herself to watch him as he watched her. It had been six months since she had last seen him. Six months since she had thrown him out, her face flushed and stinging from his neat backhand during their argument. Six months since she had closed the apartment door behind him and begun her life in Aix without him.

Six terrible months.

Six wonderful months.

She could see he was smiling now. It was that same old smile. The one that used to affect her so. The one that made her tummy flip-flop in anticipation of the moment he would take her into his arms and drill her with that all-possessing focus of his. The one that assured her she was the only one. No one else. Until, of course, there was.

Julia turned away from the sight of Jacques standing there and reminded herself that it wasn't just the slap, the lies and the other girl. *A girl!* No more than seventeen. How could she complete with that? Smooth skin, clear eyes, and eager heart. The child wore a midriff-baring top as easily and unselfconsciously as Julia did her flannel granny nightie.

No, it wasn't the lies and the infidelity. It was the undeniable, unassailable and relentlessly unavoidable evidence that Julia would never be young again—no matter how young she felt on the inside.

*A man who took that away from you,* she thought as she dropped her apron onto the couch and ran a hand through her short curly hair, *well, he should die a slow and horrid death.*

# Chapter Three

Sometimes Maggie swore she could smell the *Mistral*, that icy-cold wind that comes down the Rhône River Valley from the Alps to jolt the sun lovers of Provence back to their senses. As she sat with her laptop on the terrace of the beautiful stone *mas* she shared with Laurent, she found herself pulling her cotton cardigan tighter around her. Petit Four, her little hybrid poodle mix, was curled up next to her on the cushion of the bench where she sat.

From here she could just see the form of her husband—always the tallest figure in any grouping—walking the perimeter of his vineyard with the men he had hired to bring in this year's harvest. She loved to watch Laurent, especially when he was unaware of her. At more than six foot four, she often thought his natural grace of movement belied his size. She watched him now as he moved easily between the carefully trussed vines, pointing out this one or that to his audience.

Maggie put a hand on her stomach and directed her attention back to her laptop screen. In the time it took to bury one uncle—hers, this time, not his—and make a baby, she and Laurent had somehow managed to pull off the impossible. They—particularly one malcontented American expatriate—had taken their marriage firmly by the horns and turned it all around. Her resentment of Laurent's focus on his vineyard evaporated when she realized how important his happiness, however it was derived, was to her. Then she realized how important *she* was to *his* happiness. That, and a two-book deal for a mystery series that came out of left field, had enabled Maggie to put Laurent's passion about his grapes into perspective—and to kick start her own passion.

Her editor had sent a series of changes on the first draft of her book. And while at first she almost had to sit down and put her head between her knees to keep from passing out, with time and the sturdy good sense from her straight-thinking husband, she soon accepted that strong revision was par for the course for most writers—even experienced ones. That, and soothing and encouraging phone conversations from both her agent and editor, soon had her breathing normally again. Even so, her editor had seen the need for a lot of changes to Maggie's first draft of a murder mystery set in Paris during Paris Fashion Week.

A *lot* of changes.

Maggie scrolled down the manuscript on her computer and found herself nodding more often than frowning at what the editor had pointed out. She knew her editor was just making sure the book was the best it could be. After all, it was Maggie's name on the jacket cover. She'd told Laurent, "Before I got this email from my editor, I thought I could write." As usual, Laurent was not in an indulgent mood and she had received a Gallic snort in response that could only be interpreted as *knock it off and get to work*. She smiled at the memory.

A motion glimpsed out of the corner of her eye made her look up in the direction of Laurent again and she was surprised to see him striding purposefully back toward the terrace where she sat. It was nowhere near lunchtime, and she was sure he meant to spend the morning in the vineyards. Before Laurent was halfway back to the house, Petit Four jumped down from the bench barking and ran to the double French doors that led back to the house.

Between Laurent and the dog, it was pretty clear someone was either at the front door or was rappelling down the walls into the upper bedrooms. Maggie got up and went into the house. *Now how had Laurent known someone was here*, she wondered. She had gotten used to his knack for hearing and seeing things that only bats and some carefully attuned dogs could hear, but she still marveled at the ability. As she reached the heavy front door to the *mas*, Maggie was already out of breath. Her pregnancy left her wilted and tired these days from the simplest exertions.

She pulled open the door and was stunned to find her best friend Grace Van Sant standing on Maggie's ancient slate threshold, a Louis Vuitton bag at her feet, a pair of Prada sunglasses on her nose, and her two-year-old towhead on her hip.

"Surprise, darling," Grace said, her voice trembling just a little. "We're here."

\* \* \*

"I am surprised, is all, Grace," Maggie said after all the hugs and luggage had been dealt with, Grace comfortably scooted into the main lounge, a glass of Côte de Rhone in her hand, a small plate of crudités on the coffee table before her. "Delighted, but surprised. Why didn't you tell me you were coming? And where are Taylor and Windsor? Can you stay?"

From the minute her dearest of all friends had crossed into her home, bringing with her the ever-present whiff of Chanel No. 19 and a sense that her namesake, Grace Kelly, was trans channeling, Maggie knew something wasn't right. It wasn't just that Grace was here from Indianapolis without any advance notice at all. It wasn't the fact she had come alone, except for baby Zou-zou. It wasn't even the fact her excuses for the absence of her husband and other child were so vague. It was Grace, herself.

Grace Van Sant was rich and always had been. That kind of money for that length of time formed a person. It shaped the way they looked at the world, gave them a languor they could transfer to just about any situation they found themselves in.

Grace and Windsor had been living in Provence for three years before Laurent and Maggie arrived. Unlike Maggie, Grace had handled the language, the village, the food and the clothes as if she had been born to them. Everything was easy for Grace, Maggie had long believed. And she lived and moved like her name—smoothly, elegant, perfectly.

Which was why it was so disconcerting to see her now. The hand that held her sherry glass shook. She licked her lips repeatedly. She patted her hair as if not sure it was just right. And Grace was *always* just right. She constantly pulled out her cellphone to check the time. *Or was it to see who hadn't called?*

No, there was something definitely wrong and Maggie had a sinking feeling, a sinking, hard-to-believe feeling, she knew what it was.

"I told you I'd come for the birth," Grace said, smoothing out the nonexistent wrinkles in her Dolce & Gabbana slacks.

"That's not for a month or more," Maggie pointed out to her. "And I thought you'd let me know when and where so Laurent could come to the train station and pick you up."

"Yes, well, now I've saved him the bother."

"Is everything alright, Grace?"

"What? Don't be silly, darling! I come back to France for the first time in nearly two years and you think something's wrong? I'm not sure how to take that."

Maggie frowned, unconvinced, but Laurent entered the salon holding Zou-zou and deposited the baby into Maggie's arms.

"Lunch is ready soon, yes?" he said to them.

"Oh, that sounds divine, Laurent," Grace said, reaching out to take his hand as he moved to go back to the kitchen. "I can't tell you how glad I am to be here."

Laurent gave her arm an absentminded pat. *"Bien sûr,"* he said over his shoulder. *Of course.*

Lunch was its usual Laurent-spectacular. It was mid September, but many days were already too cool for eating out-of-doors, and Laurent deemed this was one of them. He had Maggie set the long, oaken farm table he had inherited with the house while Grace put the baby down for her nap. When she returned, he handed her a glass of wine and motioned for her to take her seat at the table.

"One of yours?" she asked, sniffing the bouquet.

*"Non,"* he said. "Much better. Well." He stopped and glanced at Maggie for a moment. "Perhaps not *much* better."

"Laurent's stuff is really good," Maggie said. "His last harvest was so, so good. Flinty and dry but a little sweet."

Grace took a healthy sip and sank down into her dining chair. "You're getting pretty good, yourself," she said to Maggie. "Learning the lingo after all this time?"

Laurent grunted and returned to the kitchen, but Maggie knew he was pleased with the interest she had taken in the vineyard and the effort she had made to learn what he did.

"Well, you know what they say," Maggie said seating herself. *"Petit à petit…"*

*"L'oiseau fait son nid." Little by little, the bird builds its nest.* Grace nodded. "You guys look like you really figured it all out in the end."

"Don't jinx us, Grace. But, yeah. We're finally happy. What with the book and everything." She waved at her very large abdomen pressing into the side of the table.

"Yes, you definitely have your distractions. I can see. What about socially? Are you two just stay-at-homes or do you go out?"

"There are a few discos in Aix if you need some excitement," Maggie said dryly. "Or were you asking if I'd replaced you yet in the best friend department?"

"Can't slip much past you. I haven't found anyone in Indianapolis yet. It's a hard town to break into. I've put in my applications for best friend but so far nothing. I understand you and Danielle have gotten close?"

Danielle Pernon was Maggie and Laurent's elderly neighbor. While it was true that after Grace left Maggie reached out to Danielle more than she had before, Grace knew well enough it could never be like what *they* had.

"I'm really too busy for palling around much lately," Maggie said. "It's a good thing you left, Grace. I would've had to dump you."

"Charming, dearest. And good to know."

Laurent entered with a large tureen of *bouillabaisse* and set it in front of the women.

"It's not fish, is it?" Maggie asked, peeking under the china lid of the tureen.

"Of course it is fish," Laurent replied, nonplused. "It is *bouillabaisse*."

"You can't eat shellfish?" Grace asked, reaching for her napkin.

"She can eat anything," Laurent said firmly, giving Maggie a raise of his eyebrow. "It is just her little joke." He placed a large basket of garlic rounds on the table with a bowl of *rouille*.

"Oh, I have missed this," Grace said, and Maggie could swear her eyes watered when she spoke.

"Just fish soup, Grace," she said. "No biggie. Right, Laurent?"

But Laurent was off to the kitchen to fetch something else necessary to make the lunch perfect.

"Well, it's a biggie to *me*," Grace said, spreading the *rouille* on a toast round. "I can't remember the last time I had French food, let alone with friends."

"Windsor working a lot?"

"You could say that. And Taylor is a full-time job. She's worse now than ever. Plus, she hates me."

"I'm sure that's not true, Grace."

Laurent returned with a large ladle and spooned the steaming and fragrant stew into three large stoneware bowls. As soon as they were served, Maggie's cellphone rang.

"It could be my editor," she said, looking at Laurent.

"You can call her back," he said.

Maggie picked up her phone and looked at the screen. "It's Julia," she said and accepted the call before Laurent could speak. "Hey, Julia. What's up?"

Laurent sighed heavily and flapped a linen napkin across his lap.

Grace nudged him with her foot under the table. "Who's Julia?"

"*Une amie*," he said. "They met last year. They have become close." He frowned and looked at Maggie, who was off the phone. "*Qu'est-ce qui'il y a?*" he asked.

Maggie looked at him as if startled out of a daze.

"Maggie?" Grace said. "Is everything alright?"

"That was Julia." She shook her head. "You're not going to believe this." She looked from Grace to Laurent. "Jacques is dead."

Susan Kiernan-Lewis

# Chapter Four

Maggie sat in the large, sunny lounge in Julia's apartment. She had bolted out the front door and into her Renault while Laurent and Grace walked down the long gravel drive trying to talk her into staying. In the end, Laurent insisted on driving her and ushered Grace back into the house to wait for them. He promised they would not be late. Now, he sat in one of the many cafés that lined the Cours and waited for Maggie to emerge from the apartment building.

"Was it suicide?" Maggie asked Julia gently. Julia was sitting straight-backed on her sofa, holding a glass of untouched wine in her hands.

"What?" Julia seemed to forcibly drag her attention back to Maggie from whatever private world she was seeing in her mind's eye. *Jacques as she had last seen him?* Maggie wondered. "No. No, I can't imagine. That wouldn't make sense. He wanted to reconcile, you know?"

Maggie nodded. "But," she said, "if you told him no, maybe he was so distraught that he…"

"No, Maggie. I mean, *yes*, I told him no but he didn't seem a bit distraught. If anything, he seemed…energized by my rejection. He was full-on for making me change my mind. He was up for the challenge. You know?"

35

Maggie didn't really, but she nodded. "When did he leave?"

"Right after dinner," Julia said, indicating the dining table with a jerk of her head. It was clear and tidy except for a glass bowl of nectarines. "He said he didn't feel well. I told you he was having problems?"

"Money problems?"

"Well, yes, that too, I think, but I'm talking about his health. He didn't feel good. I know he wanted to stay, but he left early. He looked terrible. Like he was in pain."

"How did you find out about…?"

"His bitch of a daughter called me," Julia said. Her mouth was pressed in a firm, tight line. "She called me screaming and…and…" Julia put her hands to her face and burst into tears. "She was horrible. Just horrible."

Maggie reached over and put her arms around her friend. "I am so, so sorry, Jules." She rubbed her back. Over Julia's shoulder, Maggie could see the large birdcage with the multi-colored lovebird in it. A friendly little thing normally, it seemed to be eyeing Maggie now in an indicting fashion, as if *she* were responsible for the unhappy sounds emanating from his mistress.

"I shouldn't blame her," Julia said, swallowing her sobs and trying to compose herself. "She found him, you see." She shook her head as if unable to clear the gruesome picture from her brain.

"At his apartment?"

"Yes. She was supposed to meet him there or something. I didn't get the whole story. And she found him on the floor. He must have…it must have happened last night. He was fully clothed. Oh, Maggie, I can't believe he's not in the world any more. I can't believe, it's impossible to believe, he'll never b-b-bother me again." Julia let her sobs break full force out of her and into her hands. Maggie held her and patted her back.

"I know, sweetie," she said. "I know."

The knock at the door made both of them jump. Annoyed at the thought it might be Laurent, impatient and coming to see what was taking so long, Maggie gave her friend a brief squeeze and jumped up to wrench open the door. When she did, she gave a gasp of bewilderment to find two uniformed police officers standing there flanking none other than Detective *Inspecteur* Roger Bedard—looking way too darkly handsome than any man had a right to.

"Roger!" she blurted out.

"I should have known," he said, shaking his head when he saw her. Then his eyes travelled down the front of her dress and his mouth fell open. "You're pregnant," he said, stupidly.

"And here I thought you weren't a good detective," Maggie retorted, her cheeks burning with embarrassment.

Quickly recovering himself, Bedard snapped out an order to his men and then pushed past Maggie into Julia's apartment.

"Hey, wait a minute," Maggie said. "You can't come in here without a warrant or something."

Roger moved to stand directly in front of Julia where she sat, stupefied, on the sofa. Without looking behind him, he held out a hand for the handcuffs he expected to fill it and spoke directly to Julia.

"Madame Patrick, I am placing you under arrest for the murder of Monsieur Jacques Tatois. Please stand up."

"Roger, no!" Maggie tried to reach where Roger and Julia were standing, but one of the uniformed police held out an arm to prevent her.

"Maggie, stay out of this," Roger said sternly. He spoke again to his men and the man who held his arm out against Maggie dropped it to his side, but he continued to block her from going any further.

"It's okay, Maggie," Julia called to her with a shaky voice. "It's a mistake and I'll get it sorted out." She turned to Roger. "Where?"

"Your consulate has been notified," he said. "You'll be held at the *Palais de Justice* here in Aix.

"I'm coming with you," Maggie said.

Roger and Julia both turned to her. "Maggie, no," they said, nearly in unison.

"I'll be fine, Maggie," Julia said as she turned away and allowed Roger to cuff her hands behind her back. "Have Laurent come pick me up in an hour."

Roger took Julia by the arm and shoved her past Maggie toward the door. Before exiting, he turned to Maggie. "I wouldn't bother."

Maggie could see the anger and hurt in his eyes, and something more. Shame. He knew he had no right to his feelings. In a moment he was out the door and gone, but not before Maggie thought she could hear Julia start to weep again.

\* \* \*

"What do you mean *they're holding her overnight?*" Maggie waddled over to where Laurent stood in the living room of their home. He had just tossed down his cellphone and stood staring out the French doors into the distance, as if an answer might be out there that wasn't available anywhere else.

"Just that, *ma chère*," he said tiredly. "They will not release her tonight."

"But I told Julia you would come pick her up." Maggie looked helplessly at Laurent and then over at Grace, who was sitting quietly in an overstuffed armchair watching her.

"*Je sais*," he said, reaching an arm out to draw her close to him. *I know.* "But we must wait. They are not releasing her."

"Stop saying that!" Maggie put her arms around her husband. "Does this mean they have some kind of proof of her involvement? Is that possible?" Maggie looked up at Laurent as if expecting an answer and he shrugged.

Grace unwound her long legs from underneath her and stretched her back. She crossed her ankles. "I guess the ex-girlfriend or the ex-wife always tops the list of suspects. Makes sense."

"But he was alone when he died," Maggie said, pulling out of Laurent's arms and addressing Grace. "How can it be murder when he was all alone?" She looked at Laurent as if a new thought had just come to her. "Maybe the daughter did it. Julia said she was a bitch and didn't get along with her father. *And* she found the body. Isn't that like a classic rule of thumb? The person who finds the body is most likely the killer?"

"I have never heard of this rule," Laurent said, frowning. She saw him scanning the furniture in the living room for the glass of wine he had set down.

"Yes, I've heard of it," Grace said, nodding. "First the spouse and then the person who found the body. It's a classic formula."

"It's true, right?" Maggie said.

"Yeah, except for one thing," Grace said, picking up her own wineglass. "They arrested her for *murder*, not took her in for questioning, so they must know something."

"I can't believe this is happening," Maggie said. "I was going to introduce you two today."

"Oh, well."

"Maggie?" Laurent stepped back into the room and held up his car keys. I am going into the village, yes? You are alright here with Grace?"

Maggie nodded. "Fine, Laurent. If they call you—"

"I will go immediately. You are not to worry now, yes?"

"Okay." Maggie forced herself to smile at her husband. She knew he hated to see her stressed, especially this late in the pregnancy. When she heard the front door shut, she turned to Grace. "We need to do something."

Grace raised her eyebrows. "You mean like organize a jailbreak?"

Maggie sat down on the sofa and began pulling at the hem of her tunic. She stood up again in agitation. "I don't know what I mean," she admitted. "I just can't stand this, knowing that she's down there. Damn that Roger!"

"Roger Bedard?" Grace's eyebrows arched up. "*Your* Roger Bedard?"

"Oh, stop it, Grace. I haven't seen him in over a year."

"Did he know about..." Grace gestured to Maggie's very prominent baby bump.

"No reason why he should. We don't run in the same circles. I mean, I knew he was transferred to Aix only because Laurent heard it and passed it on to me."

"Darling Laurent. So civilized about the men in love with his wife. I suppose it's the French in him."

"Stop it, Grace. If you want to know, he's not at all civilized about it but he knows he never had anything to worry about—"

"Never? Careful about the history you attempt to rewrite, darling," Grace said with a sly smile. "I was here at the time, remember?"

"Okay, *one* kiss. That's nothing to get derailed over."

"Does Laurent know about the one kiss?"

Maggie looked at her with exasperation. "Why are we talking about this? It's all water under the bridge. I'm practically ready to deliver Laurent's baby. There was clearly no harm done and all parties have retreated safely to their respective corners. And I would greatly appreciate it, Grace, if you forgot about the stupid kiss."

"Consider it forgotten," Grace said with a shrug. But her eyes met Maggie's and said otherwise.

As uncomfortable as this whole line of conversation made Maggie feel—especially with Roger showing up again in her life—she had to admit it was the first time since Grace had arrived that she had behaved in her old confident manner and Maggie hated to totally quash her teasing.

"He wasn't expecting to see me," Maggie said as she reseated herself. "And all this…" She gestured to her stomach. "God, Grace, he looked…hurt."

"Which isn't rational, right, sweetie?" Grace said, helpfully. "Whatever he felt for you or hoped to get from you was at least *mostly* all in his own mind, right?"

Maggie nodded. "Laurent and I have been getting along so well lately."

"I should hope so."

Maggie narrowed her eyes at her. "Not just because of the pregnancy, Grace. Ever since I got back from Paris and got involved with the book I'm writing, I've been able to see the things I was doing to sabotage my marriage."

"That's handy."

"Why are you being so glib?" Maggie's face flushed with annoyance. "How I was treating him *wasn't* easy to see and it *wasn't* easy to stop doing either. You act like I'm some kind of one-dimensional sitcom character. Did I not *tell* you how close Laurent and I came to tossing in the towel?"

"You did," Grace said, taking a sip from her wine, her eyes never leaving Maggie's.

"Then how can you be so flip? It was literally the scariest thing I've ever gone through."

"I'm sorry, Maggie. But like you said, you and Laurent had serious issues and I guess I'm just not buying into the whole *I solved it and everything's perfect now* scenario. Or do you honestly think having a baby will fix all that's wrong with your marriage?"

"What?!" Maggie sputtered.

"Look, I'm sorry, Maggie," Grace said hurriedly. "I just don't want you to think children will make a difference—except maybe to make everything worse. That's the truth of it and I'm sorry if you don't want to hear it."

Maggie took a long, steadying breath, trying to stay calm. She smoothed her tunic down over her tummy and forced herself to reach out for Grace's hand. "It isn't the baby that's changed things, Grace," she said firmly. "As I was trying to tell you, *I* changed the way I looked at living here in St-Buvard—in *France*—and *that* made everything else better."

"Well, that's great then," Grace said, her eyes filling with tears.

Maggie scooted over to her on the chair and Grace moved to accommodate her.

"Why are you here, Grace?" she asked quietly. "What's going on with you and Win?"

"Nothing good," Grace said, brightly, blinking back the tears. "Nothing good."

Laurent's nights out were rare and Maggie hated to begrudge him the few he did take. Besides his monthly co-op meetings in Aix where all the *vignerons* collaborated and exchanged notes, and his one night a week at *Le Canard*, the local pub in St-Buvard, he never went out after dark. Those rare times he did, normally he made her a dish of something that she either reheated or ate cold. Tonight he'd been distracted, and she found herself rummaging around in Laurent's other kingdom—the kitchen. Although Grace insisted she wasn't hungry and baby Zou-zou had already demonstrated she would eat anything in any condition at any time, Maggie still felt the need to rustle up something even if it was just cheese toast.

"I honestly don't bother at home," Grace said, shifting the chubby toddler on her lap.

"Well, that's because you have a cook, isn't it?" Maggie said from the interior of the refrigerator.

"Oh, I guess you're right. That could be the reason."

Maggie pulled out a plate of lamb slices, a tapenade and leftover potato gratin made with the gnocchi Laurent had served the night before. "I think I can do something with these." She put the dish of lamb on the counter and scooped out a piece of cold gnocchi and handed it to Zou-zou.

"Hungry, sweetie?" she asked the child, who popped the plump bit of potato and pasta into her mouth.

"She's going to be massive when she's a teenager," Grace said. "All she does is eat and those kinds of habits don't die easy."

"Oh, Grace, you exaggerate," Maggie said, laughing.

"You won't think so when she's ripping your refrigerator door off its hinges. I kid you not. The child is a bottomless pit."

"Laurent will love cooking for her," Maggie said. "He hates how I'm always watching my diet and swears he wouldn't care if I get fat."

"Laurent is about the only man I could honestly believe that about. He really loves you no matter what. How did you manage *that*?"

"I have no idea. Oh, look, he's got great tomatoes still, and this bread he brought home from Aix."

"He went shopping while you were with your friend?"

"You know Laurent. He wouldn't pass up their Wednesday Food Market if it was *me* they were arresting for murder."

"A bit of an exaggeration."

"Maybe, but only a bit. Anyway, it'll make a fine feast for us. We don't normally have good bread unless one of us has been in Aix or Avignon."

"The village still hasn't replaced the bakery?"

"Nope."

"Ah, well. Memories are long in this part of France."

"You can say that again. Here, take the wine. Just because I'm not drinking doesn't mean someone else shouldn't enjoy it. Oh, she likes the gnocchi, Grace! Didn't you, little bug? Is it weird she isn't talking yet?"

"Hush your mouth, Maggie Dernier," Grace said, putting the little girl on her feet and grabbing the bottle of wine. "The minute they start talking is the minute they start whining. I'm enjoying the peace while I can."

They settled back into the living room and Maggie spread their picnic out on the coffee table, which Zou-zou attacked with delight, grabbing up a fistful of tapenade and smearing it across her face in her attempt to get it into her mouth.

"Will that make her sick, do you think?" Maggie asked, reaching for a napkin for the child.

"I really don't know," Grace said. She broke off a piece of the bread and dipped it into the tapenade.

"Do you want to talk about it?"

"Not yet, if you don't mind."

"Okay. But that is why you're here, isn't it?"

"Is it?" Grace looked at her blankly, then away. "I suppose it is. Why else? To process it all. To say it out loud to my dearest friend and watch the expression on her face. You know, some cultures don't believe a thing is a fact until it's spoken. That's strange, don't you think? That you can keep something from being true just by not saying it?"

"I think people do it all the time."

Grace laughed but there was no mirth in the sound.

"Does Taylor know what's going on?"

Grace shrugged. "She's pretty solidly into her own little world. A normal kid couldn't help but know. But Taylor? I have no idea."

Maggie wanted to ask about Windsor. *Was he distraught? Was he fed up? Was he the guilty party?* She watched Grace as she pulled an anchovy out of Zou-zou's grubby little fist and replaced it with a carrot spear. She would talk when she was ready.

As if Grace could read Maggie's mind, she turned to her. "Tell me about your new best friend. How did you two meet?"

Maggie tucked a thin wedge of lamb into the heel of the crusty bread and spread a hefty dollop of tapenade over the top. "We met at a *fete* that Laurent's co-op put on. She was there with Jacques, the man who died, and we were the only two native English-speakers in the room."

"A natural recipe for instant friendship."

"Well, it kind of is, as you know," Maggie said pointedly. "She was English, not American, but we were both with Frenchmen and living in Provence and so we had a baseline of things in common. The more we talked…you know."

"The more you fell madly in love with each other."

"Well, Grace, we connected. Above and beyond the obvious things we have in common, we really enjoyed the time we spent together. I'm sorry you haven't made any friends in Indiana, but it's worse for me since, unlike you, I don't have a whole effing country of my own people to fall back on. It's pretty lonely over here and friendships mean more."

"Wow. Big speech, darling. And you're right. It's hard for me to complain about being friendless when I have drive-through banking and round doorknobs."

"Okay, Grace, I am not going to apologize for making friends. And if you were any kind of a *real* friend, you'd be glad I had someone to turn to after you left."

"Well, I'm sorry to be such a disappointment to you, Maggie," Grace said. "But even all the wonders of living back home again couldn't fill the hole left by the dissolution of our friendship."

"Now you're being dramatic. We Skype practically every day."

"Which is not the same as being together and solving mysteries like Lucy and Ethel the way we used to and getting into all kinds of trouble. In fact, I officially hate Skype."

Maggie laughed. "Grace, you're such a ninny. How can you possibly think there is a replacement for you in my life?"

"This Julia character certainly seems like she fits the bill."

"You are so unabashedly self-absorbed, it floors me. The poor woman is under arrest for murder!"

"You don't have to apologize for preferring one person over another, Maggie," Grace said, grabbing Zou-zou's hand before she reached the TV remote control.

"It's not a competition, Grace."

"You idiot, that's exactly what it is!"

Maggie stared at Grace with her mouth open. Zou-zou, whose hand Grace was still gripping, began to squirm away from her mother and make little grunting sounds.

Maggie shook her head. "I was in a bad way when you left, Grace."

"You're not going to blame—"

"Just listen to me. With all the other stuff going on, mostly Laurent and I doing a nosedive on the newlywed front, your leaving really kicked the stuffing out of me. I know it wasn't your fault, and that Windsor had a chance to make caboodles of money by selling his software company and then running it for the new owners in Indy. I get all that and I point no fingers. But it was really bad timing for me. And when I met Julia, it helped a lot. She was giving and funny and open and always accessible…"

"All the things I'm not."

"I *said* funny." Maggie smiled at her and Grace allowed a small one in response.

"She's not you, Grace. Never will be. But she's a dear friend and just as if something like this happened to you, I want to move earth and heaven to help her."

Grace looked up. "Aha!"

"What, aha?"

"I knew it! You want to clear her name."

Maggie looked around the room with exasperation. "We don't even know for sure that's necessary," she said evasively. "They'll probably release her in the morning."

"And if they don't?"

"Okay, yes, if they don't, I'm not going to sit here and do nothing."

"Well, then," Grace said reaching for her wineglass and holding up to toast Maggie, "I guess Lucy and Ethel are back in the saddle again after all."

Susan Kiernan-Lewis

# Chapter Five

The farmers' market in downtown Aix on the *Place Richelme* sits under the canopy of dozens of plane trees in full bloom that line the avenue. It has served as an outdoor food market since the middle ages. Laurent had left home before dawn so he would have the best pick of everything the market had to offer: peppers, glossy eggplants, tomatoes, strawberries that tasted like real strawberries, figs, apricots, peaches, plums, melons, and red currants like little glossy jewels in their tiny wooden baskets.

The first stall he approached sold goat cheeses—hundreds of different varieties, little wheels of white that looked like carefully packaged gifts. He'd gotten home late last night, and still Maggie and Grace were not in bed. Although he worried about Maggie getting too tired, he was glad to see it. He didn't know what Grace's visit meant—except that it was more than just a visit—but he was glad to see her as a distraction to the current *désastre* with Maggie's friend, Julia.

*Why do these terrible events always seem to follow Maggie? What were the odds that a murder would occur—if indeed that's what this was—the very day Maggie had lunch with the prime suspect?* Laurent shook his head and paid the goat man for several packages of good cheese. He moved on to the salami and ham stall, but took a moment to look around to enjoy his surroundings. At this early hour not every stall was stocked and ready to go, but beyond the many fruits and vegetables there were still crate after crate of olives, chocolate, herbs and spices. The air of the market was redolent with the scent of *herbes des Provence* and lemons.

As Laurent approached a table full of *calissons*, the popular and ubiquitous iced cookie of ground almonds and preserved melons that Aix is famous for, and that his pregnant *femme* had a strong partiality for, he noticed someone in the crowd that he knew. It took him a moment to place him precisely, and when he did he couldn't help but wonder if it could really be coincidental that he was running into the cousin of the murder victim the very next day after the crime.

"Florian," Laurent called, shifting his bag of cheese to his other arm in anticipation of the handshake when the man noticed him.

However, when Florrie turned to see who'd called his name, Laurent thought he did the most amazing thing. Instead of acknowledging an acquaintance—for they were no more than that—and stretching out his hand in greeting, Florrie dropped his own bag, slapped both hands to his face and burst into tears. So stunned was Laurent by this reaction, he hurriedly moved to separate the man from the crowd by pulling him out of the flow of the quickly building sea of shoppers and tourists.

"Get control of yourself," Laurent said, giving Florrie's arm a firm shake. "Are you all right?"

Clearly, Florrie was *not* alright and Laurent cursed the fact that he'd seen him at all this morning.

"I am so sorry, Laurent," Florrie said, snuffling noisily into his hands and then his sleeve. "I don't know what came over me."

"Well, you have had a shock," Laurent said, eyeing him to make sure he wasn't going to start crying again. His eyes were red and deeply bloodshot, as if he'd been drinking heavily or crying, or both. He was a good-looking man and favored his dark-haired cousin in that way, with blue eyes and very straight white teeth. But there the resemblance ended. Jacques had always been razor sharp in his manner and inclined to cut. Florrie was the soft, affable one.

"I am so sorry to hear about Jacques," Laurent said, hoping it wouldn't start him off again. "It was a shock, I'm sure."

"I still cannot believe it," Florrie said, patting his pockets in search of a handkerchief of some kind. "I just saw him yesterday!"

"And he looked well?" Laurent wasn't sure why he asked that. He glanced back at the market. He had been hoping to get a good fish before they were all gone.

"Well, no, he didn't. Now that you mention it, he was complaining of not feeling well. Did you hear they arrested poor Julia? Well, of course you would, because of Maggie, *non*?"

Laurent nodded solemnly, forcing himself not to look at the line of people at the fish stall.

"It's ridiculous to believe *Julia* could hurt Jacques," Florrie said, finally extricating a badly soiled cloth from his pocket and mopping his wet face with it. "She must be so distraught. Have you talked with her?"

"Ah, no," Laurent said.

"Will they release her soon, do you think?"

"I am sure they will. Would you care to walk with me?" Laurent could see the fish he wanted from here, a very fat John Dory that would do nicely in the soup he wanted to make today. He began to edge Florrie in that direction.

"I begged him to take better care of himself," Florrie said as he trotted to keep up with Laurent's long stride. "He smoked. He drank too much. He ate the wrong things…"

Laurent got in line at the fish stall and relaxed enough to turn his attention fully to Florrie while he waited.

"Getting back together with Julia would have been the best thing he could have done," Florrie said earnestly. "I tell you, if it *was* murder, the police should be looking at his crazy daughter, Michelle. That girl is *demented*. I have seen her physically attack Jacques on more than one occasion."

"Do you know if she saw him that night?"

Florrie blinked at him as if having trouble understanding. Laurent felt sorry for him. Clearly he wasn't prepared to have his passionate theories derailed by facts or evidence.

"It's possible she did," Florrie said.

"I'm sure the police will check into her whereabouts during the time of his death," Laurent said, then turned to the fishmonger and pointed to the fish he wanted. When he turned back around with his prize all neatly packaged up, Florrie was gone.

Maggie tried to concentrate on the beauty of the broad avenue of the *Cours Mirabeau* with its row after row of ancient fountains and cafes beneath the majestic plane trees that lined the row. She had forgotten that Laurent was going into Aix this morning, which was supremely annoying since *she* was planning on going there, too, and they only had the one car. She hated taking a taxi in France—*it was literally risking your life the way those maniacs drove*—but her errand today couldn't wait. As she stared out the taxicab window, she tried to see if Laurent's Renault was parked somewhere visible, but didn't really expect to see it. While the traffic wasn't bad this time of day, it was not yet eleven, there was still a sizable crowd of tourists and shoppers clogging the grand avenue.

During the ride, Maggie allowed herself some time to decompress and reflect on her evening with Grace. It was clear Grace had left Windsor, but whether or not that was a formal leaving was yet to be determined since Grace wasn't talking. What *was* clear was how completely miserable Grace was.

*How could this happen? Grace and Windsor were the perfect couple. And they had kids!* Maggie could not imagine what could have occurred in their lives to cause something like this to happen.

With a supreme effort, Maggie put her friend's unhappiness out of her mind to concentrate on her morning. She intended to go to the jail in Aix to see Julia. Her phone calls to the number Roger had given her had been met with a very unhelpful recording. It was time for a little face-to-face, she thought grimly. But first, she would run by Julia's apartment and pick up a few clothes for her. If Julia were released this morning as everyone hoped, then it would just be a wasted half hour. But if this nightmare was going to go on any longer, Julia would want a fresh change of clothes.

She had the taxi stop outside Julia's apartment building and instructed the driver to wait for her. "*Dix minute*," she said firmly to the driver and then exited the cab and hurried up the stairs.

By the time she reached the landing on the second floor, she had to lean against the close walls and catch her breath. By the time she reached—much more slowly—the next landing, she had gone from hopefully wondering if all the noise she was hearing from the floor above her could be the result of construction of a lift being added to the 1890 apartment building to flat not caring. As she dragged herself to the final landing just before Julia's floor, the noise was clearly more of a destructive nature than constructive, with loud thuds and the sounds of breaking glass exploding in the narrow stairwell. Julia's apartment was one of two on her floor, but only hers had the sounds of a full-scale demolition coming out into the hallway through the wide open door.

Bewildered and tentative, Maggie edged her way to the

door opening. *Was Julia having scheduled work done? Was she being broken into?* In the brief space between crashes, Maggie could hear the sounds of her own labored gasps as she fought for breath after her climb. The silence startled her, and when she heard the sound of her own struggling breaths she began to feel afraid. Whoever was in there destroying Julia's apartment —for that was clearly what was happening—might not be very welcoming of an unexpected friend of Julia's on the threshold.

A loud crash ended the silence and Maggie used the moment to slip through the front door. Inside she saw a young woman of about twenty-five in the process of hammering to splinters with a very large axe the beautiful antique table that had been a birthday gift to Julia from her long-passed father. Maggie watched in horror as the girl brought the axe down on the table full force, the table's tiny hand-placed bits of mosaic shooting out in all directions like flints of wood from a chipper.

"Stop it!" Maggie screamed. "Stop it this minute!"

The girl whirled on Maggie, the axe gripped tightly in her hands, her eyes wild with hatred and anger. When Maggie saw her face, she knew the woman had to be related to Jacques. They shared the same dark hair and brown eyes, the same olive skin coloring. It was entirely possible that the girl was pretty, probably was, but it was impossible to believe it with her current expression of insane urgency. She took a step toward Maggie.

"I am an American," Maggie said without thinking. "Think twice before you dare to attack me. Remember…Saddam Hussein," she added stupidly.

The girl stared at her as if not understanding, although Maggie had spoken in clear, plain French. Slowly, Maggie could see the energy that the manic fit had given her begin to fade and the girl lowered the axe to her side, but she did not drop it.

"Who are you?" she asked. "Are you a friend of the

English whore's?"

Maggie looked around the apartment, so much of it already destroyed. The girl had obviously been here awhile. Julia's couch had been chopped into chunks of expensive fabric and batting. Her beautiful Royal Doulton tea set, the one she had brought with her from London, was in shards. Two paintings over the couch, neither expensive, were ripped and had gaping gashes in them. The birdcage was on its side and Maggie quickly went to see if the little bird still lived.

"I am cleaning up the bastard's love nest," Michelle said, finally dropping the axe to the floor. It hit with a thunk.

Maggie saw the bird huddling in a corner of the cage. She grabbed the handle of the cage and stood up with it. "I'm leaving now," she said, shocked to hear her voice sound strong and unwavering. "I intend to call the police as soon as I'm in my car. If I were you, I'd figure out what you're going to say to them."

Michelle straightened the hem of her tee shirt over her jeans and surveyed the damage in the apartment. "I will tell them that *you* did this!" she said defiantly. "It will be your word against mine."

Maggie walked to the door holding the birdcage. "Good plan," she said. "Then we'll just see who they believe." Before she could edge past the girl, Michelle turned and bolted out of the apartment, running down the stairs. Maggie listened to the sounds of her heels pounding the steps until they receded into silence as Michelle disappeared into the street.

Maggie looked at the poor little bird, still shivering in terror, and then at the ruined apartment. A feeling of incomprehensible sadness came over her as she closed the door behind her and began her own descent to the street below. Somehow she no longer felt very optimistic about Julia's chances for returning home any time soon.

Susan Kiernan-Lewis

# Chapter Six

Grace pulled the duvet up to her chin and squeezed her eyes shut. Moments before she'd heard Zou-zou call for her from the next room, but before she could decide what to do she heard Laurent's tread as he came up the stairs and into the child's room. She listened to his soft, deep rumble of a voice as he talked to the baby. When she heard him leave, she knew Zou-zou was in his arms.

She let out the breath she didn't realize she had been holding. This was, all of it, so much harder than she ever imagined. It wasn't just the overwhelming desire to weep all the time that she hadn't expected. It wasn't even the fact she missed Windsor—which was a total shock. It was the constant state of indecision that she hadn't anticipated. That she, who was always so in control and confidant, now wanted only to hide under bedcovers and cry was a facet of her personality she never knew existed.

Her glance strayed to her cellphone on the side table, attracted by the silent vibration of an incoming call. She couldn't help herself. She had to look. She propped up on one elbow and saw the photo of Windsor on the cellphone screen. She remembered well the circumstances when she had taken that picture. Before Zou-zou was born, during one of the peaceful times that they'd found a decent *au pair* for Taylor—

one who had been able to last longer than a month—and, of course, long before Leeza the twenty-two-year-old intern who had begun work at Windsor's corporate office had moved into their world. Grace let the call go to voice mail. She would delete it later without listening to it.

*What in the world was there to say? Was he calling to tell her Taylor had fallen during PE and cracked her skull? Did he want to know where she kept the paprika in the pantry? Was he hoping they could move things along a little more quickly please?* Leeza was probably becoming impatient, and if she knew anything about Windsor she knew how accommodating he was.

As she pulled the duvet tighter around her, she could smell the wonderful aromas of Laurent making breakfast downstairs. She could also hear the sounds of her child making delighted cooing noises. Uncle Laurent was obviously letting her "help." As one particularly happy squeal came from downstairs, Grace clapped her hands over her ears to block out the noise.

*How many more people's lives did she have to ruin before she could just go off somewhere and hide for the rest of her life?*

Maggie poured herself an *espresso* from the pot on the counter and sat down next to Zou-zou at the big table in the dining room.

"Such a big girl who doesn't need a booster chair" Maggie said, handing the baby a dish of sliced bananas Laurent had prepared. The girl scooped up the contents of the entire dish and stuffed them all into her mouth.

"Dear God in heaven," Maggie said, staring at her.

"I believe she is to be handfed, Maggie," Laurent said, frowning as Zou-zou labored through the chewing of her mouthful of bananas.

"Is she starving, do you think?"

"I have already fed her scrambled eggs and *brioche au chocolat*."

"She's like one of those dogs that doesn't have a mechanism to determine when they've had enough."

"You just made that up."

"Any more of that *brioche* left?"

"*Non*, Mademoiselle Zou-zou is a girl of large appetites."

"God, I'll say. Oh, Laurent, where did you put the bird? He can't be near drafts."

"Why again is it we have a bird?"

"It's Julia's lovebird. Someone has to take care of him until she gets out. That crazy Michelle would've killed him if I hadn't come along."

"Ah, yes. And why again did *you* come along? Indulge me, *chérie*."

"Oh, come on, Laurent. You didn't think I was just going to sit back and wait for the phone to ring, did you? I need to do what I can to help."

"And so you found yourself, eight months pregnant, face-to-face with an axe-wielding crazy woman in the midst of committing a felony."

"Is it a felony? I thought vandalism was a misdemeanor."

"Not when you break and enter in order to do it, and please do not distract me from my point."

Maggie got up and lumbered over to him where he stood in the kitchen, his hands on his hips, a dishtowel thrown over one shoulder. She put her arms around his waist. "Please don't worry so much about me, Laurent. I'm being very careful, I promise." She pulled away and rubbed her stomach, smiling up at him. "We're *both* being very careful."

"Well, then will you wait until I am available to go to the jail to see Julia?"

Maggie hesitated. "Well, sure, okay. If you think that's really necessary."

"I do."

"Can you go today? I haven't seen her since the arrest and I—"

"I cannot go today."

"Okay, see, now we've got a problem. Your schedule is not very flexible because of the harvest and I understand that, I do. But I can't wait until all the grapes are picked before I go and see how she's doing. Maybe Grace can come with me?"

She saw Laurent glance at Zou-zou, happily shredding a paper napkin.

"Grace is not…" He looked away and made a noise of frustration. "That would be no better than you going alone."

"Well, good. I'm glad you're okay with me—"

"*Non*, Maggie, I am not *okay* with you going to the jail alone. *Non.*"

"What the hell, Laurent? We've been over this a million times in the past."

"And my feelings have not changed since then!" Laurent glanced at the baby again and forced himself to lower his voice. "You are very vulnerable right now. You must be protected."

"Okay, now that's just silly and you know it."

"I do *not* know it. You are *enciente* and it is very *dangereux* where you are going. And also, of course I know that Bedard is running this case."

"What does that have to do with anything? Look at me, Laurent. I'm as big as a house! Do you seriously think he wants a piece of this?"

Laurent gave her a look of incredulity and heightened annoyance. "*Bien sûr*," he said. *Of course.*

"Well, that's just nuts. I *have* to go."

"You do not."

"I do! She's my friend, Laurent. She needs me. And do not even begin to say that *you* need me because that dog won't hunt and you know it."

"I was going to remind you that you have another friend not twenty feet from where you are sitting right now who also needs you."

The energy seemed to seep out of Maggie. She knew he was right. Grace, for all her big talk, was in a bad way. She had come to Maggie for support and friendship. Grace did need her right now.

But Grace wasn't sitting in a foreign jail accused of murder.

"I know," Maggie said. "And I'm sorry about the timing of all this, but right now Julia's situation trumps Grace's. Can you watch Zou-zou?"

Laurent threw down his dishrag in frustration and the little girl snapped her head to where the two of them stood facing each other. It occurred to Maggie that maybe the child had recently heard more than her fair share of bickering adults and she felt instantly ashamed. But Laurent was faster than she was and scooped the little girl up into his arms, prompting an outbreak of giggles as she wrapped her arms around his neck.

"*Ma petite Z et Oncle* Laurent will go visit Madame Danielle, *n'est ce pas?*" he said to the child, giving her a kiss on the cheek.

"Thanks, Laurent," Maggie said.

He gave her a solemn look as he reached for the child's coat. "We are not finished with this."

Finished or not, Maggie knew she had to hurry to make the luncheon engagement she had set up with none other than Roger Bedard. Not only had she dodged a bullet by Laurent *not* being able to accompany her today, which would have been awkward, she had caught another break because he didn't need the car either.

She felt extremely guilty about the covert luncheon but, honestly, he drove her to do it. She had to find out what Roger knew about Julia's case and she had to see Julia. It was infinitely annoying that Laurent didn't appear to understand that, or if he did understand it, didn't realize how important it was.

Maggie had to admit she didn't love being this large when she met with Roger after all this time. It wasn't like he was an ex-boyfriend or anything, but when someone thinks you're hot it's depressing to then present them with dramatic evidence to the contrary.

*I'm being silly,* she thought as she parked the little Renault into one of the few parallel parking spots off of Rue Mejanes. *What Roger does or doesn't think about me is entirely beside the point.* No wonder Laurent wasn't comfortable with her seeing him.

Reminding herself that the French were different and could easily find a pregnant woman every bit as sexy as a bathing suit model (did she really believe that?), Maggie reapplied her lipstick in the car then threw her bag over her shoulder and tottered down the cobblestone street to the café on her too-tall high heels.

He was standing at the entrance waiting for her, and damn if he didn't look every bit as confident and sexy as ever. Maggie felt her heart beat a little faster. *Doesn't mean I want him,* she reminded herself. *Just means I'm not blind.*

She smiled when he saw her and she could see he was struggling to remain cool and unaffected.

*He still cares.*

He touched her elbow and leaned in to kiss her on both cheeks. She could smell the mints covering a light scent of tobacco.

"You are looking well, Maggie."

"And you, Roger. Thanks for meeting me."

"Of course. It has been a long time." He gestured to the outdoor dining area and Maggie picked out a table under a large umbrella. It could still be very warm in September, and afternoon downpours were more and more common these days.

Once they were seated and had ordered, Maggie asked after Roger's little girl and how living in Aix suited him. She could tell by the way he answered her—a faint smile tugging at his lips all the while—that he knew she was waiting for the moment when she could talk about why she was really here.

And he wouldn't make that easy on her.

"So," she said finally, sipping her Perrier. "Why is it you think Julia is involved with Jacques's death?"

"Come right out with it, Maggie," Bedard said, grinning. "I was wondering how long you could last."

"No reason to play games is there, Roger? We haven't seen each other in awhile. You've been busy. Big new promotion with the police force. I've been busy." She put both her hands out to give an unobstructed view of her very pregnant belly. "So why don't we get to it?"

Roger watched her with warm, glittering brown eyes. She noticed they lingered on her belly—and her breasts—and she couldn't help but blush darkly. *Damn him.* He would tell her in his own time, and unfortunately, in his own way.

"Well, Maggie, I see you have gotten yourself mixed up with the wrong sort again."

"Really, Roger? Was *Brigitte* the wrong sort?" It occurred to her too late that reminding him of the murdered woman who initially brought them together was probably not the smartest thing to do if she wanted to keep him malleable and open with her.

He flushed and straightened in his chair, the relaxed air of insouciance gone.

"This time, your friend is not a victim," he said. A decidedly defensive edge had crept into his tone. "I have laboratory results that prove that." Roger was well aware that Maggie knew he hadn't always been so careful with forensic evidence in the past.

"What kind of laboratory results?"

"A toxicology screening."

"He died of something he ate?" Maggie frowned. *This wasn't good. This wasn't good at all.*

"You might say that. *Agaricus* mushrooms were found in his stomach. Deadly poisonous. But actually quite flavorful, I'm told."

Maggie took a long drink of water. Her stomach cramped painfully.

"Interesting fact," Roger said, oblivious to Maggie's reaction. "Did you know women tend to use poison as their weapon of choice when committing murder?"

"Wow. Thank you, Hercules Poirot."

"I'm afraid your sarcasm will not change the facts for your friend, Maggie."

"And in light of this evidence, you decided to arrest Julia because…?" Maggie felt a tingle of heat spread across her face and upper lip as she waited for Roger to answer her.

He shrugged. "Because she served him an omelet made with poisoned mushrooms the night he died. I'm sorry, Maggie. I knew you were hoping for something else."

"Did Julia *admit* to making him a mushroom omelet?"

"She did."

*Crap.* "But that isn't proof that the *poisonous* mushrooms came from her omelet."

Roger smiled sadly at Maggie as if disappointed in her. "She served him a mushroom omelet. He died of poisoned mushrooms. I feel pretty sure that will be enough to convict. The Chief Prosecutor shares my confidence."

"Were there *non*poisonous mushrooms in his stomach?" Roger frowned. "That is irrelevant."

"But of course it isn't, not at all. If Julia served him an omelet with *non*-tainted mushrooms and someone else—"

"Oh, how I have missed your theories, Maggie," Roger said with no trace of amusement or pleasure on his face. "They are like watching a very interesting detective show. No basis in fact but endlessly entertaining."

"I guess this conviction would be a pretty big feather in your cap."

"No feathers involved. Just doing my job."

"Is Julia saying she didn't do it?"

"Of course."

"Can you at least arrange for me to see her?"

Their food arrived and Roger waited until the waiter had left before answering.

"Is your husband okay with your going to the prison to see her? It is not a nice place, especially in your condition."

"Yes, he's fine with it, thanks. When?"

Roger shrugged. "Follow me back to the office. If she is not with her attorney you may see her for a few minutes."

Annette grabbed the buzzing cellphone and slipped out of bed with it. She gave a quick glance to the large, somnolent form entangled in the bed sheets behind her before she stepped into the bath and pulled the door shut.

"*Maman?* Are you there?"

"Yes, Michelle," Annette whispered, turning on the water in the sink to cover her voice. "I am here. What did the police say?"

A sound of impatience and disgust came over the phone connection. "It was as you said," Michelle said. "They took my statement and released me. It was nothing. Who did you talk to?"

Annette sighed heavily and sat down on the closed toilet. She noticed her hands were shaking. "It doesn't matter. A friend."

"A very *good* friend, *Maman*," Michelle said, her voice heavy with sarcasm, "to allow me to walk free this morning with not even a fine after I admitted to destroying the English whore's apartment."

"You admitted it?" Annette gasped, a hand flying to her throat. *The stupid girl! Was she trying to end up in jail?*

"Why not? It was clear that I had an angel looking out for me. The police are so stupid."

"Michelle, be quiet!" Annette was on her feet in her agitation. The sudden appearance of her reflection in the mirror made her jerk her head in that direction. Not a good move. The woman looking back at her was haggard and wan, worn and *old*. She turned her head away. "Even my connections have limits. As do I! Why did you do such a crazy thing?" As soon as the words were out of her mouth, Annette regretted them. Her daughter was very sensitive to certain labels.

"Really, *Maman*? You think it insane to punish the woman who ruined your life? Ruined *our* lives? I am only sorry it wasn't the *putain's face* I was smashing with the axe."

"She is paying, Michelle," Annette said. "She will pay— with her life. That is enough."

Her daughter laughed, and the sound made Annette's skin tingle and creep. She had heard that sound before. That terrible sound, before terrible things…happened.

"It is never enough, *Maman*. You of all people should know that."

# Chapter Seven

The *cellule de prison* where Julia was being held was like any detainment center at any police facility in a midsize city. Located at the top of the *Palais de Justice* on Rue Mejanes was an ugly five-story building built in the last twenty years. The set of four minimum security holding cells looked as bleak and basic as Maggie would have imagined they'd be.

Roger had handed her off with a brief handshake to a uniformed officer, who had her empty her pockets and took her purse after itemizing its contents. It was just as well that she hadn't been able to retrieve any of Julia's clothes from the apartment—the idea that she might be able to give Julia anything was laughable.

The officer escorted her down a long, irregularly lit hallway that led to a waiting room, where another officer briefly patted her down and then unlocked the door that led to the holding cells. With all the locked doors she was walking through, it was pretty clear that any sort of unauthorized entering—or exiting—would be impossible. She was taken to a stark, bare room with two windows—both high up and barred —furnished only with a single metal table, bolted to the cement floor.

The thought of Julia having already spent two full days in this place brought tears to Maggie's eyes but she brushed them away. She glanced at the two silently malevolent video cameras that hung in opposite corners of the room. If *she* felt like crying, it was easy to imagine Julia was going to be in much worse shape than she'd feared.

When the door finally unlatched with a jarring clang, Maggie whirled around to face the entrance. For Julia's sake, Maggie tried not to cry. But when her friend entered, Maggie instantly broke into tears.

Julia wore a baggy orange jumpsuit that made her look smaller and more vulnerable than she normally did. Her gamin cap of curls was limp and unwashed, and even from across the room Maggie could see the encroaching line of gray at her part. When Julia saw her, she covered her face with her hands. Maggie ran to her and pulled her into her arms, holding her tightly, feeling her bones through the jumpsuit. The guard left the room and clanged the heavy door shut behind her.

For a moment, the two friends stood together without speaking, the sounds of Julia's ragged weeping echoing off the bare walls of the room. Maggie's own tears had quickly given away to a steely anger the moment she touched Julia. *That anyone could have the power to reduce a person to this!* Only yesterday, Julia had been vibrant and beautiful, impish and in control. She wasn't the same person today, so broken and lost.

Maggie drew Julia to the table and urged her to sit on it with her. She had nothing with which to wipe her friend's tears so she used her fingers to wipe them away, then held Julia's hands tightly in her own.

"This won't last, Jules. I swear it won't last much longer."

Julia withdrew a hand and wiped at her tears, but more took their place. Her face was lined and slack.

"Are you eating?" Maggie knew it was a stupid question but she didn't know what else to say. Julia had no control over what was happening to her, but she could at least keep her strength up.

Julia shook her head. "I can't," she said, her voice a whimper.

Maggie rubbed a hand up her friend's arm. Never before had she so accurately seen a representation of someone who was literally a shadow of her former self. The transformation had happened so quickly and so severely Maggie was having trouble recognizing the friend she had known so well for the last several months. If it weren't for the head of curls, even the graying deflated curls, she might not have recognized her.

"This won't last," Maggie said again, although her stomach twisted when she said it. Honestly, she had no idea if the current situation would last or not. Roger had told her at lunch that because Julia was English, she was considered a flight risk and wouldn't be eligible for bail. *It might very well last*, she thought miserably, looking at her friend. *It might, in fact, go on for months and months.*

"My attorney is not optimistic."

"We'll get you another one."

"I don't think it will help."

"Has the British consulate been in to see you?"

"They are who arranged for the useless attorney."

"Is there anything I can get for you?" Maggie felt so helpless. She felt guilty too, for the fact that she would be able to walk out of that claustrophobic, unhappy room when it was time.

"I didn't kill him, Maggie," Julia said, her face pinched and searching. She squeezed Maggie's hands and Maggie resisted the urge to pull away. "I swear I didn't kill him. I mean, there were plenty of times that I wanted to and, honestly, even now I'm not sorry he's dead—"

"Jules, don't talk," Maggie murmured. "The room is monitored."

"I mean, I spent about five minutes astounded that he was gone and then the rest of the time, absolutely delighted."

"Julia, shut up," Maggie said fiercely. "Are you saying this shit to your counsel? Or the police?"

"I don't know," Julia said miserably. "I'm not used to watching my words. I am an artist. I express myself."

"Well, don't. At least not while you're in here. It's all very well not to like someone, but when they fall down dead and people are pointing a finger at you don't talk about how much you didn't like them. Okay?"

"They say I poisoned him."

"I know."

"And that the mushroom omelet I made is what killed him, but that's impossible."

"How so? It would be really helpful to your defense if you can answer that with something tangible."

"I made it with Death Trumpets, not *agaricus.*"

"Is there another name for Death Trumpets that doesn't sound quite so indicting?" Maggie asked in frustration. "I mean, are you going around telling people you fed him *Death Trumpets*?"

"Well, I *did* feed him Death Trumpets," Julia said, her eyes wide and innocent. "I ate them myself."

"The toxicology report says the *agaricus* mushrooms were found in his stomach in addition to other kind of mushrooms."

"But I didn't put them there!"

"They said they found traces of *agaricus* on your clothes."

"Well, they would. I come across all kinds of mushrooms when I forage. There's bound to be spores or whatnot on my shoes or my pants cuffs. But I don't collect poisonous ones! What about my kitchen? They haven't found anything there, have they?"

"Both your kitchen and your car were open to the world for several hours after your arrest. Anybody could've come in and planted poisonous mushrooms."

Julia stared at Maggie with her mouth open. "Are you... are you telling me they found *agaricus* mushrooms in my kitchen?"

*Damn Roger and damn that stupid attorney! Were they not informing her of anything?*

"No." Maggie took a long breath. "In the trunk of your car."

"Then I'm dead." Julia spoke simply. She turned and looked at the wall and blinked.

"No, you're not dead. You didn't kill him and someone is trying to make it look like you did. Probably the same someone who did kill him."

Julia acted as if she hadn't heard. "I cannot believe this is happening to me."

"Julia, please have a little faith. I'm not going to let whomever is doing this get away with it. I promise you. Listen to me!" Maggie turned Julia's face to her and looked into her eyes. "Have a little faith in *me*."

The tears in Julia's eyes welled up again and Maggie saw the numbness begin to ebb away, revealing the depth of her tortured feelings.

"Help me, Maggie," she said, her eyes frantic and fearful. "Please help me."

"I will, Jules. I promise."

An hour later, Maggie pulled into the driveway of *Domaine St-Buvard*. The rain had held off but the cool wind, a precursor to the coming winter, whipped the dead leaves on her front porch in a whirling maelstrom. The perimeter of the drive was lined with cars, and while the harvest hadn't officially begun, she knew Laurent was only hours—if that—from making the decision of when to pick.

*Perfect timing,* she thought with resignation, *as usual.* It was still only late afternoon so she expected Laurent to be out in his vineyard. She wondered for a moment if she should have swung by Danielle's to see if Zou-zou had been deposited there for the day. Danielle was childless, and had been only too happy to act as stand-in *Grandmère.* Maggie double-checked her cellphone but there had been no text from Laurent. Not that that was unusual.

Laurent, although not exactly anti-technology, was at the best resistant to it. Half the time he left his cellphone behind at restaurants, or in taxicabs and public restrooms. He would have at least called, she reasoned, if she was needed to collect the baby. That just left Grace. Feeling a needle of guilt for having left her alone all day, Maggie collected the packages from her market shopping in town—bread, to be sure, and a large bag of *macarons* from Bechard, just because—and hurried into the *mas.*

As soon as she stepped across the threshold, she was struck by how quiet it was. Even little Petit Four, usually so quick to greet her, was nowhere to be seen.

She moved quickly up the stairs and tapped on Grace's bedroom door. Not hearing an answer, she hesitated and then pushed the door open. Grace watched her solemnly from the bed. Little Petit Four was snuggled up on the bed with her.

"Hey, I didn't mean to wake you," Maggie said. "But if you're up for it, I've got a job for Lucy and Ethel." She came into the room and held up the bag of *macarons.*

Grace eased herself to a sitting position on the bed and smiled sleepily at her. She reached out for the bag and Maggie handed it to her.

"You not been up yet?" Maggie asked cautiously. She went to the window to open the curtains but Grace moaned.

"No light yet, darling," she said, biting into one of the cream *macarons* and settling the bag on the bedside table. "I'm not feeling quite myself this morning."

"It's like three o'clock in the afternoon, Grace," Maggie said, frowning.

Grace leaned back into her pillows. Even without a stitch of makeup on she was effortlessly beautiful, Maggie thought. *Even sad and eating cookies in bed in the middle of the afternoon.*

"Danielle and I are going to Jacques's aunt's house to give our condolences," Maggie said.

"You know his aunt?"

"No, but Danielle does."

"So you're using Danielle to question the aunt."

"I'll have you know she is delighted for me to accompany her."

"So you can ditch her as soon as you're through the door and start rooting around in the aunt's attic looking for clues? I *know* you, Maggie."

"Your point?"

"Does Laurent know?"

"That's the second time you've asked me if I'm going behind Laurent's back. Maybe you should focus on your own marital dirty laundry."

"Oh, touché, darling. You really got me there. Did you ever think I might be trying to *help* you avoid the pitfalls that have brought me to such a sad state of affairs?"

"Oh, give me a break, Grace. Like you ever felt you had to hide anything from Windsor. Has he *ever* said *no* to you?"

Grace smiled sadly. "Almost never."

"So, what *was* the problem?"

"Like most complicated situations, Maggie, I'm afraid it can't be summed up in an easily digestible sound byte."

"Did you or did you not leave him? Or are you telling me he threw *you* out?"

"He's found someone else, alright? Are you happy now?"

"I don't believe it."

"Well, it's true."

"Was this before or after you gave up on the marriage?"

"Are you saying I drove him into the arms of another woman? Really original, Maggie. And supportive. Thanks a lot."

"Well, did you?"

"Look, we haven't been getting along for a while now."

"Have you gone to counseling?"

"Like that helps."

"Do you *want* to work it out?"

"I don't know. Maybe not."

"Grace, you have kids!"

"Thanks. Because I'd forgotten that for a minute."

"At least be honest, if not with me, then yourself. This girlfriend isn't the real problem, is she?"

"Well, she doesn't help."

"You were looking for a way out."

"And if I was, Maggie? Did it ever occur to you to wonder *why* that might be?"

"He hit you?"

"There are worse things."

"Such as."

"Am I supposed to live without love in my life?"

"You have two kids, Grace."

"And I know you're all excited about your own plan to add to the world population, Maggie, so I hate to be the one to tell you, but having kids is not all it's cracked up to be." Grace looked away, her face a mask of misery and hunger. "And I need more."

Maggie turned on her heel and walked out of the room, careful to slam the door behind her.

When Maggie and Danielle drove up the long, winding driveway in the village of Lignane, halfway between St-Buvard and Aix, that led to Lily Tatois's mansion, Maggie was grateful for both her friend's happy chatter and the distraction of baby Zou-zou. It had seemed easier to just bring her with them rather than risk another confrontation with Grace, who didn't appear to be in much of a motherly or babysitting mood as it was.

Besides, Z, as *Oncle* Laurent had started calling her (only it sounded like "Zed" when he said it) was *such* a good baby. As toddlers go, Maggie knew she was probably not getting a representative sampling of the typical behavior and tried not to count on it too much with her little one.

"Oh, Lily will be so distraught," Danielle said, smoothing out Zou-zou's baby-fine hair from one of the child's barrettes. Z sat on Danielle's lap. Maggie knew she should be restrained in a child seat, but she didn't have one and Grace hadn't travelled with one. It was first on her shopping list the next trip she made to Aix, if Laurent didn't beat her to it.

"Do you know her well?" Maggie asked as she navigated the long gravel drive. Several cars were parked on the grassy perimeter of the drive, pressing down the high grass and weeds to manageable levels.

"Oh, yes. We were in school together. Those boys meant everything to her. Jacques and Florrie. She never married, herself. They were her life."

"Oh, that's sad," Maggie said, her hand unconsciously dropping to her touch her stomach. "Were they close, do you know?"

"How many times Lily has told me of how devoted her nephews are to her. Especially Florrie, who I think is her favorite."

"I only met Jacques a couple of times, Danielle, but I have to say he didn't strike me as the maiden-aunt-visiting type. He was kind of a jerk."

"Maggie, I am not comfortable speaking this way about the recently departed. The poor man is passed. We should pray for the repose of his soul."

"Yeah, sure," Maggie said. "Sorry."

Maggie parked the car on the grass at the base of the circular drive. The *mas* was larger than *Domaine St-Buvard* but not as well maintained, although Danielle said Lily had servants. Maggie let Danielle bring Z while she grabbed the basket of the obligatory tarts and cookies that Danielle had prepared. She was surprised at how many people had come to offer their condolences to Jacques's aunt. Then again, the woman was quite wealthy.

The minute they stepped into the house, Maggie was assailed by the noise of at least fifty people crowded in the foyer and spilling over into the adjoining dining room and salon. Jacques may not have been the most popular man in Aix, but his aunt was clearly loved. Maggie made her way to the food table, where she set out Danielle's pies and then returned to her friend to offer to take Z.

"We are fine," Danielle said, holding onto the now squirming baby. "I just want to give my condolences and then we can leave. I know no one else here." Danielle clucked Z under the chin. "We will first just go and find a cookie, yes?"

Maggie realized she would need to act fast if she wanted to talk with Lily for more than just a few seconds. Peering into the salon, she saw what looked like a receiving line moving in the direction of a large throne-like chair in which sat a beaming white-haired woman. *Whoa. Not looking too torn up, is she?* Maggie edged into the room and plucked a glass of sherry from the tray of a passing caterer.

She didn't like the idea of asking any questions so publicly —especially with people waiting behind her in line to talk to the old lady—but a quick memory of poor Julia's tear-streaked, desperate face this afternoon fortified her conviction and she went and stood in line.

Looking around the room, it was clear that whatever fortune Lily had wasn't being spent on updating the décor or furnishings of the *mas*. The couches and draperies looked worn and in need of mending. The overall effect was shabby, but still held the essence of elegance. And Lily herself was pulling off the whole *grande dame* thing with experience and aplomb. Something about her—the way she held herself and greeted the minions there to give homage to her—reminded Maggie of Grace. She felt her stomach twist unpleasantly at the thought. She could not remember ever having a fight with Grace that had felt even close to anything like this. This *thing* that had happened between them felt divisive and…permanent.

As soon as she got close enough to smell the dowager's perfume, Maggie could see that she was flanked by family members who were also greeting the mourners in the line. A man who looked like he could have been Jacques's brother, and so must be cousin Florian, sat to the immediate left of Lily. His eyes were red-rimmed and he held one of his aunt's hands in his own.

To Lily's right sat none other than the deceased's daughter, Michelle, who was in the process of glaring daggers at Maggie. The woman next to Michelle must be Jacques's ex-wife, Annette. Maggie had assumed she might see these two here, but it hadn't occurred to her the confrontation would be so direct. It did occur to her as she edged closer to the two glowering women that perhaps this wasn't going to be the best time to do anything but say *sorry for your troubles* and leave as quickly as possible.

The thought came to her that Grace's sarcasm had been closer to the mark when she suggested that Maggie dispense with the attempt to question anyone and just slip off to poke around the house. *Too late now.*

"Hello, Madame Tatois," Maggie said, stepping forward to shake hands with Lily and deftly handing her sherry glass to Michelle, who took it without thinking. "I am so sorry for your loss."

Lily murmured something complicated in French, but before Maggie could attempt to respond Michelle blurted out, "She is a friend of Papa's *murderer*, Aunt Lily!"

When her aunt turned to her in confusion, Annette took the opportunity to clamp a heavy hand down on her daughter's arm, spilling Maggie's sherry on her sleeve. "Not *now*, Michelle," she hissed through clenched teeth.

Before a full-fledged family brawl could erupt, Maggie moved on quickly to Florrie and extended her hand. "And you must be Florian, Jacques's cousin," she said hurriedly, aware that Michelle was standing up now. "My husband, Laurent Dernier, sends his condolences, as he was not able to accompany me today."

"You are Laurent's wife?"

"Yes, and again, our deepest condolences."

"I tell you, she is connected to the person who killed Papa! Why is nobody listening to me?"

Unfortunately, it looked to Maggie as if too many people were listening to Michelle, as the noise level and rate of heads twisting to see toward the front of the line had noticeably increased.

Michelle grabbed Maggie's arm and twisted her to face her. "American whore!" she shrieked and threw the contents of her sherry glass into Maggie's face. Maggie gasped and reached out blindly, the alcohol stinging her eyes, the fumes choking her. She could feel the liquid seeping down the front of her dress.

"Michelle!" Florrie cried out. "She is a guest in our house!"

"This is not *your* house, you *crapaud*!" Michelle screamed. As Maggie struggled to see through the burning alcohol, she felt the girl grab her by the arms, her nails digging sharply into her flesh. "Get OUT!" Michelle screamed.

Maggie began to fall backwards as Michelle gripped her, and thrashed out with her arms in a panic to try to prevent the fall. Michelle jerked away from her, leaving a trail of bloody scratches down Maggie's bare arms. Maggie pawed at her face to wipe away the alcohol as she stumbled away from the group. When she opened her eyes, she saw that Florrie was holding Michelle with both hands, his face florid and stunned and looking at Maggie.

"Take her away to compose herself," Lily said to Florrie, who began to drag Michelle away.

"Are you mad? She helped plan Papa's murder! She is the accomplice to the murdering whore!" Michelle's shrieks and threats continued until they faded into the far recesses of the house.

Lily leaned over and spoke quickly to Annette who, giving Maggie a look of pure hatred, stood and addressed the receiving line. "Aunt Lily is tired now. I am sorry. If you will write in the condolences book, there will be no more visits today. Thank you all for coming." When she finished she turned to Lily, but the old woman was already beckoning Maggie to come closer.

"You knew my nephew, Madame?" Lily asked her. Her voice was kind but her eyes, now that Maggie really looked at them, seemed cloudy and vague.

"I did, Madame Tatois," Maggie said, rubbing her arms and forcing herself *not* to look at Annette, who she could feel was glaring at her. "And I am so sorry to meet you under these circumstances."

"It is true," Lily said, nodding but now seeming to talk to no one in particular. "Florrie was always the one good with money. I'm afraid Jacques wouldn't have known what to do with it."

*Okay, so that made absolutely no sense at all.*

With that, Lily turned to Annette, who began to help the woman out of her chair. Maggie didn't waste her opportunity to escape. She saw Danielle standing in the now dismissed and disintegrating receiving line with little Zou-zou in her arms. Her mouth was open in shock as Maggie motioned her to the door.

# Chapter Eight

Laurent's vineyard was as neat and tidy as a hausfrau's linen closet. Every row was weeded, every mound raked, every graceful green bough of grapes draped and staked as meticulously as a careful line of stitches in the earth. Maggie wasn't surprised that Laurent gardened they way he cooked—with organized fervor.

Their kitchen rarely had a spoon or sauce pan out of place. As she stood with him at the furthest point from the house at the north side of his vineyard, she had to smile when she thought of how his lovemaking, impulsive and passionate, was nothing like his gardening.

"You think this is funny?"

She sobered up and shoved her hands in her pockets, squinting down at the carefully raked ground in front of her as if in studious concentration. She had been careful to put on a long sleeve sweater to cover the scratch marks she'd received at Jacques's wake, but had no real hope that Laurent didn't know everything that had happened today. Somehow, he always did.

"Not at all," she said. "I am taking it very seriously."

Laurent stood next to her, his long hair thick and wild around his face, the stiff breeze pushing it without restraint. He looked a little wild himself, she thought. His eyes were flashing, and while they constantly surveyed his grapes and fields, she didn't mistake for a moment that his thoughts were anywhere but solidly on her.

"Have you seen Grace today?" she asked.

"I brought a tray up to her at midday."

"Did you speak?"

"She was sleeping. I left the tray."

"We had words," Maggie said. "Before I left with Danielle. I know Grace is upset. I'm afraid I made her more upset."

As soon as she mentioned leaving with Danielle, she knew she had made a tactical error. The *last* thing she wanted to do was remind Laurent that she'd had a drink flung in her face and a crazy woman launch herself at her. At a condolences call. While eight months pregnant.

Laurent sighed heavily. "We must come to an understanding, Maggie," he said to her, still not looking at her. "Very little do I deny you, I think, yes?"

She sighed herself instead of answering him.

"But this I must. You are to stop working on this *investigation* unless I am with you."

"Laurent, we've talked about this before—"

"*Oui!* And always the answer is the same."

"So I'd think you'd get tired of asking the same question."

"I am not asking any questions, Maggie. I am your husband. Am I not?"

"That is irrelevant to my working on this case."

He made a Gallic snorting sound that she had heard before. Usually it was over the incompetence of some groundsman or shopkeeper and it annoyed her to hear it used for her.

"If I cannot demand of you to do as I say for your own sake—and certainly not because you respect your husband's wishes—then I must demand that you stop bringing valuable items of mine along with you. Items that may become damaged or lost."

"Oh, for heaven's sake, Laurent. Are you talking about the baby? Because obviously I can't leave the baby behind."

*"Exactement."*

"Okay, nice try. You should've gone into law or something. We are at a stalemate, dearest. *Est-ce que tu comprends stalemate?"*

"I thought we had seen the last of these arguments over your *sleuthing*, Maggie." He said the word as if it had a bad taste to it.

"We had. But that was because I was led to believe you accepted my doing it under certain circumstances."

*"Oui,"* he said, tossing down a dead vine he had been holding in his hand. "Not. While. You. Are. Pregnant."

Maggie sighed and reached out to him to steady herself as she turned to face the house.

"While it's true we didn't write that particular clause into the final agreement..."

"You are being funny again. *Moi, je le deteste!"*

"If it's any consolation, I hate it, too. But where does that leave us?"

"I will go with you." He gave one last look at his vineyard.

"How can you do that? Aren't you set to start harvesting any minute now?"

He shrugged.

"Okay, Laurent, stop it. That's just childish. You can't come with me or else your whole year ends up in the crapper. It's just bad timing."

He gave her a side look from under his eyebrows, his full lips in a stubborn line.

"No, Laurent," she said firmly. "I can't let Julia rot in jail any more than you can let your grapes rot on the vines."

The two stood together for a moment, Maggie facing the house and Laurent's chin resolutely set in the other direction, toward his vines. After a moment, Maggie slipped her hand into his.

"I promise I won't take any chances, Laurent," she said softly. "I promise I won't do anything to endanger me or the baby." She watched his face and could see the battle he fought to believe her. "I promise."

Without answering, he turned and drew her into his arms. He was too tall to rest his chin on the top of her head, but Maggie squeezed him tight.

"I promise," she said again, her words muffled by his thick cotton sweater.

The next morning, Laurent left the house before Maggie. She knew he would be with the other *vignerons* in his co–op most of the day, deciding exactly when to pick and dividing up the labor as they did every year. She noticed he left her the car and she felt a rush of affection for him. She knew he only wanted her to stay safe, and it was true that a few incidents in the past had led to some very close calls for her. It was also true that this time she had more than just herself to think about.

In the end they had compromised. Maggie agreed to stop questioning total strangers about the case and Laurent agreed to allow her to continue to visit Julia in the detention facility in Aix.

She had yet to mention her meetings with Roger, and since Laurent didn't ask she felt it best to just leave it alone. After all, she wasn't doing anything wrong and she had absolutely nothing to feel guilty about. And she *did* need to know what Roger knew about the case that was developing against Julia. She was aware that possibly Laurent had a baseline assumption she would not see Roger, but she assuaged her guilt with the belief that she had no control over what he assumed if he didn't voice it to her.

She had a few hours before her first appointment, so she parked the car and walked down the Cours to the first outdoor café she came to. The plane trees, fast losing all their blossoms and their leaves, still provided gentle shade in addition to the ubiquitous blue umbrellas that stood at each table. She sat down facing the Cours—always the best for people watching—and ordered a *macchiato* from the waiter. There was a time, she knew, not so long ago, that she couldn't have enjoyed this moment without comparing it to Atlanta. She remembered how Grace used to laugh at that.

"San Francisco, maybe, darling," she had said. "But I've *been* to Atlanta. To long for it when you see this is just addled."

Maggie smiled now, remembering. At the time, Maggie had argued that Grace hadn't seen the real Atlanta: the dense heavy trees that covered most of the town, the breath-stopping dogwood and azaleas that erupted every spring making you forget you lived in a real place and not some magical Arcadia. Grace hadn't seen the stately mansions of Buckhead or Piedmont Park after the first snow. She hadn't known Margaret Mitchell Square or Midtown in its heyday. *And those were all very good arguments for someone desperately homesick,* Maggie mused as she took her first sip of her *espresso*. The beauty of the Atlanta that she knew—the one she grew up in—was tucked away in the memories she had of the special times there. Because nothing, or very little, she realized now, could compete with the beauty she saw almost every single day of her life in Provence.

From the dusty village roads to the endless fields of lavender to the dramatic evidence of Roman architecture that seemed to materialize at the oddest moments. Had she ever had her breath taken away shopping for plums in Atlanta? (Had she ever even shopped for plums in Atlanta?) That happened daily here.

After nearly five years of living surrounded by all this natural beauty—not to mention what the Romans had brought to the table over a thousand years ago—Maggie had finally gotten to the point where she was happy where she was. And all the losses she had tallied on her long list of *things she had left behind* seemed like nothing to her now when she saw all that she had.

And at the very top of *that* list was Laurent. Her hand settled on her stomach as she thought of him, a smile edging her lips. They had not even talked about having children. She had had no idea, beyond the fact he seemed to be good with kids, if he even wanted children. Truth be told, she hadn't been too sure about it herself.

She had watched Grace and Win struggle first with Taylor—a brilliant hellion of a child—and then with the process of trying to become pregnant again. In fact, Grace's agony during that bad year of injections and IVF procedures was not unlike what she seemed to be going through now. The thought surprised Maggie. Up until now, she had been focusing on how selfish Grace was to want to break up the family. She thought back to her friend's misery and desperation when it looked like she couldn't conceive again, when every attempt ended in failure. Until, of course, little Zou-zou happened. Maggie sat up in her chair as a bad thought struck her. *Is it possible that Grace and Win's present problems have to do with the question of Z's true paternity?* When they left France eighteen months ago Win had staunchly announced that it didn't matter. Perhaps, somewhere along the line, it had started to?

If a DNA test had finally put an end to the doubt and speculation, it might well explain why Grace and Z came to France alone. As Maggie was imagining this, her cellphone rang and she saw it was her editor. She had let the prior two calls yesterday go straight to voicemail, but now she hesitated.

Maggie watched as her phone continued to vibrate against the café table until it finally fell silent. She knew it was rude not to call her back, but what was there to say? She hadn't done the edits requested of her. She had no idea *when* she'd be able to get to them. If ever. It was pretty obvious she was going to miss her deadline. Her editor was probably calling to demand the return of her advance. Paltry though it was, it had already been spent months ago. And why? Why had she lost interest in the one thing that had been so exciting for her just two months earlier?

Maggie motioned to the waiter for her bill. *Was it the corrections themselves?* Her editor at the publishers was pretty smart, and most of the things she pointed out in Maggie's story needed fixing. Maggie could see that. She dropped a handful of euros on the table and stood to leave. No, it was just the feeling of being overwhelmed. Not just by the baby, but Julia and, of course, Grace. There was just too much going on right now.

*Was a stupid book more important than her best friend spending the rest of her life in a foreign prison?*

As she walked down the bricked pedestrian walk way of the Cours, the sky blotted out completely by the arching plane trees over the center, Maggie vowed to call her editor back and explain why she was going to miss the deadline. *Who knows?* Maybe she'd even be sympathetic.

She hadn't really come off like that up to now, but maybe she would understand. Maggie slowed her gait and felt a stab of sciatica in her lower back. She massaged it with her hand and caught a glimpse of herself in a store window as she passed. *Whoa. That is one big girl there.* She eyed her large, protruding stomach critically and wondered if the doctor could possibly have gotten his dates wrong. *I look like I'm about to drop any minute!*

She noticed she was on the street that led to the *L'ecole Primaire* in Aix. She remembered that Taylor had gone there for a year before more specialized education was required. Her heart beat with excitement when she realized that *this* is where *her* child would go when he or she was old enough.

The leaves from the plane trees were scattered across the sidewalk, which was lined with wrought iron fences, through which poked a colorful display of red geraniums and the pretty purple *clochette* that seemed to grow everywhere. *It's just like the school in the Madeline storybooks,* she thought, smiling. True, it was a long way to come every day from St-Buvard, but she and Laurent had already discussed it and decided it was best.

She'd stopped to give her back a break, when a disorderly queue of school children erupted from the lane off the Cours in front of her. She stood back, delighted, and watched them as they crossed the street, their teacher herding them as if they were a hoard of unruly lambs. The children were dressed in colorful scarves and caps, *tabliers* and backpacks. Their chatter came to Maggie in snatches of childish, excitable French. She grinned and put her hand on her stomach. *That'll be you someday, cherub. Speaking French like you were born to it instead of laboring over every consonant like your Maman. Mind you*, she thought, as she turned and began her walk up to the detention center, *you'll speak English like a native, too.*

The waiting room at the *Commissariat d'Aix en Provence* was sterile and uncomfortable. Maggie had an image of a French home décor designer sitting down with the Aix chief of police to get the goal for the room.

*"Well, of course, we do not want certain kinds of people to become comfortable here, yes?"*

*"Exactement! They are the family and friends of France's lowest criminal element."*

*"I can make the seats so hard they will not want to stay a minute longer than necessary."*

*"Do it!"*

*"I can paint the walls the exact color of the vomit they slept in the night before in order to ensure they will prefer not to remain."*

*"Excellent!"*

Maggie squirmed uncomfortably in the hard seat and glanced at the digital clock over the locked door that led to the warren of detectives' offices. Or they might just have opted for the cheapest possible alternative to a waiting area and this is where they landed, she thought reasonably. Although she did have to admit, she shared the waiting room with some pretty nasty looking characters—and given the intensity with which they stared at her, most of them had never seen a pregnant woman before.

"Maggie?" She looked up to see Roger standing in an open door, beckoning her toward him. She pulled herself to her feet and tried very hard not to *lumber* over to him. Perhaps because of the stares of the riff-raff in the waiting room, Roger dispensed with the cheek kissing this time and just led her back to his large, windowless office.

Maggie had been in Roger's office in Arles several times when the two of them had worked together. He'd clearly had a promotion in more ways than just his title. While still lacking a view—*such a shame in a town like Aix!*—the office was well furnished and obviously reflected his new, higher rank. He gestured to a chair across from his desk and Maggie gratefully eased into it. *Crap.* Now even her feet were starting to ache.

"You are well, Maggie?" Roger asked, not looking at her, not smiling.

"Yes, thanks, Roger," she said brightly. "And you?"

"Fine, *merci*. What is it I can help you with today?"

"Well, first let me thank you again for allowing me to come and see you. I know how busy you are, and now I see how important you are, too." She waved a hand at his office.

He looked at her from beneath his eyebrows, registering her light sarcasm. She thought for a moment he was fighting a smile, but if so he won the fight.

"Your purpose today?"

"I have some questions about Julia Patrick's case."

"I have released all pertinent information to the media."

"That's funny. I didn't read anything about the case in the paper."

He looked at her blankly.

"Oh," she said. "I see. Good one, Roger. Nothing pertinent to report."

"Is that all?"

"Nope." Maggie pulled out a piece of paper—one side was clearly a grocery list of some kind. She squinted at the other side. "Oh, yeah," she said. "The crime scene was compromised."

"That is not a question."

"Okay, Roger, I'll rephrase. How can you use evidence found at a crime scene that has been tampered with?"

"How do you know evidence was affected?"

"How do you know it wasn't?"

He shrugged.

"Someone's life is on the line here, Roger," Maggie said, fighting to keep her composure. *Why is he acting like such a dick?*

He took a breath and seemed to come to an answer on some internal struggle he had been having. "The poisonous mushrooms found in Madame Patrick's car will not be admissible as evidence," he said finally.

"Thank God!"

He looked at her quickly. "Just because a jury won't know about them doesn't mean that everyone else—the prosecution, the police, the victim's family, eventually the media—won't know. Their existence is very damning *and* pertinent to building our case against the suspect."

"Okay. Whatever all that means. Question two: what was Annette Tatois doing the night in question? My understanding is she hated him."

"That is none of your affair. Besides, Madame Tatois has a firm alibi for the time of his death."

"Well, that's the other thing. How can that be? Unlike shooting or stabbing, my understanding is that when you poison someone, you don't have to actually *be* there when the victim has his last seizure, you know? I would have thought it would be more important to nail down Annette *and* Michelle's whereabouts for about twelve hours *before* he died."

"It seems our Medical Examiner disagrees with you."

"Then your Medical Examiner is an idiot."

"Of course. As is anyone who disagrees with you, *n'est-ce pas?* Are we done?"

"Roger, you are taking the easy way out here." She forced herself not to say, *again.* "You have no confession and everything you do have is circumstantial. That's not enough to convict."

"*Au contraire*, Maggie," Roger said heatedly, his calm façade falling off him with each word. "Circumstances dictate fact and they always have. What do you Americans say? Where there is smoke, you will find the fire? Madame Patrick is covered in smoke."

"Fine," Maggie said, trying to hide her frustration with him. "It looks like I am going to be forced to do your job since you won't. I intend to talk with Madame and Mademoiselle Tatois, and anyone else who wanted Jacques dead."

Roger clenched his fists against the table. "You will not talk with them!"

"Oh, yes, I will," Maggie said. "You can't stop me. It is a free country. Which, by the way, *you're welcome.*"

Roger stood up, fists on the desk, and leaned toward her. "I will speak with your husband. Perhaps he can control you."

Maggie didn't like the sound of that, but she stood up to face him nonetheless.

"Screw you," she said, putting her face close to his. Suddenly, she was aware of his cologne, how close his lips were to her own, the electricity snapping between them, and she emitted a small gasp at the realization. He must have felt it too, because his hand came up to her face, slowly, gently. And she did nothing to stop it.

But before he could touch her, she heard the whoosh of the door opening behind her. Flushing, Maggie took a step backward and stumbled over her chair. She caught herself and stood, knees shaking, wondering what had just happened.

"Roger?"

The sound of the woman's voice—and by the form of address clearly not an underling—made Maggie snap her head to the door, where the figure of a beautiful young woman stood gaping at them. She was svelte, blonde and younger than Maggie by at least ten years. She entered the office and shut the door behind her. Maggie was impressed with her confidence. She knew she wouldn't have had as much at her age. She wasn't sure she had as much now.

"Have I interrupted something?" she asked coolly, appraising Maggie's bulky form with unfriendly eyes.

*It's true,* Maggie thought with amazement. *Even late stage pregnancy is not considered a deal breaker in matters of the French heart.*

"I was just leaving," Maggie said, refusing to look at Roger. *What had just happened?* "I can find my own way out." She hesitated in front of the woman, who blocked her exit, before she stepped out of the way and allowed Maggie to slip out the door. As Maggie hurried down the hall and across the disease-pocked waiting room, she thought she could hear raised voices behind her.

Michelle couldn't believe the *gall* of that woman. From where she sat in the outdoor café of the Rue de la Masse, she could easily see her as she pranced about in her provocatively bare running shorts and bra top. *Did she think she was in Houston?* She was clearly American. *Why did Aix have so many? Why weren't they in Paris? Or Nice?* She was probably a student here. Michelle literally felt her stomach turn when she saw the woman lean against a tall tree and pull her leg up behind her to stretch out her muscle.

"Did I keep you waiting, babe?" He came up behind her and kissed her on the cheek before she even knew he was there. Michelle struggled to regain the good mood she'd had before she'd seen the American whore. *Maman said they were all whores. Even worse than the English.*

He seated himself across from her blocking her view of the runner and she had to force herself not to twist in her seat to continue watching. Instead, she smiled at him knowing the smile would eventually reach her eyes if she kept at it. *Although he probably wouldn't know the difference.* She sat a little straighter in her chair, knowing the effect of her increased bosom would distract him from her wooden smile, if that was necessary.

"*Oui*," she said. "Don't you always? It is a little game you play, *non*?"

"No, it is not," he said, frowning in a clearly inauthentic way, his bottom lip protruding to form his idea of a pout. *Was he authentic about anything?* In a flash, an image developed in her mind of him on top of her, panting and sweating. *Yes, there were times.*

"You know how difficult it is for me to get away."

"So you insist."

"I can't just leave in the middle of the day, you know. You French may be used to taking three hour lunches, but I can tell you that wouldn't fly with my company." He looked around the café until he caught the eye of the waiter.

"Well?" she asked, peeking over his shoulder to see that the Lycra-clad American student had gone. "Can you stay for lunch?"

"Of course," he said easily. "That's why we're here, isn't it?"

"Have the police talked with you yet?"

His handsome face lost a shade of its luster. "Why in the world would they talk to me?" he asked, his voice guarded, eyes wary.

"You knew him."

"Many people knew him."

"You threatened him."

"And you know *why*." She saw his good mood was gone, replaced by a nervousness and agitation that had him plucking at the menu and tapping his ring—his *wedding* ring—against the ceramic ashtray on the table.

"The police don't really consider justifications, David," Michelle said, "when they look at their suspects."

"I thought you told me they had someone in custody."

"They do." Michelle shrugged and reached for her glass of rosé.

"Well, then why would they talk to me?"

"You're right," she said, shrugging. "No reason."

"I hope you weren't expecting me to be all sorry and full of consolation attempts, were you? Because you always said you hated him."

"I never said that."

"Well, maybe you just behaved that way, but the fact certainly remains. Christ, Michelle, why are we talking about him? Didn't he cause enough damage while he was alive?"

Michelle reached across the table and touched his hand. "You're right. Let's forget him. And let's forget this." She gathered up her purse and cellphone. "Throw some money down. My apartment is just around the corner."

From the stifling interior of her parked car, Maggie watched the two leave the café. Except for the brief hand touch they didn't look like lovers, but while menus had been delivered to them, they left the café without ordering. She fanned herself in the driver's seat and had to admit *that* sounded like the behavior of lovers.

*But what did that mean? So Michelle has a boyfriend. So what?* She waited until they were out of sight before she opened her car door to allow a breeze in. Her thighs were rubbing uncomfortably together, and while the late September weather wasn't exactly hot, neither was it cool and crisp. She felt wilted and clammy. A quick glance into the rear view mirror showed her face was an unattractive blotchy red.

*Roger ought to see me now. Or his girlfriend. She would definitely not be feeling jealous.*

*So Roger has a girlfriend.* Not sure why it surprised her, Maggie focused instead on the more salient fact, which was that she disliked the idea. *Was I just hoping he'd pine for me forever?* What kind of a torch was he carrying that allowed a girlfriend on the side? Knowing she was being ridiculous, Maggie tried to banish thoughts of Roger and his gorgeous girlfriend from her mind. She left the car, locked it, and began to walk in the direction Michelle had gone. With this section of *Cours Mirabeau* being one wide, long pedestrian walkway, she felt fairly sure she'd be able to keep Michelle in view without being spotted herself. Assuming the two were heading for a little afternoon *tête-à-tête*, Maggie didn't bother hurrying. She pulled out her cellphone and glanced at the time. It wasn't even three o'clock. She had plenty of time to wait out Michelle's tryst, talk to her, and get back to St-Buvard before dinner.

She watched the pair turn off of the *Cours,* and when she got to the corner she was just in time to see them enter an apartment building. She glanced around and spotted a bistro across the street. She would have felt too exposed in an outdoor café and was glad for the extra cover. As soon as she took a seat at a table by the window, however, she saw the man she thought was Michelle's companion burst out of the apartment building, his face like thunder. *Uh-oh. Lovers' tiff.*

That probably wouldn't bode well for Michelle's mood during Maggie's questioning.

Maggie waved away the approaching waiter and pulled herself out of the table. She wasn't sure exactly what she intended to do. She only knew she had to talk to Michelle because Roger wouldn't—or if he had he wasn't sharing. And as much as she wasn't looking forward to the next fifteen minutes—her arms had yet to scab over from her last meeting with the girl—all she really had to do was bring Julia's tear-stained and stricken face to mind to galvanize her into taking the next step.

And right now, the next step was crossing the street and punching the button to Michelle's apartment. Right after she used the bistro's facilities.

*That bastard! Did he really think she was so stupid she didn't see what he was trying to pull?* Michelle snatched up her cellphone and punched in her mother's number. As she listened to it ring, she padded into the kitchen and jerked open the refrigerator and extricated a Diet Coke. Her eyes glanced at the boning knife on her kitchen counter. *The worm was lucky we were in the bedroom when he got the call from his wife. Otherwise…*

"Michelle?"

"Oh, *Maman*. You are not going to believe what he's done now."

"Who? David?"

"He is still screwing his wife! He virtually admitted as much to me. You were right. You were right all along."

"Where are you, *chérie*? Are you home? I will come at once."

"No, don't bother. I am not staying here. I need to go out. I just wanted to tell you that I ended it finally."

"That is good, *chérie*. I know it hurts now but it is for the best. Are you sure you don't want me to come?"

"*Non, Maman*," Michelle said, her eyes still on the boning knife. "I don't want to see anyone right now. Oh, fuck. I have to go. Some idiot is buzzing me from downstairs."

Susan Kiernan-Lewis

# Chapter Nine

"I wouldn't for the world disturb you during your time of grief, except I thought you might want to know several hundred thousand euros were found in Madame Patrick's apartment, and I know for a fact they aren't Julia's."

Maggie had rehearsed the line so many times on the walk over to Michelle's apartment that she prayed it didn't come across wooden and mechanical. The girl already didn't trust her. On the other hand, it was entirely possible—and she was counting on this—that *what* she had to say would distract Michelle from *how* she said it.

Maggie forced herself not to look at the wicked looking kitchen knife that Michelle came to the door holding. *Expecting the return of her boyfriend, maybe?* She took a long breath and willed herself to look confident and sure of herself.

Michelle stood looking at her. "Say that again," she said finally, her lip curled in a snarl. "In English, this time."

"A small fortune in cash was recovered in—"

"Who recovered it? The police?"

Maggie tamped down the smile that wanted to burst through.

*She had her.*

"No, I found it after you left. Is it yours, then?"

Michelle took a step back into her apartment, which was all the invitation Maggie needed. She stepped forward.

"I didn't bring it with me today," Maggie said, "because I fear the rampant pickpockets in Aix. I, myself, have been a victim on two separate—"

"Yes, it is mine," Michelle said, practically licking her lips when she spoke.

"Very good. I'm glad to hear it. And I also wanted to take this opportunity to tell you that I am not, in fact, a friend of Julia Patrick's. Far from it. I am an animal lover, only, intent on the care and—"

"What were you doing at my Aunt Lily's home yesterday?"

Maggie was ready for that one. "That was a total coincidence," she said. "I am only a friend of a friend of your aunt's. My neighbor, as it happens—"

"Yes, yes, whatever. When can you bring me my money?"

"Immediately, Mademoiselle Tatois. I would be only too happy to do so. But as you can see, my burden is great and I was wondering if I could trouble you for a glass of water before I—"

Michelle emitted a snort of impatience and whirled on her heel. For a moment, Maggie wasn't positive she wouldn't come back with an even bigger knife, but when she returned she had a large plastic cup in her hand. Maggie took it gratefully and drank as slowly as she could, careful not to observe the girl over the cup as she did. Eventually, she was rewarded when Michelle slumped to a sitting position on the couch, and Maggie took the opportunity to sit, too.

"Thank you so much," Maggie said. "I have been tracking Monsieur Tatois for several months now and he—"

"*Tracking* him?"

"Well, my organization," Maggie said, placing the cup on the coffee table in front of her. "We are an anti-cruelty to animals organization, which is why I knew that Madame

Patrick possessed a lovebird that would need rescuing. We have been watching the two of them for quite awhile."

*Was the girl really crazy enough to buy this nonsense?* Maggie dearly hoped so.

"My father abused animals?"

"Oh, my heavens, yes! Very much so! Dogs, cats…that bird I rescued. Pigeons in the park. He has been on our watch list for a long time now."

"Well," Michelle said crossing her arms and glaring at Maggie. "I am not surprised. The man was despicable. It is well that he should have been monitored for his disgusting behavior."

"Monitored, yes." Maggie said. "My organization was very close to gathering the necessary evidence to ensure that Monsieur Tatois never bothered another one of God's gentle creatures again."

"So *you* killed him?"

"What? No! That's not what I meant. We believed we could be the authors of his incarceration with the state. It is against the law, you know, to abuse animals."

"Why did it take your organization…what is the name of it again?"

"Uh, the Anti-Abuse of Animals League."

"Why has it taken you so long to move against my father? And in the meanwhile, he has committed untold damage. Not just to stupid animals but to *people*! Did you know he was arrested last winter for the attempted rape of one of your countrywomen?"

Michelle shook her head vigorously.

"I can see you do *not* know! Yes, it is true. My father was a disgusting pig who deserved to die the painful, ignoble death he did—emptying his bowels on the Venetian tile of his foyer. A foyer, by the way, that he stole from my mother when he took our home from us. A home I grew up in…"

Maggie could see Michelle momentarily warring with herself about something before she reversed course. *Was this the psychosis she was seeing, or was Michelle really attempting to curb her words?*

"The husband of the woman my father attacked? His name is David Armstrong. He works here in Aix at an American software company. He threatened to kill my father."

"Well, I imagine he was very upset."

"He said it on numerous occasions. And I am not the only one to hear him."

"A software company?" Maggie frowned as if confused, hoping the girl would elucidate.

"X-Trad Corporation. They are based here. The police are dolts not to have questioned him."

"They haven't questioned him?"

"He says not."

Maggie worked to keep the look of enlightenment from appearing on her face. *It appears the errant boyfriend was taking a pair of pinking shears between the shoulder blades.*

There was one very important item on the list of things Maggie wanted to know, and she wasn't exactly sure how to get that information from Michelle.

"At least," she said, hoping this didn't get her thrown out —by way of the window— "you will have the satisfaction of Monsieur Tatois's estate to assuage your shame of having such a vile father."

"Estate?" Michelle looked perplexed.

"You are his only heir, I presume?"

The laugh that erupted from Michelle's face was like the cawing of a depraved crow, ugly and strident.

"He had nothing and left me nothing! The bastard couldn't even die when he should! Just three more months…" But now Michelle *did* stop herself and eyed Maggie with distrust, as if she had been tricked into saying as much as she had.

"It doesn't matter," Michelle said firmly. She stood up, ready to see Michelle out. "All that matters is that the English whore who destroyed my family will pay for it with her life. It's my one constant. My one joy." She held the door open and waited for Maggie to struggle to her feet and walk into the hall, slamming the door before Maggie could say another word.

On the drive home, Maggie tried to process what she had learned. Maggie could swear—unless the girl really was certifiably crazy—that Michelle had really thought for one moment that Maggie's fictitious organization had put a hit out on her father. And if she thought *that*, even for a second, then *she* didn't kill him. It was truly annoying to go to this kind of trouble only to have it result in the *clearing* of one your prime (and favorite) suspects.

Maggie reminded herself that eliminating potential suspects was crucial to finding the murderer. And possibly, she thought with some optimism, Michelle was so crazy that she really *did* kill him and just couldn't remember it.

As Maggie pulled onto the long drive that led to *Domaine-St-Buvard*, she found herself wondering what Michelle meant when she said, *He didn't even die when he should?* Was that a reference to an inheritance that was coming to *Jacques,* and therefore, eventually, Michelle? And what did she mean by *just three more months*? What was going to happen in three months? Maggie's head was definitely starting to ache, and she was relieved to turn off the car and just sit in the silence for a moment before moving into the house.

As she stared out over the horizon of Laurent's vineyard in an attempt to clear her mind, it occurred to her—as it had several times on the drive home—that she needed to talk to David Montgomery. She frowned. Technically, he was a "stranger." And she had promised Laurent she wouldn't talk to strangers. Damn. She *had* to talk to him. What if he was the murderer?

Was it believable that someone could repeatedly threaten to kill someone, and then when that person was murdered, not be questioned at all? *Obviously, yes. Especially if Roger Bedard was in charge.*

She took a long breath and released her seatbelt. Plenty of time to noodle the details of how she could talk to Montgomery later. *Maybe Grace? Grace* hadn't promised Laurent she wouldn't talk to strangers. Grace also wasn't, at the moment, speaking to Maggie, but that was just a detail to be sorted out.

She walked up the slate walk to the massive front door of the ancient *mas*. She hadn't touched the doorknob before it wrenched open. Laurent stood there with Zou-zou in his arms.

"Finally! You are here," he said as he pushed the child into Maggie's arms, making her drop her purse.

"What? No, Laurent," Maggie said, hoisting the child onto one hip as Laurent picked up her purse and tucked it under one of her arms. "I don't have time for this."

"Is your cellphone turned off?" he asked, edging past her toward the driveway. "We've been waiting for you. I'll call if I have any news." He trotted to the car in the drive and was in and backing it down the long driveway before Maggie could respond.

She turned when she caught movement out of the corner of her eye at the front door. Danielle stood there and held out her arms for the child. She wasn't smiling.

"Danielle, what is it?" Maggie handed Zou-zou to her. "Has something happened?"

"It is Madame Van Sant," Danielle said, kissing the baby's forehead, her eyes distant and sad. "She is gone."

There weren't many places to go. Not in St-Buvard. And of those few places, Grace knew them all better than most. Hadn't she nearly died here not three years ago, herself nearly as pregnant as Maggie was now?

She turned up the collar to her jacket when she felt the first few drops of rain. She knew she should have headed for the hotel bar. Not that that wouldn't be the first place they would think to look for her. But she couldn't bear the feeling of being hemmed in. It was partly the reason she had fled in the first place.

She signaled the waiter for another bottle of champagne. So stupid to drink champagne of all things, especially when the last thing she was doing was celebrating. But it was her signature drink, rain or shine, in good times and bad. What she really needed, she thought ruefully, was a Rusty Nail.

*Why not make them worry?* She could do nothing about all the damage she was causing. Not a single thing. She couldn't spare Zou-zou her inevitable tears. She couldn't erase the disgust and anger from her best friend's face. She couldn't stop the hurt she was causing Win. Or herself. So why care about running away? Her friends were civilized. Maggie was already mad at her, so that was a wash. Laurent was too very Laurent to say a cross word to her. And Danielle clearly wanted to adopt Zou-zou and would hardly regret her absence.

The desire to break free had been overwhelming. She smiled bitterly, thinking of the three-mile walk to the village—the last half-mile in the rain, ruining her best shoes in the process. *I would have crawled it to get away.*

*I am such a bad person,* she thought as she allowed the boy to open her bottle and pour her glass. *A bad mother—that goes without saying. A terrible wife. A bad friend. Was there ever something I was good at? Before I started destroying all these people's lives? Daddy never even looked in my direction. Smart man. He must have known how much grief I would cause.*

"This is not a very good hiding place."

She was glad it was him and not Maggie. She didn't have the energy or the wit to fight.

"Maybe I wanted to be found," she said.

"*Je sais.*" He sat down opposite her and she watched the waiter scurry to bring him a clean glass. She watched him over her glass, grateful she hadn't started weeping before he showed up. It had been close.

"I hope I didn't worry you." She didn't really give a shit, but it was what people said. She watched him pour his glass and hold it up to her as if to toast. If it were anybody else but Laurent, she would have thought he was mocking her.

*God, I hope Maggie knows what she's got in this guy.*

"For all that you do have," he said, and then drank.

"Okay, I'll bite."

He gave her a confused look that made her laugh. "It's an American colloquium," she said. "I would have thought Maggie would have taught you all of them by now. It means, *sure, tell me.*"

"You are still beautiful."

Grace nearly choked on her sip and Laurent had to stand up to pound her on the back as she coughed painfully. "I thought you were going to say my kids or my wonderful husband or something. Oh, my God, leave it to the French. Thank you, darling Laurent. I needed that."

When he sat back down, he sat down in the chair next to her, and before she knew what she was doing she was in his arms crying as quietly and as helplessly as she could. A part of her brain knew how painful this kind of public display must be to someone like Laurent. *The man used to be a Côte d'Azur conman, for crying out loud*! The only thing he *did* run from was public attention. She struggled to control herself, but only succeeded in producing loud hiccoughs in addition to the sounds of her muffled wailing.

"I'm so sorry, Laurent," she said, snuffling into his chest. "I can't believe I'm putting you through this."

He made soothing clucking noises and patted her on the back. When she finally pulled away, he handed her a clean handkerchief and she mopped her face the best she could.

"I'm a mess," she said, shaking her head. "A total, drunken, mess."

"*Non*," Laurent said, his hand on her back, large and warm and reassuring. "You are never that."

They sat without speaking for a moment, and then Laurent poured champagne in both of their glasses and placed hers in front of her. He signaled for the waiter and ordered two large coffees and cake. Grace wanted to protest but didn't. She knew that most of Laurent's solutions to any situation involved food.

"Grace," he said, solemnly. "It is too late?"

She took a long, rattling breath and fortified herself with a sip of the champagne before answering. "It is."

"*Je suis desolée*," he said. "Is it Windsor?"

She closed her eyes tight and shook her head. "No, it's me."

"Ahhh."

The coffees arrived and Laurent took her hand. The two sat quietly, side by side, while they finished their coffees.

"You want this now," he said. "But a year from now? Will you be glad you left?"

"I don't know. How can I know?"

Laurent accepted that. The unanswerable question.

"I can talk to Windsor."

"Thank you, Laurent. He'll need a friend."

She laughed at his eyebrow raise. "Yes, it's true he has one of *those*, but he'll need a *guy* friend."

"You will be fine, Grace. Not just because you have to be for Zou-zou and Taylor. You are strong."

"I know. It just hurts. And I don't feel like I have the right to come to anyone for sympathy since I'm the one causing all the problems."

"Maggie is impulsive," he said. "You know that."

"She's only saying what my family and everyone else is thinking. I don't blame her for being disgusted with me."

"Not disgusted, Grace. Frustrated. She will go around."

"*Come around,* I think you mean. I hope so."

Both of them looked up in time to see Danielle and her husband, Jean-Luc coming into the café.

"I guess Maggie is on solo baby duty," Grace said, watching the two as they chose a table in the dining area.

"It will give her some practice for later."

"They're coming over," Grace said. "I should try to look a little ashamed in the presence of the woman I abandoned my child to."

"Danielle is not like that." Laurent reached out and patted Grace's hand. "She has lived a life of much disappointment, herself. As you know."

"*Salut*, Laurent! Madame Van Sant!" Jean-Luc was the first of the two to reach their table and he had his hand out to shake with Laurent, even though Grace knew for a fact the two had spent the day together. "If I had known you wanted to eat out, we could have made plans. Where is Maggie?" Jean-Luc looked from Laurent to Grace and then back to Laurent and his face took on a sudden look of horror.

"Don't be an *idiot*, Jean-Luc," Laurent said gruffly. "Maggie is home with *l'enfant. Bon soir,* Danielle. *Ça va?"*

"*Oui, ça va,* Laurent," Danielle replied, her eyes friendly and open. "Madame, we were worried about you but I see you are well."

"Yes, sorry about that, Madame Pernon," Grace said, gathering up Laurent's handkerchief and carefully folding it on her lap.

"*Pas du tout,"* Danielle said. For a moment no one spoke, and then Danielle approached the table and touched Grace's shoulder. "I am going to the toilet. Would you care to come too?"

Grace looked at the older woman with relief and for a moment, thought she might start crying again in the face of Danielle's unexpected kindness. "Yes, Madame Pernon."

Danielle waited for her to stand and then took her almost literally under her wing.

"Call me Danielle, please, yes?"

As soon as the women disappeared inside, Jean-Luc took Grace's seat.

"Forgive me," he said. "Danielle says I often make hasty calculations."

Laurent waved away his apology and Jean-Luc edged closer to him across the table. "Is it true that Maggie visits the condemned murderer in her cell in Aix?"

Laurent snorted. "I believe there must be a trial before one can be condemned."

"A formality, surely? Have you wondered how is it that your wife knows so many murderers personally?"

"Are you coming to a point, my friend?"

Jean-Luc looked over his shoulder in the direction the two women had gone. "My own beautiful wife talks of little else. She knows Lily Tatois, you know. They were girls together. This tragedy has served as opportunity for the two of them to reconnect."

"Lily Tatois is at least a decade older than Danielle, is she not?"

Jean-Luc nodded. "But friendless as a schoolgirl, I understand. And you know my Danielle. So kindhearted she would befriend a monster."

*And had done so,* Laurent thought, thinking of Danielle's first husband, now in prison for arson and murder.

"It made me think of Jacques; what a *putain*, eh? Did *anybody* like him? And that made me think of the time last year when he publicly accused his accountant, Yves Briande of swindling him out of his money. Right in this very café!"

Laurent frowned. "Why did I not hear of this?"

"It was last January. You were in America with your wife. Anyway it was widely known that Yves hated Jacques for the humiliation. He confided to me that his business had fallen off as a result of the slander."

"Did he?"

"What? Swindle Jacques? Who knows? I didn't know Jacques had any money to be swindled out of after…well, you know." He gave Laurent a knowing look. "I, myself, am still recovering. But the look I saw in Yves's eye that day? It was definitely murderous."

Later that evening, after Grace and Laurent returned to the *mas*, Maggie took a long contemplative bath before slipping between the cool sheets of her abundant king-size bed. Laurent was already in bed reading. "So it sounds like Grace is still going through with it?"

"You understand she is in crisis, yes?" Laurent said tiredly. "If she had committed a terrible crime, she would expect you to stand by her. As would I."

"Are you drawing a connection to this situation with Julia? Because you know I believe Julia to be *innocent*."

"So you would not stand by her if she committed a crime?"

"No, I didn't mean that. Of course I would. If it turned out she were guilty, I wouldn't abandon her."

Maggie picked up the tube of fragrant body lotion she used to keep her heels and elbows supple. She read somewhere that lotion was good to rub across pregnant bellies to avoid stretch marks. She glanced at Laurent. "I've always believed that children are the glue to marriage," she said.

Laurent put down his book. "Children are not the glue. They are the cracks that force one to search for glue."

"Laurent, are you serious? You think children are the thing that cause stress in a marriage?" Maggie's eyes widened.

"Of course. Well, that and worry about money." He turned to face her. "Maggie, there is no one thing that will prevent a marriage from failing. Not locks on a bridge or having babies or being Catholic." He shrugged. "You look for insurance when there can be none."

"Then why do you want kids at all if you think they're just going to cause trouble for us?"

"Because I like the glue so much." He smiled and touched her knee gently with his large hand.

Later, when the lights were out, Maggie was too wide-awake to sleep. From her cuddled position in his arms, she held up her hands in the dark to tick off her suspects.

"Help me with this, Laurent," she said. "Okay, I've got this guy David Armstrong who threatened to kill Jacques but, of course, the police haven't even questioned—"

"And who you will not go see."

"Yes, Laurent, I already told you I wouldn't. And then there's Michelle, the victim's daughter, who found the body so that's suspicious right there."

"But who Bedard says has an alibi."

"And, of course, Annette. The ex-wife."

"The number one suspect of all."

"Exactly. Thank you. Who nobody's questioned."

"She has not been questioned?"

"Well, okay, I don't know if she has. Bedard doesn't really share with me, you'll be happy to know. And now this Yves character, who definitely had a motive for wanting Jacques dead."

"A weak motive."

"Why do you say that?"

"The moment of his anger was long past, *tu sais*? Now if he stood to benefit *financially* from Jacques's death..."

"Everyone says Jacques had no money."

"True, but he was heir to Lily Tatois's fortune."

Maggie twisted around in his arms and snapped on the light.

"Maggie..." Laurent groaned as the light flashed on.

"How do you know that? *Jacques* was Lily's beneficiary?"

"Jean-Luc told me. Please, Maggie, turn off the light."

"So that's what Michelle meant when she said he couldn't even die when he was supposed to. He died first so someone *else* will inherit. Laurent, did Jean-Luc say who Lily's new beneficiary is?"

"I will only tell you if you turn off the light. And perhaps do that thing you sometimes do when you are in a very good mood and you are particularly glad to be married to me."

Maggie laughed and kissed him. "I promise," she said. "Who is it?"

"Jacques's cousin, Florian."

# Chapter Ten

The next morning, Laurent had a table full of females at breakfast. Grace sat next to Zou-zou, her face alternately flushed and wan as her moods came and went. He noticed that Maggie was quieter than usual and assumed that was because she was debating about how to approach her friend. Hopefully, how to *apologize* to her friend, he thought as he slid an omelet onto her plate.

"Thanks, Laurent," she said picking up a fork and glancing over at Grace, who was only drinking coffee. She cleared her throat. "Did you sleep okay?"

Grace looked at her and set her cup down. "Are you talking to me?"

"Well, since I already *know* how Laurent slept, obviously I was talking to you."

Grace shrugged. "Fine, thanks."

"Look, Grace," Maggie said, putting her fork back down on the table. "I'm sorry, okay?"

Grace looked at her for a moment and then nodded. "Okay."

Laurent picked up a piece of bacon with his fingers and placed it in front of Zou-zou. The baby grabbed it as if she hadn't already eaten a large wedge of quiche and a bowl of grapes this morning.

"Did you get the message from your editor, *chérie*?" Laurent asked from the kitchen.

Maggie got up and followed him into the kitchen. "Where is the *Texas Pete*

"You are going to put hot sauce on my omelet?"

"I believe we transferred possession," she said sweetly, standing on tiptoe to give him a kiss on the cheek. "Where have you hidden it?"

With a long-suffering sigh, Laurent opened a cabinet door and extricated the bottle of hot sauce and handed it to her. "You are going to ignore your editor? Is that wise?"

"I'm not ignoring her," Maggie said as she returned to the dining room. "I'll call her back later. The time difference, you know."

"That's your New York editor?" Grace asked.

"It is. We're having trouble connecting lately."

"Because of the time difference."

Maggie gave Grace a quick look to try to ascertain if there was any sarcasm or hidden element in the statement but there didn't seem to be. Grace innocently sipped her coffee.

"That's right. She sent me a bunch of edits she wanted me to do and she's calling to see what the status is."

"Because they're late?"

"No, because she's just interested in knowing what stage they're in."

"What stage are they in?"

Maggie sighed and looked at Grace, and then glanced at the baby, who was happily chewing on a paper plate Laurent had given her. "They're not at a very advanced stage," she admitted. "I've been distracted."

Laurent entered the dining room and tossed down his kitchen towel. He clapped his hands together and held out his arms to Zou-zou.

*"Est-ce que tu es prête, ma petite?"*

Zou-zou immediately began squealing and clapping her hands. *"Oncle Laurent! Oncle Laurent!"*

Grace dropped her cup in the saucer as Laurent scooped the child up. "Oh, my God, Laurent," she said, her mouth open in astonishment. "You got her to speak."

"She got her own self to speak, *n'est-ce pas*, little one?" Laurent said to his squirming armful.

The sounds of tires crunching on the gravel front drive had been obvious all through breakfast. A quick look out the window showed that the pickers were right on time this morning. At least ten of them—a scraggly looking bunch of unemployed youths—stood outside smoking and waiting for Laurent.

Grace took her coffee and went to the kitchen window. "Are you picking later than usual this year?" she asked.

Laurent hoisted Zou-zou over his shoulder to her squeals of delight. *"Oui,"* he said as he grabbed his cap from its hook by the kitchen door. "But still first before everyone else in France."

"Because the southern grapes ripen faster," Maggie said to Grace, proud that she knew something about Laurent's harvest. "How long will it take it pick our fields?"

"A week, I think," he said. "I will take *petite Z* to Madame Pernon, *oui*?" He stepped back into the kitchen to give Maggie a hearty kiss on the mouth before exiting through the kitchen. Maggie heard him greet some of the pickers as he joined them.

"You used to hate this time of year," Grace said softly. "How things have changed." She turned to Maggie. "However, on the ever increasing good-news front, Win will be delighted to know the baby's first words were *Oncle Laurent*."

"Is Zou-zou the reason you two are splitting up?" Maggie didn't know the question was coming until it was half way out of her mouth.

Grace's smile dissolved from her face. "Zou-zou?" A look of grim comprehension quickly replaced the confusion. "You mean because of not knowing who her real father is?"

"Sorry, Grace," Maggie muttered, looking away. "I'm not used to editing my words with you."

"No worries, darling. Please speak freely. No, Zou-zou has nothing to do with it. Win's grand gesture aside, he snuck off and had a DNA test done almost as soon as we were back in the States. The results are in and, drum roll, please…she's officially his."

"And by *his*, you mean…" Maggie knew she was making it worse.

"Windsor's."

"Oh. Well, good."

"Yes, isn't it? I'd hate for him to pay support for a child that wasn't biologically his. Much tidier this way."

"He loves Zou-zou."

"He loves her even more now."

"Was it because he got the test?"

"Darling, what a simplistic world you live in. It must be very black and white to be Maggie Newberry Dernier."

"I thought we were trying to be friendly."

"Sorry. No, it wasn't because of the test." Her voice caught. "It was because of everything else." Grace put a hand to her face and released a stifled moan. Maggie could see she was trying to get her emotions under control. She jumped up and put her arms around her friend.

"I'm sorry, Grace," she whispered. "I am so, so, so sorry."

Grace reached up and squeezed her hand without speaking. After a moment, Grace disengaged and patted Maggie's arm. "I'm okay, darling. I'm good."

Before Maggie had a chance to reply, she saw her cellphone light up where it lay on the dining room table. She didn't recognize the number.

"*Allo?*" she said.

"Maggie?"

*Roger.*

"Wow. To what do I owe this earth-shattering event?" She said a silent prayer of thanks that Laurent was out of the house.

"Just a courtesy call, as you Americans would say," Roger said. But Maggie could hear the excitement in his voice. Something had happened that he was taking credit for and he wanted her to be the first to know.

*Something good for his case, not hers.*

"What's up?"

"I wanted to let you know there was a break-in at the laboratory that handles our toxicology work."

*A break-in?* Maggie's hopes soared at the thought of something lucky finally leaning in her direction. She willed herself not to speak lest the littlest thing dam up this valuable flow of unexpected intel.

"Someone attempted to destroy the samples of poisonous mushrooms taken from our victim's stomach."

Maggie felt her mood begin to deflate.

"Fortunately, the security guard at the lab was vigilant and the perpetrator was quickly apprehended. I thought you would want to know."

"So the samples were compromised?"

"No. Unfortunately for Madame Patrick, the samples remain intact and viable."

"The person who tried to destroy the samples—is he a new suspect in the case?" Maggie could see Grace's eyes widen as she listened to the conversation.

"*Non.* He is only a person of interest." Roger's voice became clipped and Maggie could just see him beginning to pout as he reacted to the fact that Maggie did not appear as impressed as he hoped she might be. "He was arrested and released on bail. He had no priors—"

"Roger, why are you not treating this as the act of a guilty person? *He broke in to destroy evidence!* That in itself is proof of—"

"It is proof only of being an idiot." Roger huffed on the other line. "If anything, it is even stronger proof that we have the right person in custody."

"What are you talking about?"

"The man was trying to destroy evidence of the crime committed by Madame Patrick—"

"So you said, but I don't understand how that—"

"He admitted that he's her lover."

Maggie turned her shocked face to Grace and then sat down in her chair as if her legs no longer had the strength to support her.

"*Her lover?*" she whispered in disbelief.

Two hours later, Maggie sat in her car on the Rue Mejanes and waited for the phone to ring. Roger had made it clear that a visit to the detention center would not be possible at this time, but had agreed, if Julia wanted to speak with Maggie, to arrange for a phone call between the two later that morning. Although she knew she wouldn't be able to see Julia, Maggie opted to drive to Aix to take the phone call. She felt closer to her friend here. And she now had an errand in Aix that couldn't wait.

*What had Julia been thinking? She has a boyfriend?* How was that even possible without Maggie knowing? *What did it mean in all of this?*

She hadn't even had time to process the news that *Florrie* was Lily's new beneficiary. *Did that even matter?* Even if Florrie killed Jacques in order to take his place as next in line to Lily's fortune (*did that make sense?),* why kill Jacques *now?* Besides, lots of people stood to gain when a rich relative dies. Maggie, herself, would split a sizeable fortune with her brother when their parents passed, but she hadn't been plotting to kill them in the meantime.

It wasn't actually motive in this case, she realized. More like, Florrie being the next heir was just one more interesting fact to add to the growing pile of other interesting facts that now constituted a confusing mess that pointed in no particular direction at all. She sighed and glanced down at her cellphone at exactly the moment it began to ring.

She recognized the number as a New York City area code and hit the "decline" button on her cell. Of course she wanted to talk to her editor, but not when any second she was waiting to hear from Julia.

The next call that came through Maggie recognized as the Aix prison exchange number. She punched *accept* on the phone face.

"Julia?"

"Oh, Maggie, thank God!" Julia's voice came over the line reedy and shrill. Her throat sounded rough, as if she had been crying. "They lie to me so much I wasn't sure you'd really be there."

"Julia, are you okay?" *Stupid question.*

"Maggie, you've got to help me. Nobody is telling me anything. They won't answer my questions and my attorney is out of town at a wedding or something. Do you know what's going on?"

"Well, probably not as much as your attorney, but *Inspecteur* Bedard called me this morning to say they'd caught some guy trying to destroy the samples in your case at the lab where they're—"

"I know! Do you know where he is now? They won't tell me whether they're still holding him or if he's released or anything."

*So it's true,* Maggie thought, her shoulders slumping against the warm back of the car seat. *She's with him.*

119

"I...I heard he was released," Maggie said.

"Oh, thank God. Thank God."

"So who is this guy, Jules? I didn't know you were seeing anyone."

"I'm sorry, Maggie. I know it looks like I didn't trust you but you have to understand that after my last fiasco, I felt I needed to hold my cards close to the vest for awhile. Do you see that?"

"Sure, Jules. So how did you meet him?"

"He lives in my apartment building. We just kept bumping into each other when we were taking out the garbage and one thing led to another. You know how these things go."

"That must have really shocked you to hear he'd broken into a police toxicology lab to destroy evidence pertinent to your murder case."

There was silence on the line and for a moment, Maggie wasn't sure the call hadn't failed.

"What are you saying, Maggie?" Julia asked quietly. "Are you suggesting that *Mathieu* killed Jacques, or that *I* did it and my lover is trying to cover for me?"

"Did he know Jacques was trying to get back together with you?"

"Of course. I showed him the notes."

"And the police have those notes now?"

"I assume."

"Did he know Jacques was coming to dinner that night?" Maggie was sure she already knew the answer to this.

There was another brief silence on the line, and then, "If you do anything to implicate Mathieu," Julia said, her voice cold and flat, "in some misguided attempt to free me, I promise you I will never speak to you again. He had nothing to do with Jacques's death. Nothing."

"How do you know that?"

"We're done, Maggie." The line went dead in her ear, and when Maggie pulled her head back to look at the screen she saw that the hand holding the phone was shaking.

In the space of the very brief conversation, something repulsive and finite had happened to her conviction and to her faith in her friend. Maybe it had been building on the drive over from St-Buvard, ever since she got the phone call from Roger that morning. Ever since she realized that her good friend had kept a serious boyfriend a secret for God knows how long. When Maggie pulled the phone from her ear after Julia hung up on her, her stomach was roiling with nausea.

*That fact was, it didn't make sense for Mathieu to break into the lab to destroy samples—if that is what he was trying to do—in order to protect himself. The only reason would be to try to help Julia. And why does he believe those samples are so damning to Julia's case?*

The answer to that came unbidden and immediately to Maggie as she sat in the stifling confines of her compact car: *Because they really are proof of her guilt.*

Susan Kiernan-Lewis

# Chapter Eleven

"*Maman!* Can you talk?" Michelle sat in the window seat in her apartment and stared out onto the residential street. It was early and only school children and their parents and *au pairs* were moving about. Michelle couldn't help but notice how the little wretches all looked like chimps dressed in human clothes. The way they ran and skipped and thumped on one another reminded her of the last time she had been dragged to the zoo as a child.

She wondered why no one else but her seemed to see it. One boy actually stopped and vigorously scratched his crotch, and she half expected to see him begin to pick lice out of one of the other boys' hair.

"Yes, of course, my sweet. Is everything all right?"

Michelle turned from the revolting street scene to the interior of her apartment and began to chew on a nail. She hadn't slept last night. She wasn't sure she had slept the night before either. "No, *Maman.* Everything is not *all right.* Are you mad? That woman who came to Papa's service at Lily's? You know the one? The one who made Lily force me to leave?"

"Yes, of course, *chérie.* The pregnant American."

"Well, she came to see me."

"What?"

Michelle took satisfaction at the level of agitation in her mother's voice.

"What did she want?"

"She tried to tell me she had money for me. She said she wasn't really the whore's friend."

"Well, she lied to you, Michelle. My…friend says that she is very definitely connected to the murdering whore. Closely connected."

"I know, *Maman*. When I thought about it later, I realized how she tricked me. And I will ensure that she is never able to do that to anyone else again."

"Michelle, do not do anything. Promise me."

"Didn't you hear me? The bitch tricked me! She came into my apartment and lied to me. She will not walk away from that!"

"Please, *chérie*, let me handle it. I have friends. I can hurt her. I *will* hurt her. You do not want to endanger yourself."

"How can I not? Even the lying bitch knew how desperately I am in need of money. Even she could see. How is it that my own mother is so blind? I don't have the money for this semester. I don't have last month's rent!"

"Oh, Michelle, what of the money I gave you last week? I know it wasn't much…"

"It was worse than nothing! Enough for a meal out, that's all. Why do you torment me like this? If you cannot help your only child, please just say so."

"Michelle, you know I have no money myself——"

"But you can get it! And now that goddam Florrie will inherit what should have been mine! Can you not go to him and shame him into sharing it with me? He is like a thief in the night to swoop in and steal my inheritance. Is he so stupid, that he doesn't realize the crime he has committed against me?"

"I will talk to him, my love. I will ask him to see reason. You are his cousin."

"It is revolting. That old woman has always hated me."

"That is not true, Michelle. She is just old and ill."

"Well, then, can we not argue that she is mentally incompetent? To give all her money to that fat weasel—and he has so much!"

"He has been managing her estate for years, Michelle. The courts will not see it as bizarre for her to make him her beneficiary."

"Why are you saying this?!" Michelle stood and looked wildly around her room, as if trying to find something to break or throw. "Is it possible you don't care that the fat wretch is taking money that should be mine? Where am I to go when I cannot pay my rent? Will you tell me that?"

"We will somehow get the money for your—"

"Bah! You are as weak as Papa always said you were. I don't want a few euros here and there. I want the fortune that should be mine!"

"I know, Michelle. I know, but—"

Michelle couldn't hear any more of her mother's pathetic mewing on the other line. She had been a fool to call her. *She never helped. Never!* She threw the cellphone across the room and felt the thrill and satisfaction of hearing it smash into the useless antique wall mirror that her grandmother had given her.


Annette quietly disconnected and sat on the bed in a rumple of sheets and blankets holding the cellphone in both hands. She took a long breath and tried to visualize in what manner her daughter had terminated the conversation. She hoped it wasn't into the television screen like last time.

"She doesn't know?"

Annette turned to the man in her bed. He had been smoking and listening as she spoke to her daughter. She replaced the cellphone on the nightstand. "I thought it best at this point."

"You are probably right. Although she hated him almost as much as you did. She would probably not even care, my love."

"I'm not worried about that. He was a pig and Michelle is better off without him."

"*C'est ça.*"

"I'm only afraid she won't understand why I kept it from her. She'll think I don't trust her."

"And why are you keeping it from her?"

"Maybe I just want something for myself. Just once I want it to be about me and what *I* need. Can you understand that?"

He chuckled and drew her closer to him on the bed. "If not I, then who?" he murmured, pulling the drawstring that held her *peignoir* gathered in a scrunch at her throat. His eyes glittered as the thin top collapsed into a silken puddle in her lap exposing her breasts.

Annette slipped under the sheets next to him, but her eyes stared unseeing out the window over her lover's shoulder. "I'm afraid I must admit to not liking my daughter very much."

The three tractors inched slowly down the winding routes of the hillsides, each one loaded with crates of the grapes of *Domaine St-Buvard* and bound for the presses at the co-op. Laurent would have liked to have begun picking at least a week earlier but had held off at the request of his local federation of vintners. The quality of the wine from the region was a reflect on them all. Although it had taken years to learn the lesson, Laurent knew the value of working together as a team—even if the results were often less than could be done independently. He watched the army of young people moving, hunched over, through the rows of vines. Their youth was the only thing that would prevent permanent damage to their postures, he mused. Unless they came back year after year, harvest after harvest as so many would. But labour in the grape fields was not work for any but the young. Exhausting, bent over, tedious work—

usually in the punishing heat of late summer—and long days to match the longer periods of light.

This was his fifth harvest. The first had been poor due to lack of experience on his part, and as the result of ground that had not been cultivated in decades. The second year, all three fields had burned to the ground a week before they were due to be harvested. And then came the recovery years. Last year had been good, but the rains had bleached the sweetness from the grapes. And, of course, there had been the *Mistral*. This year promised to be better. Laurent smiled to himself. The life of a *vigneron. Always thinking to the next harvest, the next season of wines.*

His phone vibrated in his pocket and he grimaced in annoyance. He preferred to leave it at home so that he couldn't be reached. There were very few things more important than the harvest right now. Maggie at eight and a half months pregnant was one of them.

*"Allo, chérie?"*

"Laurent, do you know anybody by the name of Mathieu Benoit?"

Laurent squinted at the horizon, watching one of the temporary workers stop to drink from his water bottle. "Is that the name of Julia's boyfriend?"

"It is. Can you ask around to see if anybody knows him?"

*"Oui.* Did you talk to Julia?"

"Oh, Laurent, she hung up on me!"

*"Incroyable."*

"Okay, I know you meant that as sarcasm, but it really upset me."

"Did you accuse her boyfriend of killing her other boyfriend?"

"Not really." There was a pause on the line. "Maybe."

Laurent watched the temporary worker pop a handful of grapes in his mouth and pretend to be strangling on the taste.

He could hear the laughter of the other workers from here. He frowned. "Is Grace with you?"

"She said she wanted to take a nap."

Laurent grunted. *There was too much napping from people who needed to be kept busy.* "And are you coming home now?"

"Are you making lunch?"

"*Non.* I am in the fields until late."

"Well, don't worry about me then. I have one quick errand to run and then I'll be home to check on Grace."

"What errand?"

"Laurent, don't worry, okay? It's just a female thing and I'll be right home."

"You will not try to contact this boyfriend of Julia's?"

There was the briefest of hesitations on the line. *Clearly, that was exactly what she had intended to do.*

"Not if you don't want me to." He could hear the frustration in her voice.

"*Bon,*" he said. "Then I will see you tonight."

The worker seemed to have returned to his backbreaking task and Laurent motioned to the head tractor as it crept its way toward him. He would examine every precious crate before it went to the presser. He found his heart lightening with each foot that the tractor advanced.

*Well, that was annoying.*

It wasn't that she had planned to interview Mathieu Benoit this afternoon (although she had thought about it), but she certainly intended to find out a lot more about him before calling it a day.

*Was there anyone in Aix who might know of him?* As she walked to the outdoor café facing Julia's apartment building, it occurred to her that she could talk with Julia's neighbors without danger of breaking her agreement with Laurent. *What constitutes a stranger anyway?* She had probably said hello in the narrow hallway and landings to every person who lived in Julia's building at least once. If they saw her and recognized she was a friend of Julia's, surely that meant they weren't really strangers?

She took a seat at one of the tables which gave a clear view of Julia's building and ordered an iced coffee.

Sometimes sleuthing was just a matter of sitting and waiting. She had learned that a long time ago. *You had to talk and talk to people until you just happened to talk to just the right person—the one person who knew something or who had seen something—and you have no idea who that person is. Not really*. While it was true Laurent had said don't talk to people, he didn't say *don't watch people*. And that, Maggie knew, was half the battle.

As she sipped her coffee she watched everyone who came into the little café, or the apartment building across the street. She watched the waiter (who was watching her) and the young mother with the carriage, and the two students who argued furiously with each other but were clearly lovers. She watched the old man who looked grumpy and miserable, probably because he'd been coming to this café for years and now he couldn't smoke in it and it was crammed full of tourists and students.

Maggie shifted her weight in her chair but it was no use. She wasn't going to find a position that was comfortable. She might as well give up on trying until after the baby was born. Just when she was about to ask for the bill and head to her appointment, she saw him. In truth, she didn't know *what* she was looking at for at least the first thirty seconds of seeing him, only that, of everyone on the street, he was the most visually arresting.

*And not in a good way.*

At least six foot two—unusually tall for a Frenchman. He had a shining, bald head,  long handlebar mustache, and both shoulders—bared in his sleeveless leather vest—were covered in dark tattoos. It couldn't be anyone else. Maggie watched in openmouthed wonder as the man strode down the sidewalk to the front door of the apartment building. He looked mad. He looked beyond mad. Maggie could practically see him foaming at the mouth from where she sat forty yards away.

*It had to be him.*

He punched his door code into the keypad on the front door panel and jerked the heavy double wooden doors open as if he'd prefer to rip them off their hinges in the process. He disappeared into the building, the doors slowly, almost reluctantly closing behind him.

*Dear God, Julia,* Maggie thought in bewilderment as she watched the doors close. *Do I know you at all?*

\* \* \*

Julia sat on a bare mattress on the floor of her cell at the detention center in the *Palais de Justice.* She stared at the chipped paint on the wall opposite her. Another woman sat next to her on the mattress, her shoulders shaking with her silent sobs. She was Muslim judging by her robe, but it was torn and stained. If the woman spoke French it wasn't a dialect that Julia had ever heard before. They had brought her in last night. She had wept most of the time since then.

Julia estimated that her cell measured less than twenty feet by twenty, yet she shared it with five other women, including the sobbing Muslim. The floor was filthy, and while there was a sink in the cell, it didn't function. Neither did two of the four showers in the communal bathroom. The orange jumpsuit she wore had clearly not been laundered since the last inmate had used it.

Two weeks. Two interminable weeks, broken only by a daily hour long visit from her lawyer, a man who sat opposite her in the visitor's room and wrote notes, and rarely spoke. Julia was convinced he worked on someone else's case while he was with her. She had stopped asking him questions after the first week.

One thing she didn't need to ask anymore, which had become very clear to Julia, was the fact that she was going to die in this festering hellhole and all the people who cared about her were powerless to do a damn thing about it. She thought of Mathieu and the rising sounds of her weeping companion triggered a sudden urge to cry, too. *Stupid, stupid man. What was he thinking? Did he think attempting to destroy the State's proof would make her look less guilty?* She reflected on her conversation with Maggie and was engulfed in an irrepressible resurgent wave of anger. She clutched the fabric of her orange jumpsuit, kneading it until both knees were wrinkled and dirty. *Does she not realize he's all I have left? Would she have me lose him, too?*

An invasive odor of defecation filled the little cell and the other women groaned. Julia breathed through her mouth and edged away from the woman on the mattress, although she had no reason to believe the smell was coming from her. In the two weeks she had been held in this place, she had done her best to remember how much worse it could be and to be grateful for how less bad it was. She thought of her great aunt, who had died in a German concentration camp during the war after having been captured and tortured.

The story was that Sybil Patrick had volunteered to travel behind enemy lines delivering messages between the French Underground and British Intelligence. Intrepid and beautiful, she was killed, or died of disease, her family never knew which, before she was twenty-four years old—six months before the war ended.

Although Julia never knew her aunt, she had nonetheless trotted out her story at parties and dined off her relentless, timeless heroism for as many years as Julia had been an adult. And it was thoughts of Sybil that kept her sane now. When

Julia thought of how her kinswoman must have died, brutally hurt and alone, and then compared it to the simple benign neglect of an antiquated, underfunded French prison system, she forced herself to believe her trial was small.

Down the hall and through the bars, Julia could hear the sounds of someone being beaten. The soft thuds of fists against flesh and the muted grunts of the victim filled the hallway as the entire cell wing fell silent to listen. Julia dug her nails into the palms of her hands and found herself wondering how Sybil had kept herself sane those last brutal weeks of her life. Or if she simply hadn't bothered.

*  *  *  *

*Jacques's accountant must be doing well*, Maggie thought. His offices were ensconced comfortably at the top of an old—but not *too* old—mixed-use office building on the edge of the oldest section of Aix. Grateful for the smoothly functioning elevator, Maggie took a moment to enjoy the view from the sixth floor. From her vantage point in Yves Briande's waiting room, she could see the *Cours*—majestically shaded by two perfect rows of stately plane trees—as it dissected the town. She watched the tourists and the shoppers meander up and down the famous boulevard, looking like colorful ants on a mission.

She was the only one in the waiting room, and for that she was grateful. It was still a struggle to speak French—even conversational French, where the other party might be prone to lapse into colloquialism or the difficult to understand dialect of the region. While she had learned through tapes and Laurent—who spoke Parisian French—it was the unmanicured *patois* of St-Buvard's shopkeepers who had largely taught her the bulk of what she knew of the language.

"Madame Dernier?"

Maggie shook herself out of her thoughts and stood to greet Yves Briande, Jacques's accountant and the man who had every reason to want him dead. If ever she was grasping at straws, she thought as she stuck her hand out to shake his, this was it.

"Yes, thank you, Monsieur Briande for seeing me. I'm afraid I probably need to make clear that I am not here for advice on my finances and I know it must have felt like that when I set up the appointment.

Briande, a squat, florid man with stark white hair that he kept combed in a slick swath across his crown and forehead, frowned but motioned for her to take a seat in the waiting room. Maggie was relieved he wasn't throwing her out.

"What is it I may help you with, Madame?" he asked politely. He sat and steepled his hands together, resting them on his knee.

"I heard that you were the accountant for Jacques Tatois and I was hoping I might discuss your dealings with him."

Maggie had decided on the walk over that revealing she was a friend of the accused who was looking to find out more about his accountant's motive for killing Jacques was probably not her best opening gambit.

"I see."

Maggie had to admit that Briande didn't look like the kind of hothead who would nurse a grievance for months and then set up an innocent woman to take the fall while he took his revenge. Besides, as Laurent had pointed out with some impatience earlier in the week, typically acts of revenge demand the emotional satisfaction of watching your enemy die. Poisoning Jacques was as passive an act of murder as there was. He died alone, even the exact time of his demise undetermined. *If you hated someone, what kind of satisfaction was there in that?*

"I'm not sure if you know that this is still an open investigation, Monsieur Briande?"

"I was under the impression that the police had settled on a suspect."

"Yes, that's true, but until she is convicted, the case remains open."

"I have to say I was amazed to hear that Madame Patrick had killed him," Briande said, smoothing his comb-over with large, fat fingers.

Maggie forced herself not to respond to his words. If he found out she was friends with Julia, he would certainly refuse to talk with her.

"I guess everyone was. The police are investigating whether or not there was a financial benefit to the murder," she lied.

Briande frowned. "Financial? That would surprise me. Jacques was broke."

"Well, maybe the killer…Madame Patrick…wasn't aware of that. It could be the reason she…you know…"

Briande laughed. "I am sure Madame Patrick—who had a personal relationship with Jacques—had many other reasons why she might want him dead. As would anyone who knew him very well. But ignorance of his financial situation wasn't likely."

"Oh, yes? And why is that?" Maggie smiled encouragingly at him. She was trying so hard to get him to reference Jacques's public accusation against him. She had to admit, he was smooth. If he *was* the killer, he didn't seem a bit concerned that anyone was probing about this very damning incident—*a powerful motive if there ever was one.*

"Like so many people last fall, Monsieur Tatois—how is it you Americans so delightfully put it?—lost his shirt on the *Mistral Promis.* I, myself, bet and lost, but unlike Monsieur Tatois, I know restraint and did not wager more than I could afford to lose."

Annoyed that the conversation was going down a road other than the one she had planned, Maggie reminded herself how much gold she had often uncovered when interviews took on a life of their own and rerouted her expectations.

"The *Mistral Promis*?" she prompted.

"Ahhh! How can it be that you have not heard of it?" Briande shook his head and clapped his knees with both hands in as close an approximation of delight as Maggie had ever seen in a grown man. "Well, as I am sure you must know, a Frenchman will bet on anything. And in winegrowing country, the bookmakers here enjoy a long and profitable history of climate betting."

"People bet on when the weather will turn or when is the best time to harvest?"

"Yes, certainly there are always bets like that, but the *Mistral Promis* was very special. Created by bookmakers in Marseille, it made its way to Aix last year for the first time and was received with much enthusiasm."

"So what exactly is the *Mistral Promis*?"

"It was an attempt to guess the exact date the Mistral would come to Provence in last year's harvest."

"And when was it?"

Briande shrugged. "I don't remember. It was, however, much later than anyone had any memory of it ever happening before."

"So everyone in town bet and everyone lost."

*"C'est ça." That's right.*

"And Jacques bet all his money and lost it all."

"I am sure I break no client privilege by confirming that to you."

"Were you his accountant at the time of his death?"

A look passed over his face. "No, but I was his accountant at the time he lost all his money and surely that is more pertinent?"

"And you're saying it was this wide-spread betting phenomenon that was responsible for Jacques losing all his money."

"It was on the news. On the television. There was virtually no one who escaped—*many* people were ruined that day. I am, in fact, reliably informed that your own husband bet significantly on the *Mistral Promis*. His losses must have been considerable. *Tu sais?*"

Maggie's hand flew to her mouth to stifle her gasp before she could stop it.

*Laurent? Gambling?*

"I see this is news to you, Madame," Briande said, a coy smile on his lips. "We men must not tell our wives every little thing, *n'est pas?*"

"You know my husband?" Maggie was astonished to hear her voice sounded normal. Her heart was racing and she had a nearly uncontrollable urge to call Laurent straightaway to find out if this was true.

*If it was, it meant he had lied to her. Lied by way of omission. The time-honored road to dishonesty practiced by…*a niggling image of herself attempting to re-define the connotation of a stranger in order to circumvent her promise to Laurent came uncomfortably to mind.

"We are not acquaintances in that way," Briande was saying. "I have met him upon occasion, but there is no one in St-Buvard—or indeed in Aix-en-Provence—who does not know the *vigneron criminel* and his *Americaine* wife."

If Maggie hadn't already been sitting, she would certainly need to now. *Did Laurent know this? Did he know they were infamous in the region? Did he know his criminal past was widely spoken of?*

In any event, the interview was over. Maggie struggled to her feet. She felt a trickle of perspiration inch its way down her back and, autumn or not, she felt overly warm and breathless.

She shook hands with Briande, noting his amusement at her discomfiture. She had come with the intention of putting him on a list of possible suspects that might edge Julia out of pole position.

She left with a very big bone to pick with her husband.

Susan Kiernan-Lewis

# Chapter Twelve

Annette watched the pickers stroll down the long winding rows of the vineyard. It was well past lunchtime but they were obviously breaking for a meal in one of the clearings at the north perimeter of the old stonewall that enclosed the vineyard. It had not surprised her to discover that the American woman owned a large *mas* in Provence.

It was practically a cliché—the English and the Americans swooping in to buy great tracts of land in order to impress their friends; living in quaint stone houses that had stood, some of them, for hundreds of years. Bragging rights. *To have that kind of money!*

She watched the large man move among the workers. At first she thought he was the foreman, normally an owner didn't need to get so dirty, but she could see by the way they deferred to him—all of them—that it must be his vineyard.

She knew who he was—who they both were. *Wealthy outsiders. Here to pretend to be a kind of people that they were not. Playing a game for their own amusement.* The size of the estate was considerable. To play such a game of this magnitude, they must be rich indeed. And the rich always commanded the tune and the dance. Her thoughts flitted briefly to Michelle. *Would money really solve her problems? Could money possibly make her less angry at the world?*

She lit a cigarette and tossed her lighter on the car seat next to her. However rich or powerful these people were, they would not be allowed to interfere with what had been put into motion. She heard the crunch of gravel from a long distance away and turned her focus away from the fields and to the end of the estate's driveway where she would be able to clearly see the American as she approached. In her rear view mirror, she could see the big man in the field was standing with his hands on his hips, looking in her direction. She smiled. As well he might. He saw a strange car in his driveway. He would be wondering.

As the American's car came into view, Annette threw her cigarette out of the window and stepped out of the car. She would need to be quick. The master of the house was indeed curious, and with a very pregnant wife likely overly protective too. She kept the keys firmly in her hand as she waited for the car to come to a stop next to hers. The American was out of the car almost before it was completely stopped. She was younger than Annette had thought, and prettier.

It didn't matter.

"Madame Dernier?" she said, her voice imperious and cold.

The American came around the car to face her without their vehicles between them. Annette couldn't help but notice that she glanced to the fields where her husband must still be watching.

"And you are?"

*The American's French sounded like crows fighting over a chicken bone. It was physically painful to hear her speak.* Annette held up her hand. "I know enough English to spare both of us any more discomfort with your attempts to speak French. I will be brief. I am Annette Tatois, the wife of the man your English friend murdered."

The American made a most unpleasant—almost comical—face and said, "You mean ex-wife, I think."

*The effrontery! Michelle was at least right about one thing. This cochon would ruin everything if given the chance.* Annette forced herself to ignore the comment.

"I must insist that you stay away from my daughter and my aunt, Lily Tatois. If you refuse, I will have no recourse but to have you arrested."

The woman made a very unladylike sound. "On what charges? You can't have me arrested for speaking to people."

"No?" *How was it the cochon was so bold?* She looked ready to deliver her *vache* at any moment, yet she faced Annette as confidently as if she had just stepped down from a Paris catwalk. "I have friends in the police." She noticed that Madame Dernier's eyes had caught a movement over Annette's shoulder. *The husband must be approaching.*

Annette turned and slipped into the driver's seat of her car and jammed the keys into the ignition. From this direction she could see confirmation of what she had suspected. Dernier was striding toward the house and would reach them within seconds. Annette started the car up with a roar, making the American jump. As she turned to back the car up the long drive, she spoke loudly out of the open driver's side window.

"If you do not care for yourself, Madame," she said. "Perhaps you will care for your friend. As bad as you think it is for her right now, I promise you, I can make it much, much worse for her."

Just as he reached them, Annette sped backward down the drive, enjoying the sight of gravel from her tires spraying the two figures as she did.

The night had not begun well at all.

When Grace walked to Danielle and Jean-Luc's farmhouse next door—nearly a mile from *Domaine St-Buvard*—to retrieve

Zou-zou, she had been invited to spend the night. It was clear to any and all who could see that the child had become attached to Danielle and no doubt had begged to stay. Grace, probably thinking Maggie and Laurent could use some *alone time*, accepted the invitation.

Now Maggie sat alone in her dining room, fuming, with nothing to distract her from the showdown she had every intention of having with Laurent as soon as he returned from the field. The pickers were staying later and later each day. Often they worked long into the evening, as it was cooler and more pleasant to work at night. Laurent had set up outdoor lighting along the outer perimeter of the vineyard.

When he finally came into the kitchen, well past ten o'clock, his face sunburned and his shoulders sloping from his long day, she was ready for him. Before he even had a chance to throw down the cloth that he had used to wipe the grime of the day from his face, she confronted him.

"Can you talk to me about the *Mistral Promis*?"

"*Comment*?" He frowned. The confusion—if there was any—didn't last long. She could see the work going on behind his eyes as he quickly assessed the situation. "What do you wish to know?" he responded drily before turning to the sink to wash his hands.

"It's true, then? You gambled on the weather? You wagered a lot of money guessing on when the mistral would come through last year?"

Laurent took his time to dry his hands and reach for a clean wineglass before answering. "*Oui*. So?"

"Did you lose much?"

He poured his wine and held it up to the light to examine its color. He looked at her over the rim as he drank. "Why are you asking me this?" he asked, regarding her coolly.

"You don't think this is information that might be important for me to know?"

Maddingly, he shrugged. "If it was, I would have told you."

"You don't think losing whatever princely sum you lost, *gambling*, involved me?"

"I think I just answered that. Maggie, I am tired. It has been a long day."

A needle of guilt touched her. Whenever *she* was late getting home he always had a hot meal ready for her. Always. She glanced at the cold oven, still spotless from his ministrations this morning. "Are you hungry?"

He smiled at her. "*Non, chérie.* I ate in the field."

"Can I ask you how much we lost?"

Laurent sighed heavily. "Has your lifestyle changed? Did we not still fly to Atlanta this year? Are we not still doing renovations in the house for the baby's room?"

Feeling like her concerns were being batted away like an annoying fly, Maggie fought down the frustration that was building in her chest. "It's not the gambling as much as the fact that you kept it a secret. I heard today that this *Mistral Promis* was a huge deal and that practically everybody in Provence was ruined by it."

"That is obviously an exaggeration."

"I heard that it wiped out the fortunes of many men. Is *that* an exaggeration?"

"From whom did you hear this?"

Maggie hesitated. She stared at him as if she hadn't understood his question.

"Maggie?"

"It doesn't matter from whom," she said. "The point is you kept a secret from me. You understand the concept of lying by omission?"

"I more than anyone," he said.

"What is that supposed to mean?" But her indignant tone was softened by her untimely realization of her many attempts in the past to circumvent Laurent by not telling him the whole truth. The look on Laurent's face plainly showed he was thinking the same thing. "Okay, fine," she said instead. "But it's still upsetting. To be told by a total stranger something so significant about my husband—and I knew nothing about it."

"Again, who was this total stranger?" Laurent looked a lot less playful now and Maggie realized the showdown had taken a nauseating U-turn.

*Crap.* If she said *no one*—which was her first and strongest inclination—she would be caught in a bald-faced lie and there it was. She pulled up a kitchen chair and sank into it. Maybe the baby was stealing blood from her brain or something. She used to be a whole lot faster than this.

"I met with Yves Briande today."

Laurent raised an eyebrow.

"Jacques's accountant," she said.

"The one Jean-Luc told me about," he said. His brows knit together and she could see he was not pleased. "Doesn't he qualify as a stranger? And did we not agree you would not approach strangers related to this case?"

The argument she had assuaged herself with earlier—that Briande was a professional services provider and therefore somehow not to be considered a stranger in the sense that Laurent had meant—sounded ludicrous to her now as she stood before her slowly smoldering spouse.

"I'm sorry, Laurent," she said meekly. "I met him in his office in broad daylight and I just didn't think you meant *stranger* in that way."

"It appears that next time I will have to carefully define my words," he said, his eyes narrowing.

"No. I'm sorry, Laurent. I knew what you meant. I just had to see for myself if he wasn't a better candidate for Jacques's killer. I don't have an excuse for going back on my word."

Laurent set his wineglass down on the counter and reached out for her, drawing her slowly to him. She felt like she could melt into him, so strong and capable was he. He made her feel like he could take care of everything. It occurred to her that their child would get that very same feeling from these arms and the thought made her smile. He tilted her head back and kissed her mouth and then pushed her hair from her face.

"So we have both had our indiscretions with the truth, yes?" he said.

"Yes," Maggie said, enjoying how easy it was to lose herself in the depths of his dark brown eyes, the curve of his full lips, so close to her face.

"And going forward," he whispered, kissing her neck and moving his hand down her back to cup her bottom, "we will be better to always tell the truth, the whole truth."

"And nothing but the truth," she said, smiling into his neck and loving the smell of him mixed with sun and sweat and somehow even lemons.

"*Bon*," he said, kissing her deeply.

An hour later, they lay in bed together with the remnants of a lovers' picnic on the bed with them. It hadn't occurred to Maggie until they had an evening without Grace in the house that her presence had been somewhat oppressive. Living with a depressed person, Maggie thought, doesn't do much for the rest of the household. She felt guilty for being so grateful for the respite, but she couldn't deny that she and Laurent needed this connection—now more than ever.

"How long do you think we have before these lazy nights of love and food are behind us?"

Laurent looked at her and frowned. "Why would that be?"

"When the baby comes, Laurent. We won't have the energy for anything like this until he goes off to college."

"*Vraiment*?" Laurent looked around the bed with its covering of saucers of cheese and tapenade, aioli and crusty bread.

"Grace says *forget* ever having a moment to yourself after the baby comes."

Laurent shrugged and removed a small saucer of olives to the bedside table. It pleased Maggie that he didn't seem to care how the baby might disrupt their lives. He was so affable (about most things anyway), it was hard to imagine a little thing like a crying baby derailing his schedule *or* his usual good mood.

"You haven't asked me anything about that horrible woman's visit this afternoon."

Laurent sighed and brushed crumbs from the duvet. "Always I am putting up with these things when you are investigating your little mysteries. A strange woman comes to my house to threaten my pregnant wife? How can I be surprised?"

"Well, I certainly did nothing to provoke her visit!"

"Then why did she come?"

"I have no idea! Or, I mean—if I were to make a wild guess—it might be because I spoke with her daughter, that equally horrible Michelle, and before you get started, Laurent, this was *before* we agreed that I wouldn't talk to strangers, although, I'd already met her so technically she wasn't really a stranger."

"The woman today was Jacques's ex-wife?"

"Yes, and she threatened to make life worse for Julia if I talked to Michelle or Lily again. Can you believe that? She said she knew someone high up in the police department."

"As do you."

"Except *my* contact in the police department doesn't talk to me, let alone do special favors for me."

"Is it too much to hope it will remain so?"

Maggie snapped off the bedroom lamp and snuggled down with Laurent in bed. He wrapped his arms around her.

"I wonder if there's something specific she's afraid I'll find out?" she mused sleepily.

Laurent yawned. "Perhaps she is not as uncaring as you think. Perhaps she is trying to protect the old woman's peace in her last days."

Maggie sat up and snapped the lamp back on. "What do you mean *last days*?"

"Maggie, the light…"

"Is Lily sick?"

Laurent rubbed his face and gave her a long-suffering look. "I heard it from Jean-Luc," he said, stifling a yawn, "who heard it from Danielle that Lily has cancer of the throat. The doctors say she is terminal and it will be not much longer now."

Maggie stared at him. "How *much* not longer?"

"Three months."

The next morning, Laurent woke Maggie in bed with a kiss and a steaming cup of *café au lait*. She pushed her pillows up behind her to sit up and see out the bedroom window. From this vantage point, she could see the pickers combing the vineyard outside like somnolent locusts, creeping along and methodically stripping the vines as they went.

"Have you been up long?"

"*Oui*," he said from the doorway. "Grace came home early this morning and went back to bed. She said that Zou-zou will stay with Danielle and Jean-Luc for a little while."

"I suppose that's probably best. She's not in really great shape."

"*Non*. Make her a tray before you leave, yes? *Chocolat* is good for sadness. I have *des pains au chocolat* for her."

"I will. Where is it I'm going?"

Laurent grinned. "*Je ne sais pas, chérie*, but I know it's somewhere. *Fais attention*, eh?" *Be careful.*

"I will." Maggie took a luxurious sip of her coffee and sank a little further into her pillows. "Love you, Laurent," she said as he vanished from sight.

"*Je t'aime aussi*," he called from the hall.

Maggie looked out her window until she saw Laurent's familiar form moving steadily through the throng of workers in the field. If this wasn't his favorite time of the year it was pretty close. Not only was it the culmination of a year long cultivation of his grapes—the hours of tending, staking, feeding, watering and weeding—not to mention the hours of talking and arguing about the grapes with the other vintners in the area. Just organizing the all-important construction of the best supports for the vines was an ongoing project. *If a French vineyard was a high school, then harvest time was the prom,* Maggie thought with a smile.

She put a hand on her very pregnant belly and felt the movements and flutters of the little one inside. Your birthday will probably come right around harvest time. So your Papa will always be in a state of high excitement. A little foot seemed to kick her hand in answer. *God, I hope you're a boy.* As soon as the thought was in her head her mouth fell open in surprise. She had no idea that thought was even there.

She never thought she had a preference one way or the other. And the way Laurent falls all over Zou-zou, it was clear the man was *born* to have a little girl. So where did the thought come from? Her eyes went out the window again where she picked out his form again. She saw him clapping a worker on the back. Laurent was such a man's man.

Was she hoping to give him a boy to share his passion? A boy to trot at his heels and keep his name? Well, it's true, she thought. A girl to wrap him around his little finger, to make his eyes fill with pride and tears at her strength, her poise, her beauty. A little girl to sit on his lap and call him *ma Papa*.

But first, a son.

After a long hot shower, Maggie pulled on one of the last sundresses she owned that still fit her and was aghast that she appeared to now be getting larger by the day. The dress pulled across her bust and her belly making her look like she squeezed into it—which she had. Before she even made it downstairs she was feeling tired and hot, and it wasn't eleven o'clock yet. She tiptoed by Grace's room first and confirmed by the sound of soft snoring that she wasn't up yet. In the kitchen, she put a tray together containing three *pain au chocolat* and a sliced pear. She debated between a glass of milk and coffee and finally opted for the milk. She didn't know how long Grace would sleep and the coffee would cool too quickly.

She left the tray and moved into the living room, where she and Laurent kept their desktop computer on an old battered desk that had belonged to Laurent's uncle. He had never met the man but the desk was one of the few pieces of furniture that hadn't been rubbish, and Maggie knew Laurent had been pleased to keep something of his family, his past.

She lay down her own *pain au chocolat* on the desk and wiped her fingers on the cloth napkin. Laurent would fuss at her for not using a plate so she was careful to pick up all the flakes from the delicate croissant that she left on the desk. She opened up a browser and typed in "poisonous mushrooms." It took only a few moments to see that *agaricus* mushrooms were common in the area and looked not at all deadly. She studied the picture on the website showing them nestled in a clump at the base of a tree.

She printed out the picture on their wireless printer, polished off her breakfast and went to pour Grace's milk in the glass.

*Were the deadly mushrooms really that commonplace? Could anyone collect them pretty easily?* She picked up the tray and walked carefully upstairs with it. *What I wouldn't give to see the history on Michelle's computer!* She wondered if the police had taken Julia's computer and assumed they probably had.

She stood outside Grace's door and listened. She didn't hear snoring anymore, but she didn't hear anything else either. She hesitated, wondering if she should knock or just leave the tray. Finally, she set the tray down. Even if Grace was awake, she probably wanted to be alone, Maggie reasoned. She tiptoed away from the door and back downstairs.

As she collected her purse, the photo from the printer, and the car keys from the hook in the mudroom outside the kitchen, she noticed the mail had been delivered. It had been poked through the mail slot which perched over an old wicker basket that had probably served the same purpose since the days when the mail had come by horse and wagon. She glanced in the basket in passing and saw her name on a long white envelope on top.

A very formal long white envelope. Curious, she picked it out of the basket and looked at the return address label. It was from the Aix Police Department.

*Whatever in the world?* She quickly opened it and pulled out a short piece of paper that, in essence, informed her that she was required to show up for a hearing in two weeks time on a charge of jaywalking. For a moment she just stood in the mudroom and frowned in confusion. *Was it a joke?* She looked at the return address again and saw that it was embossed. It was legitimate.

*Jaywalking?*

And then it came to her: *Son of a bitch.*

*Roger.*

She stuffed the letter into her purse, refraining from ripping it into two neat pieces first. Whatever his game was, she couldn't do anything about it and she would not let it emotionally derail her in the process.

*What a jerk!*

Taking deep breaths to restore her calm, Maggie settled into the driver's seat of the car and placed both hands on the steering wheel to steady herself. When she looked up, she saw Grace standing in the window of her bedroom. As soon as Maggie saw her, Grace moved away.

Maggie felt a wave of helplessness wash over her. Grace had come to *Domaine St-Buvard* to heal, to answer questions, to rest before the big battle—whatever. And she had landed, if not on a rocky bed of disgust and anger from her best friend, then certainly not in the warm and loving support of friends. A part of Maggie wanted to rush upstairs and tell Grace that she loved her no matter what and to beg her to tell her everything —every horrible, spider-crawling, fantasy-killing confession she needed to make in order to survive this terrible passage. But the other part of her just wasn't sure.

Maggie stared up at the empty window and realized she wasn't sure about why she and Grace were friends. Or why she had chosen Julia to take her place. She wasn't sure if the baby was such a great idea, especially as different from each other as she and Laurent daily proved themselves to be. When it came right down to it, she wasn't sure her best guesses weren't usually just wildly wrong and ultimately damaging to everyone around her.

*Face it,* she thought, as an unbidden image of Julia came to mind, *If you can't trust your instincts about something so basic as the people you choose as your friends, what other kinds of mistakes in judgment are you making?*

In the end, she decided not to go back inside and put the car in reverse and backed up the long drive. She knew the forest where Julia went most often, and if she had any hope of getting there and back before dark, she needed to go now. As soon as she was on the highway, she steered her thoughts away from Grace and Julia as much as she could and tried to focus on what she hoped to find this afternoon.

First, a clue or some evidence that proved someone else—Michelle or Annette would work nicely—had been to the area, possibly to dig up poisonous mushrooms would be ideal. Failing that, Maggie didn't really know what to expect beyond the fact that this was a place that Julia went to. A lot.

*So. Three months. Poor Lily. But what a vulture Michelle was!* Michelle, who cursed the timing of her father's dying because he failed to hang on long enough to inherit—so that Michelle could then inherit. Did Lily have any idea of the monsters around her she called family? And now Florrie was next in line. Well, at least he seemed like a decent guy. Too bad he was related to such scumbags.

An hour from St-Buvard and just before the outskirts of Aix, Maggie saw the sign for *Indian Fôret Sud.* Julia had mentioned it many times to her. She was sorry now that she had never taken the time to come here with her. The memory of her last conversation with Julia came back to her as she parked the car. *So much anger. And fear.* Maggie shook her head. It was like she wasn't the same person who Maggie had known and lunched with, gushing on about her mushroom cookbook and teasing her about how motherhood would leave Maggie with no time for girlfriends.

Maggie tucked her purse under the seat and grabbed the picture of the poisonous mushrooms she had printed out from the Internet. The parking lot held three other cars, which surprised Maggie. All three vehicles looked like they might belong to farmers—they certainly weren't rental cars. *Why would farmers come to the forest?* Making sure her cellphone was in her pocket, Maggie left the car and took the first path that led from the parking lot into the woods.

The ground was scrubby and brown but punctuated with bright pockets of rosebay and the pretty yellow Spanish broom. She imagined Julia must have walked this same path every time she came here. She looked around and she couldn't help but think of Julia in this place.

This was her world. It was her Zen, her church, her *milieu*. This was where she made her discoveries. Maggie could just imagine her friend's laugher and squeals of delight as she uncovered this fungal jewel, or that one.

Maggie left the trail, holding on to the long saplings and eased herself down an easy incline. She was aware that there were wild boars in the area and she hoped they would react properly to pepper spray—as in *run in the opposite direction*.

Her breathing was coming a little hard and she cursed the fact that Laurent was probably right; the late pregnancy was slowing her down and she should be resting more. The heat of the early fall day was dissipated by the canopy of leaves that had yet to fall and Maggie was grateful for the shade.

Stepping through the thick bushes off the trail—and praying they weren't riddled with poison ivy—she spotted a clump of mushrooms at the base of a withered banyan tree. Pulling the printout from her pocket, she edged closer to the grouping. She knelt down next to the mushrooms and tried to compare what she saw on the ground with what was in the picture. They looked identical. But they also looked very much like the mushrooms that she and Laurent bought from the market in Aix each Saturday. *Hell, they looked like the mushrooms she used to buy from her local Kroger back in Atlanta.* She sank to one knee in the damp dirt, unable to balance easily at her new heavier weight.

"Crap." She pulled herself up using the side of the tree by grabbing a low hanging branch, which promptly broke off in her grasp nearly sending her over backward. She caught herself in time and leaned against the tree, taking a moment to regroup. *Could Julia possibly have made a mistake?* They look so much like the poisoned mushrooms in the picture. Could she have *accidentally* fed Jacques the wrong mushrooms? She shook her head. But Julia ate the omelet, too.

*She said.*

Maggie hated the kernel of doubt that seemed to be interfering with every theory she developed lately. *Could Julia have done it? Could she have planned it?* Reminding herself that she hadn't known her all that long, Maggie stooped again to look at the mushrooms and, although not sure why, snapped a photo of them.

As soon as she stood up she heard somewhere close by the sound a dry stick makes when a heavy foot treads on it. Whirling around to see who or what was approaching, Maggie was struck full in the face by a hard, wide hand that grabbed her harshly, covering her nose and mouth.

# Chapter Thirteen

Maggie fought for breath as she clawed at the hand over her face. At first she could only smell and feel what was happening to her. Her sight seemed to have failed as she grappled with her assailant. Even at eight months pregnant, she felt light and inconsequential in the punishing grasp of the much larger man.

She struggled to free herself from his tightening grip. At the exact moment she knew she was losing the fight for breath, he took his hands from her face. He held her at arms' length from him. She stumbled against him, gasping, her knees weak and doing nothing to support her weight. He held her in her standing position, his arms shaking with either exertion or anger.

When she had gotten her breath back enough to register her surroundings again, she saw that it was *him.*

*Mathieu.*

He looked even more terrifying close up. His bottom lip was punctured by several hooks and piercings. His lips were pulled back in a grimace in what looked like barely-controlled revulsion. For one mad moment, Maggie thought he intended to bite her.

"What are you doing here?" he growled in guttural French. She could barely understand him, the languorous weight of the difficult *patois* of the region stretching out his syllables, distorting the words she should have known so well. He shook her and repeated his question.

"I'm here for Julia," she said, her voice rasping in fear even to her own ears.

A mixture of distrust and guilt seemed to cross his face, but maybe she imagined that. If he killed Jacques—and he certainly looked like he could have—he would have no problem killing her, too. *Was he trying to protect Julia? Or was he using her to cover his own tracks?*

"M-many people know I am here today," she said, trying to hear her own words over the pounding of her heart in her ears. "If…if you hurt me…"

Abruptly, he let go of her and she fell to her knees on the damp ground, her cellphone, which had been clutched in her hand, falling into the mushrooms at the base of the tree. She looked up at him, her fear evolving to a strange numbness. *Was she going to die here…in the peaceful forest…in Julia's special place?* Maggie looked past him into the verdant dark interior and felt a strange peace come over her which blocked out the vision of the towering form of the angry man.

Suddenly Mathieu threw something in the bushes and ran toward the parking lot. Maggie didn't turn to watch him go. She could hear the sounds of breaking branches and crushed brushes that heralded his departure. Depleted, physically and emotionally, she sank against the tree and waited to get her strength back, her glance falling on the little burlap bag floating atop the bushes beside her.

It took Maggie nearly a quarter of an hour to make her way back to the parked car. She could see that all the cars in the parking lot were gone now. She wondered who the other people had been and if they had witnessed the assault. If so, they certainly hadn't done anything to help.

She picked her way gingerly to the car from the trail. She had only been about five minutes into the forest, but from where she lay after Mathieu grabbed her, it had felt like much more. Her dress was ruined, streaked with mud, and she'd scratched one leg, which bled, when she fell into the bushes, but otherwise no real harm done.

The baby was kicking merrily along, she noticed as she slid into the driver's seat of her car, so clearly he hadn't been negatively impacted by her adventure.

But she knew it had been a close all. From the comfort and safety of her car, she tried to imagine what Laurent would do or say if he knew that she had been physically attacked in the woods today. Suffice to say, he could never know. Today Laurent's worst fears had nearly been realized. She had taken a chance and she had suffered the consequence of it. She pulled down the visor to examine her face in the mirror. *What if Julia really was guilty? What if she and that thug had committed murder? And here I am going around jeopardizing my life— and the life of my baby—for someone who doesn't deserve it?*

That thought stopped her because of course it wasn't a matter of *deserving,* and she, of all people, should know that. She wasn't doing all this to free Julia because her friend had somehow proven herself worthy. She was doing it because she believed she knew Julia well enough to know she wasn't capable of this crime.

She smiled into the mirror, ignoring the dirt. *Julia didn't kill Jacques.* Not like this. Not by planning it, finding the mushrooms, preparing them, inviting him over and feeding them to him. No way. Maybe in the middle of a terrible argument with a quickly grabbed up steak knife to the heart... but that was not how Jacques died. *And this way, the way he did die, well, there was no way Julia Patrick could have done that.* Maggie knew it as well as she knew anything. And had always known it.

Feeling more at peace than she had in days, she started the car. She assumed she had plenty of time to bathe and change clothes before Laurent was home from his long day in the vineyard, but she would feel better when she was cleaned up. She glanced briefly at the burlap bag in the passenger's seat next to her. Inside were a variety of different kinds of mushrooms—none of which looked anything like the deadly ones in Maggie's Internet photo. If Mathieu had been in the forest foraging for mushrooms—as it now appeared he was— he was either very bad at telling the deadly ones from the good ones, or he didn't currently have anybody else he wanted to kill.

\* \* \* \*

He stared at his hands until they stopped shaking. In the past, he had trained himself to control the shaking, even willed himself to lower the numbers when the corpsman strapped on the blood pressure cuff. It could be done. He had done it. *If you were disciplined. If you knew your own strengths, you could conquer your own weaknesses.* He dropped his hands and slumped against the steering wheel, resting his head on his arms.

*How close had he come to hurting that woman?*

It had all happened too fast. One minute he was alone and the next she was there—there where she shouldn't be. *Damn!* He had just wanted to stop her from being there, to make her leave, but he could see how frightened she was. And *he* had done that. Attacking the woman in the forest today…that made three major lapses in a week. Allowing himself to be caught at the laboratory was particularly galling. *And then, of course, the other. With Julia.* He cringed to think of it. To think of her. He had to face it now. There was no good in pretending otherwise.

He was no longer in control at all.

And he knew better than anyone what hell that promised.

Desperate to use the bathroom, Maggie was dismayed to see that the driveway of *Domaine St-Buvard* appeared to be blocked. Upon closer inspection, her dismay turned to nausea and a churning stomach when she saw that the vehicles blocking the drive were police cars.

While it had been years since she had any real worries about Laurent's criminal past, she was sickened to realize as she drove slowly up the driveway that in some ways they had always been right below the surface. Seeing the police now at her house—two cars with four police officers standing in the driveway—she knew without knowing that they were here for Laurent.

She parked her car on the grassy side of the driveway and hurried toward the grouping. One of the men was smoking. He watched her approach with a frown, as if annoyed to have to deal with her. Maggie could see that the few pickers who still remained to do the last little bit of work had stopped and were watching the proceedings with apparent fascination. She saw Laurent as soon as she rounded the curved bend in the driveway. It was hard not to. He was the tallest of the five men and he stood among them, his back ramrod straight, his thick dark hair tousled and flying about his face. His hands handcuffed behind his back.

"Laurent!" she cried out as she trotted toward him. He turned toward her and his look wasn't one of welcome or relief. *He probably hoped to be gone before I returned,* she thought helplessly.

She confronted the smoking cop, the first one she came to. "What is the meaning of this?"

He took a long drag on his cigarette and eyed her from head to toe. "Your name, Madame?" he said in the thick accent of the region.

*Bumpkin!* Maggie thought with frustration, turning from him to where the other police were putting Laurent into the back of one of the cruisers.

"Can someone tell me what's going on? Laurent, where are they taking you?" Maggie knew she sounded close to tears and she hated that. It was hard enough on him without his having to soothe her, too.

"*Cela ne fait rien, chérie,*" he said. *It's nothing.* "Go inside. I will call you later."

"Laurent, no," Maggie said. "Are you under arrest?" She turned to the two policemen who were sliding into the front seat of the cruiser. "What are the charges?" she asked them.

"Go inside, *chérie,*" Laurent repeated, his face creased with dirt from a day in the fields, his voice pinched with tension.

Maggie watched as the two cars backed out of the drive and disappeared. She turned and bolted for the house.

Grace was sitting on the couch in the living room with Petit-Four on her lap. She looked like she had just awakened although it was well after four in the afternoon.

"There's a lot of noise going on outside," Grace said without looking up at Maggie. "It woke me up."

Maggie ignored her and raced upstairs to the bathroom where, after using the toilet, she quickly washed her face of any telltale dirt of her encounter in the forest and hurried downstairs.

"Where's Z?" Maggie asked as she fumbled for her cellphone and her car keys in her purse.

Grace shrugged. "With Danielle, I imagine."

Maggie hesitated. "Are you going to be okay? I have to go to Aix."

Grace leaned down and hugged the little dog. "Petit-Four and I will be fine, won't we, pet?"

Afraid that Grace was either losing her mind or on drugs or both, but knowing she didn't have time to deal with it in any case, Maggie turned and, for the second time that day, fled the house.

Once in the Renault, Maggie adjusted her seatbelt across her belly and slammed the car into reverse. She backed up the driveway. It would take thirty minutes to get to the A8 and another thirty to reach Aix. She put on her earphones and punched in Roger's number. She didn't expect him to answer—he'd stop taking her calls days ago—and particularly not today, but it didn't matter. She had sixty minutes—or however long his voice mail could hold—of venting that he could listen to at his leisure.

When the recorded message finished, she ratcheted up the volume and began. "This is a low move even for you, Roger," she said, feeling her fury build the moment she started speaking. "This is harassment in any language. What's the matter? Was I getting too close to some important answers? Were you afraid of being shown up by the pregnant American? *Again*? I thought better of you, Roger. Seriously. Ask your model girlfriend if she's impressed with this kind of behavior. What is it, exactly, that you think you're—"

"I would stop now before you find yourself in very big trouble, Madame Dernier." Roger's smooth voice slithered across the connection and Maggie was so surprised that she was momentarily speechless.

"You...you know this is harassment, Roger," she said finally. "You can't just arrest people because you've got a bur under your saddle."

"I didn't. Your husband was brought in as a result of a complaint made against him by one of his pickers."

"That's a lie," Maggie said hotly. "Laurent's workers love him. To a man."

"You are misinformed as to the character of your husband, Madame Dernier," Roger said unctuously. Maggie imagined him rubbing his hands together with glee. "Many wives often are, I am told."

"What kind of complaint?"

"Physical abuse."

"No way. Laurent would never hit anyone."

"Even if he were defending your honor? That's quite a statement. I'm not sure I could attest to being so restrained myself under that circumstance."

"I do not know what kind of bullshit game you're playing, Roger, but it is beneath you. This is the behavior of jealous maniac."

"So you think my girlfriend is a model? She is beautiful, isn't she?"

"I'm worried about you, Roger. Seriously. You used to be somewhat normal. What you're doing is wrong and you know it."

"I'm sorry if you thought that our acquaintance would afford you privileges that I don't feel comfortable offering you, Madame," he said smoothly. "Your husband must pay the price for his crimes like anyone else. It would be an unspeakable breach of my position for me to interfere. I hope you understand."

"Oh, trust me, I do," Maggie said and broke the connection before she could add anything that might not help Laurent get released as soon as possible. "*Dickhead*," she said, accelerating.

Forty minutes later when she reached Aix, she was forced to park two blocks away. Cursing the fact that it was now well after five and full into the Aix rush hour with people racing about doing their marketing for dinner, Maggie hurried to the imposing police station, dodging shoppers and office workers on the broken and uneven sidewalk. When she turned the corner to the station she ran up the steps of the building and found Laurent sitting out front in one of the rusting café chairs.

"Laurent! Did they just release you? Are all the charges dropped? What *were* the charges? Why didn't you call me when they let you go?"

Laurent stood up and patted his shirt pocket. He shrugged. "I must have left it in my other shirt."

She shook her head and grinned. She knew he hated public displays of affection—and that was probably especially true in front of the police station—so she resisted the urge to throw her arms around him. But seeing him free with no harm done from the experience filled her with immense relief. She felt the clenched tension that had fueled her drive to the city drain from her shoulders. "So they just drove you to Aix and let you go?"

"Pretty much." Laurent took her arm and guided her down the steps to the street as if she hadn't just vaulted up them with the agility of a non-pregnant teenager. "The so-called complaint vanished by the time they brought me in."

"Who complained about you?"

"No one," he said. "Or if there was someone, he recanted before the charge could be formally made."

"This is Roger's doing*,*" Maggie said. "It's harassment, pure and simple."

*"Peut-être."* Maybe.

When they reached the street, Laurent stopped and held her at arms' length for a moment. He frowned. "While I am happy to see you under any circumstances, *chérie,*" he said, "do you want to explain why it looks as if you have been combat-crawling through the vineyard in your best dress?"

"This is not my best dress, Laurent. It's just the only one left that still fits at this stage of the game."

The look he gave her was easy to translate.

"Okay, look, I had a little hike in the forest where Julia goes for her mushrooms. That's all."

He continued to look expectantly at her.

"And I might've slipped in the mud at one point. Not a biggie. I didn't even fall all the way down."

He looked at the side of her dress which was caked in brown mud from hip to hem.

"Okay, I did fall a little bit but the mud was soft, Laurent. And even though I bruise really easy these days, I didn't fall hard enough to do that."

He reached out and touched her jaw and frowned. "Then how is it you have a bruise on your chin?"

"My chin?" As Maggie's fingers flew to her face, she could feel the tenderness where Mathieu's hand had gripped her. Her mind raced, and just when she was settling on the inevitability of telling Laurent the whole painful truth, she saw that he was no longer looking at her. Instead, he was staring, with an expression as close to shock as she had ever seen on him, over her shoulder at the parking lot. She turned to follow his gaze to where their car sat—exactly where she'd parked it —with the front windshield a demented spider's web of cracks and blood coating the grill and front bumper.

"Holy shit," she said in a low whisper.

Laurent strode to the car and walked around it without speaking. He plucked a note from the battered windshield wipers and read it before handing it to her.

"For a moment," he said looking at the damaged car, "I was afraid you had driven to my rescue with a little too much enthusiasm."

The note read: "*Since you care for the wellbeing of animals so much, you will be glad to know only chickens were murdered for this message. Next time the joke will be on you.*"

"Is she crazy?" Maggie held the note up. "This is a written confession that she's vandalized our car. *And* she's threatening me."

Laurent gave her a weary look. "*Qui?*"

"Michelle," Maggie said. She cleared her throat and looked away. "I might have mentioned to her in passing how much I like animals."

"*Vraiment*, Maggie?"

Maggie pretended to concentrate on the note in her hand.

"*Bon*," he said. "Get in. Be careful of the broken glass on the seat."

\* \* \*

In the end it had taken very little.

Julia was surprised at *how* little was required. For weeks she watched the others barter and trade for protection, for pleasure, for relief. At first, it had felt impossible—insurmountable—the amount of wealth needed to assuage the daily fear. But then, Julia had been thinking in terms of food, of warmth, of a respite from the pain and the humiliation. When it came right down to it, the thing she really needed—and had needed right from the start although she didn't know it then—was very cheaply had.

She didn't need to ask Maggie to give her money or slip her cartons of cigarettes. She didn't need to determine which guard could be bribed to be kind. She didn't need to attach herself to any group of women in particular—the terrifying or the more terrifying.

In the end, it was a simple act of friendship, honestly given, that made her ultimate deliverance possible. *Who would have thought?* When she finally came to the point where she knew what she wanted, *what she needed*, it was really only valuable to the buyer. For Julia, it had cost nothing. Less than nothing.

*A shiv for a kiss. Poetic, really. And such a chaste kiss.* On the cheek but freely given with care and sympathy and human feeling. There could be no doubt of that from either party. *And really, when you thought about it, what could be more valuable in this place of horror than that?*

Julia smiled bitterly, the knife tucked carefully into the front of her jumpsuit, its sharpened edge against her skin a promise of rescue and peace. She huddled on her damp mattress shoved up against the wall of her cell and waited.

*Who could have imagined that all it would take was a simple act of kindness?*

# Chapter Fourteen

The cobblestone square in front of *Le Canard*, the village café in St-Buvard, was littered with crisp, brightly colored leaves. As a brisk autumn breeze picked them up and tossed them into an intricate vortex of activity, Grace couldn't help but think it an animated metaphor for her own life. The thought made her smile. *So inane*. And if her life was a convoluted crazy-quilt of events and happenings as volatile and random as the wind, then surely she could absolve herself of the very real part she had taken to create the disturbance?

"You're smiling. What's up?"

Grace turned to look at Maggie. They sat with Danielle Pernon in slowly deteriorating wicker chairs on the café's terrace, their food market purchases in string bags at their feet, cooling cups of *espressos* on the table.

"Nothing," she said. "Just thinking about my life."

"Glad that makes you smile," Maggie said.

Grace looked back at the dancing leaves in the square. "Why not?"

"Your color has come back," Danielle said.

That made Grace smile even more. It was such a maternal thing to say. Grace decided she loved the older woman for it.

"Yeah," Maggie said, "you blondes can't afford to lose any color. You'll have to wear chartreuse, and I know how that would kill you."

"I must be feeling better," Grace said, "if you're teasing me again." She picked up her *demitasse* and brought it to her lips. She had to admit, she felt better. Lately there were a few hours in the day when she actually didn't feel like shit. And today, not but a few moments ago, she had felt a ghost of a memory of what happiness felt like. It was gone quickly, but it had been there. A memory of sunny days and wine and laughter with good friends. It was hard to have that memory without thinking of Win, too. She wondered if she would ever be able to think of sunny days and wine without thinking of him.

*And wanting to cry.*

"Okay, now you're starting to lose it again," Maggie said, watching her over her coffee cup.

"Take me out from under the microscope, darling," Grace said, allowing an edge to come through in her voice. "I am what I am. And please, no Popeye references." She turned to Danielle. "How is Lily Tatois doing? I heard she was ill."

Danielle hunched in her thin coat and Grace wondered if she and Jean-Luc were having money problems. The coat was old and unattractive, but perhaps that was just Danielle's lack of taste showing. It did look like it was a label at least. Just not one from this decade.

"She is not doing well, I'm afraid. I hate to say that the death of her nephew has been the occasion for us to renew our acquaintance with each other, but that's the truth. And now that she is dying, she is open to resuming our friendship."

"Were you close before?" Maggie asked.

Danielle shrugged. "We were school girls together but not from the same class. Lily was beautiful and confident and rich. I wasn't."

"But she wants to be friends now?" Grace said as she redirected her gaze across the courtyard to a van laboriously unloading heavy pipes on the sidewalk.

"I don't fault her for that," Danielle said. "It breaks my heart to see her like this."

"So is she really going downhill? I thought the doctor gave her three months."

"I'm afraid recent events have worn on her."

"Yeah, I'll say," Maggie said. "Just having Michelle as a member of my family would wear on me, big time."

Grace noticed that Danielle seemed to give Maggie a disapproving look and it amused her to see it. In any case, it didn't seem to bother Maggie, which surprised Grace not one bit.

"How are you coming on the case?" Grace asked her.

Maggie's face brightened. "Well, not great," she said cheerfully. "I have more suspects than I know what to do with and none of them are of interest to the police, which of course is not a shock, but still." She turned to Danielle. "Have you ever heard of anyone in town by the name of Mathieu Benoit? He's truly a dangerous character. I would tell you, Danielle, of how I know that to be true from personal experience but I know how you hate to keep secrets from Jean-Luc, who then hates to keep secrets from Laurent…"

Danielle put her coffee cup down with a clatter. "If you are doing *anything* to endanger yourself or that little baby, Maggie Dernier—"

"I'm not! Jeez, Danielle, take a chill pill."

"Maggie is teaching me American idiom."

"God, Danielle, I didn't know you had a sarcastic bone in your body until just this moment," Grace said, laughing. "I'm glad to see it."

Maggie put her hands up as if to defend herself. "I just need to know if you know this guy, Mathieu. Jean-Luc said you know everyone in town, including Avignon, Aix and half of Marseilles."

"Mathieu Benoit is the son of a friend of a cousin of mine," Danielle said primly. Grace could tell Danielle didn't always know how to react to Maggie. Frankly, Grace thought that that was part of Maggie's charm.

"And?" Maggie prompted. "Star student at his high school? Rap sheet a mile long? Come on, Danielle. He looks like he's already a headliner with Interpol. What's the gossip?"

"I don't listen to gossip, Maggie," Danielle said, "but Mathieu, I believe, has in fact been a disappointment to his family."

"This is like pulling teeth from a chicken."

Grace patted Danielle's hand. "She said *chicken,* Danielle, because chicken notoriously do not have teeth."

"I am aware of Maggie's legendary impatience," Danielle said. "But I will not say more than what I know."

"Yeah, that's fine," Maggie said. "So if I were to tell you that I'm meeting Mathieu tonight behind the old abandoned *boulangerie*, just him and me—"

"You wouldn't dare!"

"Okay, so spill it. What's his story?"

"I never said he was innocent." Danielle looked at Maggie with real aggravation. *Yep,* Grace thought with an inner smile. *That's our Maggie. She can make a saint cuss.*

"He is a hothead," Danielle said. "And very jealous. In fact…I believe he is prone to violence."

"Wow, when it rains it pours," Maggie said, nodding her head at Danielle's admissions. "Let it all out, Danielle. Could he have killed Jacques?"

"Do you mean is he capable of it?" Danielle's face relaxed and Grace saw the faintest hint of a smile coming through. "Aren't we all?"

"Some more so than others," Grace said. "What's your theory, Maggie?"

Maggie scooted up to the table as much as her expanded stomach would allow and Grace could see a pink flush of excitement on her face.

"Okay, here's how I see it. Julia and Mathieu met in their apartment building. Julia's lonely and she's had a bad experience with her last guy, Jacques, so she's vulnerable."

"I thought you said Mathieu was this big hulking brute with tattoos and piercings and a buzzed head."

"That's right."

"Well, then were you not totally flabbergasted to learn that your dear friend Julia chose someone like that?" Grace felt herself relaxing. The tension was draining out of her shoulders, her face, her arms.

"Well, sure," Maggie said, frowning. "I mean I would've been shocked to hear that Babette the village tramp was dating him, okay? He's an ape. But like I said, she was vulnerable. May I continue?"

Grace lifted one shoulder in a shrug.

"So I figure they get together, and after a few bottles of wine she tells Mathieu the whole story of how Jacques was such a rotter—and then puts the cherry on the cake with the fact that he hit her—*and* that he's trying to get back together with her—"

"*Vraiment?*" Danielle looked unconvinced. "Monsieur Tatois was attempting a reconciliation?"

"Yes," Maggie said, "and it's kind of a secret. I mean, as far as I know only Julia, Mathieu, Jacques and the murderer knew that. And I think that's significant, don't you?"

Grace watched as Maggie regained her enthusiasm at Danielle's interest. "And you, of course, darling."

"Of course."

"And Laurent? Because that would make it you, Laurent, Julia, Jacques, Mathieu, and the murderer. And of course myself and Danielle."

"*Anyway*," Maggie said, ignoring Grace, "so Mathieu—a known hothead—hears that Jacques is coming to dinner and he figures a genius way to off him is to switch the mushrooms in the omelet that Julia is preparing—"

"Whoa, wait a minute," Grace said. "How would he be able to do that? How would he know how to acquire poisonous mushrooms in the first place?"

"It just so happens," Maggie said, "that I have proof that Mathieu accompanied Julia on her foraging trips in the woods to find fresh mushrooms. He knew exactly where to go to find poisonous mushrooms."

"Because, presumably, Julia pointed them out to him? The poisonous ones?"

"Well, she's the expert."

"You admit that?"

"Look, I never said she didn't know good mushrooms from bad. Of course she does. She forages. How else would she make sure she didn't pick poisonous mushrooms?"

*Or make sure that she did,* Grace thought. "And you also admit that Tatois died eating the mushrooms she put in his omelet."

"That *Mathieu* put in his omelet."

"Okay, *whoever* put them there…you admit that he died from the omelet he ate at her house."

"What's your point here, Grace? Are you being deliberately obtuse? I *get* that the whole world thinks *Julia* poisoned Jacques. My theory turns on the same facts but points to a different person. Mathieu. He had motive. He had opportunity."

"His motive was jealousy?" Danielle asked.

"That's right."

"What do you mean you have proof that he went foraging with her?"

Maggie hesitated a moment and smoothed her long tunic over the mound of her belly. Grace could see the baby kicking from across the table.

"That's not important," Maggie said. "The point is, he knew where to get the mushrooms."

"So your contention is that he'll let Julia swing for a murder *he* committed? Kind of defeats the purpose, doesn't it? He gets rid of his rival, but loses his girlfriend in the process?" Grace felt her handbag vibrate and reached in to look at her cellphone.

"I'm working out the details," Maggie said. "Obviously I don't have access to all the information I need to fill in the blanks."

"Obviously. Maggie, is your phone turned off? Because I've got two phone calls here from Laurent and I don't think he's trying to get a hold of *me*."

Maggie pulled her phone out of her bag and frowned at the screen. "Yeah, he's called me, too. I wonder what's up." Suddenly her phone vibrated in her hand. She stared at the screen for a moment. "I don't recognize the number," she said and then, shrugging, accepted the call. "Hello?"

Within seconds, Grace watched the color drain from Maggie's face. Danielle must have seen it too for she reached for Maggie at the same time that Grace did.

"Sweetie, what is it?" Grace asked. *Was it Win? Taylor? Was Zou-zou hurt?*

Grace saw Danielle's grip tighten on Maggie's wrist but Maggie's face remained stunned and unaffected by her friend. In mounting panic, Grace watched as tears filled Maggie's eyes.

"Maggie, for God's sake, what is it?" Grace said sharply, her hand over her mouth.

Maggie dropped the phone on the table with a clatter, then grabbed it up and pushed the off button. She tossed it back down and looked at it as if it were radioactive.

"*Qu'est-ce qu'il y a?*" Danielle whispered. *What is it?*

Maggie visibly brought herself under control, even reached out to pat Danielle's hand. "It's Julia," she said, her voice hoarse as if she'd been screaming. "She tried to kill herself last night."

"Dear God," Grace said in thanks to prayer that her family was safe, and then felt a wave of guilt at Maggie's stricken face.

"Was that Roger?" she asked.

Maggie gave a disgusted laugh. "No. No, that was Annette Tatois calling to tell me in person the kind of power she has to ruin my world."

"She took credit for the suicide attempt?" Danielle extricated a tissue from her purse and dabbed at the perspiration on her top lip.

"Oh, my God," Maggie said. "Poor Julia. I can't imagine what she must be feeling to have tried something like this. I need to go to her." She stood up without knowing she was doing it, and Grace reached across the table and pulled her back down into her chair.

"Maggie, no. She'll be in the hospital under heavy guard. You're not family. You won't be allowed anywhere near her."

"She is right," Danielle said softly.

Maggie looked at them with misery and acceptance. "Annette said it was because Julia was moved into general population—something Annette is taking credit for. How can one person be so full of hate?"

The three were silent for a moment and Grace noticed that Danielle had caught the eye of the waiter. He nodded as if he understood perfectly her visual shorthand and disappeared into the café.

"I've totally let her down," Maggie said.

"Nonsense," Grace said. "You're working on it. These things take time."

"Julia almost ran out of time last night."

The waiter approached and set out three wineglasses. He decanted a bottle and poured the glasses, then silently retreated.

"I guess it's that time of day," Maggie said sadly as she lifted the glass to her lips.

"I thought we could use something a little stronger than coffee," Danielle said. "Did Madame Tatois threaten you?"

"No. She was just gloating. Horrible woman." She turned to Grace and then to Danielle. "It occurs to me that *Annette* knew that Jacques was trying to get back together with Julia. Remember how I said that was something only a few people and the murderer knew?"

"So now you think *Annette* is the murderer?" Grace asked, lifting her wineglass. It was a white wine, unusual for Provence, and she wondered how in the world Danielle had ordered it without ever mouthing a single word.

"I don't know," Maggie said, biting her lip. "But I'm telling you she knows stuff only the forensic police lab or the killer knows. And here I sit with nothing. Roger won't even take my calls."

"Have you been calling him?"

"Well, not lately," Maggie said. Grace noticed she squirmed uncomfortably, but that could just be the late stage pregnancy. "But he's my only contact on the case. Can you believe I heard about Julia's suicide attempt from her alleged victim's ex-wife? Why couldn't Roger have let me know?"

"Maybe because he's too busy having your husband arrested and fining you for jaywalking?" Grace relaxed into her chair and wondered where the fear had come from a few moments ago when she thought it was her family in danger. *So much for believing she couldn't feel anything any more.*

"I know! Can you believe that? If the head cop in France has a personal beef with someone he can just ignore her rights?" She looked indictingly at Danielle. "And everyone just accepts that?"

Danielle sighed heavily. "If you are asking is it only France where people abuse their power, I would venture to guess no."

"Okay, fine. Whatever. But I can't just sit here. The last time I talked to Julia she hung up on me. She must be feeling so alone."

"Have you talked to her attorney?"

"I tried. He won't take my calls. Poor Julia. I still can't believe this nightmare is happening to her."

"Your purse is ringing, Maggie," Danielle pointed out to her.

"It's probably Laurent," Maggie said picking it up. "No, it's another number I don't recognize. If it's Annette again, I swear...Hello?"

Grace watched Maggie frown in annoyance, so obviously it wasn't Annette.

"What did you say your name was?" Maggie listened for a moment and then made a face. "And how did you get this number? I see. Have you been in touch with Julia? Did you hear about her...accident?'"

Grace could see the impatience bristling off Maggie. Her fingers drummed the table and Danielle surreptitiously pushed her wineglass toward her.

"It's a pre-trial detention center, not a prison," Maggie said. "Have you talked to her?" Maggie's fingers stopped drumming. She looked at Grace and her mouth fell open. She spoke into the phone: "Are you shitting me?"

Grace exchanged a puzzled look with Danielle.

"Do you know that because she *said* you could have them, or because you figure she'll be in a French jail for the next fifty years so you *might as well* have them?"

Danielle covered her mouth as she listened.

"That's right," Maggie said to her caller. "You *don't* need to explain yourself to me, but you might want to try explaining the coat hanger you have stuck up your ass. I think you totally suck, Miss Patrick, and I can see why Julia never mentioned you. But don't worry, I'll see to it that the antiques you're talking about are carefully taken care of until Julia is released. And in the unlikely event that she isn't, I'll make sure they take center stage in the huge goddamn bonfire I intend to build in my back yard! Hello? Hello?"

Maggie held the phone away to confirm that her caller had, indeed, hung up. She looked at Danielle and Grace, but before she could say a word Grace laughed and said, "Do not even begin to tell us what that was about, darling. I feel sure we got the picture."

At which point Danielle joined her in the first good belly laugh she had had in over a year.

Susan Kiernan-Lewis

# Chapter Fifteen

That afternoon, after dropping Danielle off at her home, Grace and Maggie came back to Domaine St-Buvard for a quiet evening. Maggie could tell that Grace's spirits were vastly improved. As she reheated the quiche that Laurent had made earlier in the day and compiled salads, she watched Grace play a simple game with Zou-zou in the living room. *Children help*, Maggie thought as she watched Grace's face. *When you're forced to act happy for their sake, you end up feeling happy.*

She glanced at the kitchen wall clock and was surprised that it was as late as it was. Laurent was off at his weekly meeting with the other vintners in the area to discuss the processing of the recent grape harvest. Maggie knew that business had probably concluded by this time and the men were likely all just drinking and relaxing.

She didn't begrudge Laurent that. She smiled to think of him and wondered if he ever really did relax? Partly due to his criminal past and partly because of just who he was intrinsically, Laurent never seemed to let his guard down. Or just the opposite: he did *seem* to let it down.

*He just never did.*

"I don't know, Z. Why don't we ask Aunt Maggie?"

Maggie looked up to see Grace standing in front of her with Zou-zou in her arms. Grace's face was flushed pink from her exuberant play with the toddler and the thought occurred to Maggie that Grace would have no trouble attracting another husband. Maggie always knew Grace was stunningly beautiful. Her classic good looks were as much a part of Grace's personality—and the reason for most things she did—as anything else about her. But the agony of her recent depression had obscured that fact for a bit. Now Maggie could see that when the time came and Grace was fully back to being herself, when she was over all of this as much as she ever would be, she would be as beautiful and magnetic as ever.

It was a shock to realize that one could survive something so devastating as the loss of one's marriage and the happy cohesion of the family you created, and outwardly—at least eventually—there would be few if any changes at all. The light in Grace's eyes when she looked at her daughter told Maggie that. *Ha!* she thought. *Do not tell me children don't help.*

"Ask me what?"

"When dinner is ready. It's not for me, mind you, but Z is not used to going more than fifteen minutes before *Oncle* Laurent pops something tasty in her mouth."

"Yeah, I know the syndrome. It's why *Tante* Maggie is a full pants size larger than last year."

"*One* pants size?"

"Now *why* is it I thought I missed you? Help me remember." Maggie smiled as she handed Grace Z's plate. "Y'all go on in. I'll bring our plates."

After an exhausting meal of mopping up the child, the dining room table and the floor—with help from the ever vigilant Petit-Four—Grace went upstairs to give Zou-zou her bath and put her to bed. Maggie stacked the dishes in the sink, intending to deal with them later and went to feed the dog, who, not surprisingly, was too full from the baby's dinner droppings to care.

With another quick glance at the kitchen clock, Maggie sat on the living room couch, pulled out her phone and punched in the number she had found on the Internet earlier that day. With any luck, Laurent would be gone for another hour or more. As she waited for the line to connect, she could hear Grace upstairs singing over the sound of Zou-zou's bathwater.

*It's all going to be fine. Grace is going to be fine.*

"Hello?" The voice on the other end of the line was cool, clipped and American.

Maggie figured it must be the wife. "Uh, yes, my name is Maggie Dernier." *It's always good to identify yourself right off the bat when calling women whose husbands are known to be big fat cheats.* "I was hoping to speak with a David Armstrong?" *Along those same lines, it was also always good to try to make it appear as if you don't know the husband personally since wives who have been cheated on are typically a little sensitive about strange women calling to talk to their husbands.*

Clearly she needn't have worried. Without responding to her, the woman yelled away from her phone, "David! It's for you." Maggie heard the phone being set down with a clunk. She waited.

"Hello?" A reluctant, almost sullen, but definitely American voice.

"David Armstrong?"

"Who's this?"

"My name is Maggie Newberry. I am a friend of Julia Patrick, who is a suspect in the murder of Jacques Tatois." *Might as well just come out with it.*

"Okay." He was obviously waiting for more. He was curious. Maggie thought that was a good sign. People who killed people in cold blood like Jacques was killed tend to like to see the media releases on their handiwork. If this guy were the murderer, he would be interested in seeing how much of the case Maggie had put together.

"I'm calling you because I had a conversation with Michelle Tatois, who is the victim's daughter."

"I know who she is."

Maggie detected that he had dropped his voice a level. The wife must still be nearby. "She said you might be able to help me in reconstructing the events of Jacques's last hours." Okay that was a stretch, but Maggie had hoped the conversation would have taken on a life of its own by now instead of her being forced to drive every inch of it. This David guy was cool and he was giving her nothing to sink her teeth into.

"Why in the world would she say that? I didn't even know the guy."

"That's not what Michelle says." Maggie willed herself not to say more. She bit her lip to let the statement do its magic without her talking it into meaninglessness.

It worked.

"Yeah, okay," he growled. Maggie could hear an agitation in his voice that made her think he was walking with the phone —moving somewhere away from the ears of his nearby wife. "I had a run-in with the bastard and I'm sure Michelle told you all about that, too."

*Shit! So Michelle was telling the truth? What run-in?*

"I'd love to hear your side of it," Maggie said, holding her breath.

"The only side that matters is the one where that turd attacked my wife at last year's company Bastille Day picnic and then went about as if nothing had happened."

Maggie's mind raced. Last Bastille Day Jacques and Julia had still been together.

"Michelle thinks you decided to provide your own brand of American justice by killing her father."

"She doesn't think that."

"I assure you, she does. She says she has proof." That last part was a lie, but Maggie hoped it might trigger a slip up, or even a confession. Crazier things had happened.

"Well, then she planted it or made it up. Michelle's pissed because we…" He dropped his voice to a whisper. "We broke up last week. Shoulda done it a month ago but the sex was decent and my wife is still shook up from what happened to her."

Maggie felt her skin crawl. *This low-life went looking for sex outside his marriage because his sexually-assaulted wife wasn't providing it?*

"What did happen to her?" Maggie asked. "I was told the attack was unsuccessful." *It was amazing the things people would tell you if you just probed a little with stuff you were absolutely just making up off the top of your head.*

"Michelle didn't tell you? Never mind. She probably lied about that, too. Her father was drunk and ran into my wife in the garden after the picnic was dying down."

"Your wife was alone?"

"Well, I was there but she…we were having problems and she was upset…about something. Anyway, that doesn't matter. He caught her alone and took advantage of her.'

"He raped her?"

"He was in the process of it when they were interrupted."

"You're sure it was rape?"

"Now I *know* you were talking to Michelle. Yes, it was *attempted rape*. My wife even filed a complaint with the American consulate the next week."

"Why so long?"

"I don't know. I guess all the crying and thoughts of suicide in the meantime took up too much of her time to get around to it."

Feeling like she was starting to lose his cooperation, Maggie hurried to the question she really needed to know.

"Can I ask you if the police questioned you in Monsieur Tatois's death? Michelle said you talked freely in your office about wanting to quote *kill the bastard*. End quote." *Which is really rich considering you're a cheating wad of pond scum,* Maggie thought as she waited for his answer.

"They only needed to ask one question. And when I answered that they checked it out and haven't called back since."

"Can I ask what the question was?"

"You say you're a friend of Julia Patrick's?"

"That's right."

"Let me just say that if there was anyone Michelle hated more than Julia Patrick, it was her father. She could talk for hours about how much she detested him. Why aren't the police looking at *her* as a suspect?"

Maggie ignored the question. "Any idea why she hated her father so much?"

"Oh, I don't know, I suppose the fact that he screwed her best friend in high school might have been a major reason."

*Holy shit.*

"*While* she and Michelle were both in high school. But, personally? I think it was the relentless hate campaign waged by Michelle's mother against Jacques. Pretty hard to have a decent opinion of dear old dad when your mother is telling you on a daily basis what a bastard he is."

Maggie realized he was talking about himself now. Between his infidelities and his wife's trauma, things were probably pretty shaky on the marital home front. She wondered if he had kids.

"Can you tell me what the question was the police asked you that made them drop you from their list of suspects?"

"Because that's exactly where you'd like to place me, huh? Never mind. I'd probably be doing the same thing if I had a pal in trouble. Sure, I'll tell you, although I can't imagine it'll help you. They asked me where I was during the time of the murder. And I did them one better. My wife and I were back in the States for the two weeks prior to and during the time Jacques was killed. It was pretty easy to confirm. Anyway, sorry I couldn't help you out." His voice was light and indicated he was not at all sorry.

"Well," Maggie said. "Thanks for talking to me."

"Yeah, sure. Good luck with your friend."

Maggie disconnected and sat on the couch for a moment staring into space. *The world was full of some seriously screwed up and unhappy people.* She put a hand on her large belly and was instantly rewarded with a solid kick from a little foot.

She turned to watch Grace come down the stairs, a faint smile still on her face.

"Baby all tucked in?" Maggie asked, scooting over on the couch to make room for Grace.

"Did you notice at dinner how much she's starting to talk?"

"I did."

"I hate that Win is missing it," Grace said. "But I suppose that's the future for both of us."

"Grace…"

"Never mind, darling. Distract me. I heard you on the phone. More people calling to piss you off or was this constructive in some way?"

"I called David Armstrong. He's Michelle's ex-lover and he was heard threatening to kill Jacques last year."

"My goodness, that's helpful."

"Not so much. He has an alibi for the critical time."

"Well, pooh. Do you want to bounce a theory or two off me? I know I haven't been very helpful in other ways but I'm happy to listen."

Maggie tucked her feet up under her and then groaned and pulled them back out. "It's impossible to get comfortable," she said.

"I remember this stage very well. It'll be over before you know it. No, I take that back. It seems like it will never end." She leaned over and squeezed Maggie's hand. "But of course it does. No woman ever carried a child to her sixtieth birthday. This time next month, you will have joined the ranks of mamas everywhere."

"Grace, do you worry about Windsor badmouthing you to the girls?"

Grace frowned and Maggie watched her seem to physically retreat at the question.

"Of course not. You know Win. He's as honorable as they come."

"I only mention it because the guy I was just talking to said that one of the reasons Michelle hates her father is because Annette made it a full-time job to blacken his name every chance she got."

"Yes, well, I'm sure Jacques helped with that, too."

"I know. But still." Maggie visibly shook herself out of the morose reflection and tossed her cellphone onto the coffee table. "Okay," she said. "So I've got two guys—David Armstrong and Yves Briande—who publicly threatened Jacques. But he was such a weasel that's probably not significant. Both of them have good alibis." Maggie looked at Grace as if for guidance. "I should probably cross both of them off my list, but I've had suspects in the past with so-called good alibies and they ended up being the murderer."

"You have not."

"Okay, but I've heard of it happening before."

"Is there more wine?" Grace got up and walked to the kitchen. "Let's assume for our purposes," she said, "that alibis actually mean something. What if you were to eliminate suspects on the basis of no opportunity—just to make things easier."

"Okay, fine. Then on my no-alibi list I've got Florrie, Mathieu, Annette, Julia and who knows whom else. It's very possible the killer is someone I don't even know yet. I mean, before last week I didn't know Mathieu existed."

"Annette doesn't have an alibi?" Grace returned to the living room with her glass and resettled on the couch.

"She supposedly does but no one can tell me what it is."

"Michelle?"

"Iron-clad."

"Too bad."

"Yeah, I know. But patricide is pretty serious stuff, even for a nutcase like Michelle."

"Well, add the fact that she's crazy to her being French, too."

"Yeah, I'm still not seeing it. Her alibi is too good. She was at a defensive driving class at the time."

"I'm shocked to learn France even has such a thing. But also, I didn't realize the police were able to narrow down the parameter on when he could've been poisoned. I thought I heard Laurent say that *agaricus* mushrooms can poison you immediately or they can take awhile to work."

"They *did* take awhile. The police are saying they took however long it was for Jacques to say goodnight, drive to his own flat and collapse."

"Looks like they're pretty serious about making your friend Julia fit the crime time line."

"Yeah, looks like."

"Your editor stop harassing you?"

"What?"

"Your editor. Has she stopped calling you? I don't remember you having to dodge her calls this week."

Maggie sighed. "Yeah, she's stopped. Worse than that. When I had a moment yesterday to call her back, I had to leave a voice mail."

"What's wrong with that?"

"Nothing, except my emails are going unanswered, too."

"That's not good."

"I mean, we have a contract so I'm not really worried."

"Maybe that's what *she* was saying all those weeks that you weren't answering *her* calls and emails."

"Yeah, maybe. I really hope I haven't screwed this up. It's just that there was no way I was going to get those edits done in time."

"You could have just told her. Asked for an extension."

"I should have," Maggie said, feeling weary. "I just didn't want to deal with it, you know? I felt overwhelmed by it. And the publisher had made such a big deal about how much they loved my work that when it came back all bleeding and ripped to shreds, I think I lost confidence."

"You didn't expect your work to be edited?" Grace frowned. "I thought that was the whole point of a having a publisher."

"Yeah, but I almost didn't recognize the book after they got through *editing* it."

"You need to write her back, apologize and request as professionally as possible for a time extension."

"I know. That's what Laurent said, too."

"So do it. And whatever happens, happens."

"Great philosophy," Maggie said sarcastically as she stood and gathered up her phone.

"Actually, it is," Grace said with a laugh. "And nobody's more surprised about it than I am."

*They should have done this right from the start.*

Even in the beginning, their relationship had always been about shopping. Why hadn't Maggie remembered that? It hadn't taken thirty minutes into a full day of shopping in the boutiques and clothing stores of Aix before Maggie remembered what it felt like to have a best girlfriend. The shorthand between the two of them, the inane comments and the giggles, the comfortable roles they'd both adopted years ago—Grace as the fashion mentor and Maggie as the hopelessly inept but willing pupil.

It worked wonderfully for both of them.

*Talk about retail therapy,* Maggie thought as she glanced at the bags and packages at her feet. She sat with Grace in a very upscale *brasserie* at the end of a perfect lunch of wine-poached salmon with black truffles.

"I'm in heaven," Maggie said, rubbing her stomach contentedly, the remnants of a chocolate *gâteau* on the table in front of her.

"I know," Grace said, sipping her coffee. She had already reapplied her lipstick after having eschewed dessert. Maggie couldn't help but notice how much more relaxed Grace was these last two days. A shopping trip in Aix appeared to be pretty much the topper on Grace's emotional rehabilitation. It wasn't going to fix everything, Maggie knew that. Her love for clothes and jewelry aside, Grace was the least shallow person Maggie knew. But it was a baby step in the right direction.

"I guess I didn't feel good about doing stuff like this while Julia was still in jail," Maggie said thoughtfully. "It didn't feel right when I know she's suffering."

"I can see that," Grace said. "But you know the two have nothing to do with each other."

"Well, intellectually I know that," Maggie said. "But I can't help how I feel."

"Well, you know that's not true," Grace said, signaling the waiter for the check. "Did I tell you that I called Windsor last night?"

Maggie pushed her dessert plate to the side and sat up straight. "Really? How did that go?"

Grace sighed. "It had its ups and downs. But for the most part, it was good."

"I'm glad."

"This is really hard on him, too. Even with a girlfriend to dry his tears."

"Of course."

"I should've done it days ago. He said Laurent called him last week."

"Really?" Maggie frowned. Laurent hadn't mentioned it to her.

"He was able to give a good report on Zou-zou which, of course, Win was starved to hear. He loves her so much."

Maggie thought she could see a glimmer of tears in Grace's eyes but it was gone before she could be sure.

"But mostly it seems he let Win know that there are no divided camps over what we're doing. The Derniers, he said, aren't taking sides. They are loving and supporting the badly screwed up Van Sants equally."

"But probably not those exact words," Maggie said, smiling.

Grace replaced her credit card and snapped her wallet shut. "Ready, darling? I promised Danielle I'd be back to collect Z before supper."

"We can pick her up on the way home," Maggie said, collecting her purchases from the floor next to her chair. Knowing that Win had spoken to both Grace and Laurent made Maggie feel, irrationally, that they were all one big loving group again. It may not fix things or bring Grace and Windsor back together, but at least they weren't pretending they had never been friends in the first place.

As she stepped out of the restaurant, the bright sunshine in the fall day made Maggie blink. She shivered inside her light jacket against the brisk breeze. Autumn was definitely here.

*Would Julia be free by Thanksgiving? By Christmas?*

Because of Maggie's size—she was eight months and two weeks now—she was grateful to be able to hand the car keys over to Grace. It amazed her how she had gone from comfortably driving without a problem to not at all in just a few days.

Maggie settled into the passenger seat of her Renault as they drove out of the city and allowed herself to enjoy her surroundings. *Aix was so much more visual than the other cities in Provence.* Maybe that was due to all the majestic fountains—one on each corner of the city it felt like—but it was also the way Aix-en-Provence seemed to be able to blend the old and the quaint buildings with the new and the streamlined architecture. Somehow it worked.

Maggie always thought that if she and Laurent ever moved in from the country, she would want to live in Aix. The thought made her smile because the very idea of Laurent leaving his vineyard—and his sometimes leaky but definitely beloved one hundred year old *mas* in the country—was hard to imagine.

"You okay over there?" Grace asked. Maggie noticed that Grace was squinting through her sunglasses and it occurred to her that Grace might need glasses. The thought of them all getting older, day by day, brought a shadow into the sunny pleasant day.

"I'll be better when this little bugger is in a car seat in the backseat," Maggie said, rubbing her tummy.

"Yes, well, be careful what you wish for," Grace said. "Next thing you know he'll be walking, and then asking to borrow the car. I turn here, right?"

Maggie directed her out of the city and onto the D7n, the highway that dissects that part of Provence, separating Aix from Avignon and Arles. She fell asleep on the drive back, awakening only with the press of the newest Dernier-to-be on her bladder. She looked around and saw they were still a good thirty minutes from home.

"I need to make a pit stop," she said, rubbing her eyes. Pregnancy naps were so hard to wake up from. They were like a functioning coma that you could lapse into at any moment of the day. Once when she was standing in line with Laurent at the *boulangerie* in Arles, he swore she nodded off.

"We're not really close to anything," Grace said, looking over at her as if trying to gauge just how desperate she was.

"There's a place off the road up here," Maggie said. "It's actually a pretty decent little restaurant. In fact, Florrie Tatois owns it."

"You're kidding. Really?"

"Well, not really a restaurant. More like a bar with not bad food."

"No, I meant out here in the middle of nowhere?"

"Yeah, you have to know it's here. You can't see it from the highway. Laurent goes there now and then. I think his vintner buddies meet there sometimes. There's the turn off. Don't miss it, Grace."

"Got it, darling. No worries. The sparkling toilet facilities of a dilapidated French country bar in the middle of nowhere await you. Oh! I see it. Looks abandoned."

"That's the décor. Just park."

Grace pulled into the parking area next to an older model Citroen. Maggie was out the door and walking into the bar before Grace had her seatbelt off. She glanced around the main dining area and saw two men at the bar, neither of them Florrie, and nobody behind the counter.

A couple sat in the dining room, but they appeared to be drinking more than eating. Maggie hurried down the narrow hall to the toilets. She could hear Grace coming in the front door as she did.

Like most French toilets in the country, the facilities at Florrie's place, while cleaner than she had any right to expect, were old and dark. Maggie always thought these sorts of places boasted the original plumbing and that made her feel a little nervous, like she was about to fall into a deep dark hole of human waste, and probably undiscovered corpses.

She quickly relieved herself and decided to skip the hand washing exercise. There didn't seem to be any soap or paper towels in any event. A quick look into the ancient, wavy mirror confirmed what she had already guessed; she had better deliver this baby pronto if she didn't want to be drafted into a traveling carnival as the circus fat lady.

Amusing herself with silly thoughts, Maggie wasn't watching where she was going as she pushed the door open into the hallway.

"Ready for a few more tricks, bitch?"

The woman stood directly in front of her, wearing a short skirt and a shorter top that showed a wide expanse of her bare midriff. Maggie couldn't see the expression on her face in the darkened hallway, but she had no trouble recognizing Michelle standing between her and the door to the dining room at the end of the hall. She also had no difficulty in making out the heavy cricket bat that Michelle held tightly in both hands.

Susan Kiernan-Lewis

# Chapter Sixteen

*There was no way Michelle wasn't full-on crazy.* That was the first thought that ran through Maggie's head, and it was one that gave her a whole lot less comfort than if she hadn't thought anything at all. She licked her lips and wondered what she could say that wouldn't trigger Michelle to strike.

"You came to my apartment and lied to me," Michelle hissed. "You think I'm stupid? You think I'm crazy?" Maggie could see Michelle was actually spraying foam from her lips as she talked. An inane thought floated into Maggie's head that Michelle was literally foaming at the mouth.

"How did you find me?" she asked, hoping that engaging the insane woman was at least a possible way to forestall the attack.

"I followed you. You think that's hard? You really must think I'm stupid, don't you?" Michelle swung the bat hard and slammed it into the wall in the narrow hall.

Maggie screamed.

"I watched you and your friend buy everything in Aix and then eat a three-course lunch before getting in your car to go home to your country estate. I know how rich you are. Americans think they can buy their way through the world."

Maggie's brain couldn't decipher all of Michelle's rant. The contorted French and the rage made that impossible. Obviously Michelle had been watching her and Grace in their shopping today and followed her here. If Maggie hadn't slept all the way from Aix she *might* have noticed someone behind them, but probably not. It hadn't occurred to her to be afraid or careful. It hadn't occurred to her that someone was watching her, that someone wanted to hurt her.

But by the way Michelle was edging up closer for the kill shot, it was clear that the next swing would be into Maggie's body. As she got closer, Maggie could see Michelle's eyes were wild and unfocused and Maggie realized she was probably on some kind of medication—or off it. Grace appeared from behind Michelle and promptly did the only sensible thing anyone could do in the situation.

She started screaming.

Michelle jumped at the sound but didn't turn around. She didn't need to. She was the one with the weapon.

"Look, Michelle," Maggie said, "I don't think you're stupid, so I know you know how this goes. As much as you want to hurt me, you do this and you'll hurt yourself far worse."

"Shut up!" Michelle roared. She raised the bat over her head, as if smashing Maggie's body was no longer enough. "Nothing hurts more than this! Nothing!"

Maggie could hear Grace's screams bouncing off the narrow walls, but she couldn't wait any longer. Knowing she would trigger the attack but not knowing what else she could do, Maggie turned back toward the toilet and darted inside, pulling the heavy door behind her. She fumbled at the doorknob but there was no lock. The impact of the bat hitting the door sent painful vibrating shock waves up the arm that was still holding the door handle. Maggie threw her body against the door to keep it shut but she knew, even as large as she was, that Michelle was younger and stronger.

And she was crazy.

The second crash as the bat hit the door made her ears ring and her shoulders lurch away with the impact. The floor of the toilet was wet, and when she jerked she slipped. Grabbing desperately for the sink to keep from falling, Maggie heard the door opening behind her and Michelle's insane crow of victory. Looking wildly around the room for anything that could be used as a weapon, Maggie waited for the blow she knew was coming.

But it never came.

She turned around to see Michelle standing in the doorway facing her, arms by her sides, the bat falling to the ground. At first, Maggie thought Michelle was having some kind of fit. Maggie scrambled to grab the bat and held it in front of her with both hands like a sword. It was then that she realized she had been screaming the whole time.

With a convulsive jerk, Michelle, who was howling threats and profanity at the person holding her, disappeared from the opening of the toilet and Maggie saw that she was tightly in the grip of her cousin, Florrie, who was wrestling her down the hall. Grace entered the bathroom and Maggie dropped the bat as Grace drew her into a tight embrace. They both stood quietly, their hearts pounding in their ears, their breaths coming in ragged pants.

Finally Grace pulled away and looked into Maggie's eyes. "You okay?"

"I need a drink, "Maggie said, her voice shaky.

"Is that wise?"

"Water will do."

They left the toilet arm-in-arm and slowly walked down the hall to the dining room, which had been vacated by the few patrons who had been there. Florrie stood next to Michelle. She was unrestrained but he was still near enough to grab her again if he had to. They both turned to Grace and Maggie as they entered.

"You bitch!" Michelle said. "This isn't the end."

"Be quiet, Michelle," Florrie said with what looked like exasperation to Maggie. She noticed he had deep scratch marks down his face. He had obviously paid a price for coming to her aid.

"Don't you tell me to be quiet, you *putain*," Michelle said, whirling back to face Florrie. "I am not surprised that you take her side. You are not a man but a worm to steal my money from me."

Grace approached the bar and pulled a glass from the shelf under the counter. She watched the two without speaking as she filled the glass with water and returned to Maggie.

"What are you talking about?" Florrie said. "What money do you think I've stolen from you?"

"My inheritance! Aunt Lily intended that money to go to my father. To *me!*"

"And you think that money goes to me now?" Florrie shook his head as if unable to encompass how mad that idea was.

That stopped Michelle. She glanced at Maggie as if tempted to pick up a chair and go after her, but the thought that Florrie was possibly *not* the heir after all was apparently too great. "You lie," she said, her eyes searching his face in an attempt to determine whether he was or not.

"I'm not next in line, Michelle," Florrie said, his voice a warning growl. "I am not Lily's heir."

"Everyone knows you are. If not you, then who?"

Florrie turned toward the bar and reached for a bottle of *pastis.*

"It *is* you!" Michelle said, her voice becoming shrill.

"It isn't." The voice that answered wasn't Florrie's. All four people in the bar turned to face the source, and saw that Annette had entered unnoticed through the front door. She stood now, her purse over her arm, a ridiculous bouquet of flowers in her hand. Maggie thought she had aged ten years since she last saw her.

"*Maman*! What are you doing here?" Michelle frowned and looked from Florrie to her mother and back again. She appeared to have totally forgotten that Maggie and Grace were even there. "Why are you here?"

"I am here because I had an appointment with your cousin. It's you who shouldn't be here." Annette glanced in the direction of Maggie. "What has happened?"

Michelle clenched her fists and stared at Maggie with loathing. "I saw them in town," she said. "I followed them here."

"I told you I would deal with her," Annette said quietly. "What happened, Florrie?"

Florrie poured his glass and drank it before clapping the glass to the counter. "Michelle tried to kill Madame Dernier," he said. "With a bat."

"Dear God," Annette said and looked at Michelle. "What is wrong with you?"

"Me? What about him?" She pointed to Florrie and Maggie could see her other hand open and close spasmodically into a fist in her agitation. "You said yourself he has stolen the inheritance of an orphan!"

Florrie looked at Annette. "What is this she keeps saying about my stealing her inheritance? Is it possible she doesn't know?"

Annette glanced at Maggie. "We will not have this discussion in front of strangers."

"Oh, hell, no," Maggie said. "I'm not leaving."

Grace pulled Maggie gently by the shoulders toward the door. "Come on, Lucy," she said under breath. "Before you start competing with Michelle for who's craziest."

"Do *what* in front of strangers?" Michelle asked, taking two steps toward her mother. "What do you and Florrie know that I do not?"

"Tell her, Annette," Florrie said. "Tell her the truth."

"I was going to tell you," Annette said in a soothing voice. Maggie could see the girl was getting even more flustered. She licked her lips continually and stared at her mother.

"Tell me what?"

"*I* am Lily's heir," Annette said. "It was unexpected...for all of us," she said hurriedly as she watched Michelle's face contort into incomprehension.

"I'll say," Florrie said with disgust. "I have attended Lily's affairs for nearly ten years. I have visited her every Sunday for the last five..."

"What are you saying?" Michelle glanced at Florrie, as if reluctant to let him go in her stream of comfortable vitriol, and then at her mother. Maggie could see the wheels moving in her brain as she tried to figure out if this was a good thing or a bad thing. Since Annette was not an old woman, the time when *Michelle* would inherit from her—if there was anything left by then—would be many years hence. Michelle seemed to come to the same conclusion at about the same time.

"You lied to me!" she snarled at her mother. "You said you were broke and you couldn't help me."

"I *am* broke," her mother said. "Your Aunt Lily still lives."

"Not for much longer. You'll be rich by the weekend!"

"Michelle, please stop yourself from saying these vile things."

"Vile? It is *you* who is vile! You disgust me!" She ran up to her mother and slapped the flowers out of her hands to the floor. "Did *he* give you these?" she shouted. "Is he wooing the new heiress? Is that why he's wearing a new shirt?" She turned to look at Florrie who, Maggie had to admit, was beginning to look decidedly guilty. *Was Florrie with Annette?*

"*Mon chou*," Annette said pleadingly to her.

"Oh, stop, *Maman*," Michelle said pushing past her to the door. "Marry him or drop dead. I don't care which!" She stormed out the door, followed by the piercing squeal of a car's engine as it roared to life, then slowly diminished as she sped away.

Annette turned to Maggie, her face a mask of composure, her lip pulled back in a sneer. "I would not think of reporting this so-called attack to the police if I were you," she said.

"Oh, really?" Maggie said, her breath coming in sharp pants.

"Come on, Lucy," Grace said. "Time to go."

"I would listen to your friend, Madame," Annette said, stepping around the tangle of broken stems underfoot. "If you know what's good for your *other* friend." She turned her back on Maggie as if the conversation were over. Maggie hesitated for only a moment before grabbing Grace's arm and staggering to the door. Once out, she leaned heavily against the bumper of the Renault, her hand on her stomach.

"Sweetie, are you okay?" Grace came around to touch her shoulder.

"You know what? I don't think I am."

"Shit, darling, you're not allowed to go into labor on my watch. Laurent and I made a pact."

"Sorry, Grace. I think you're up." Maggie's face twisted into a grimace of pain as she waited the contraction out.

"Holy crap, Maggie, are you serious? Get in the car! Get in the car!"

An hour later, Maggie sat in a wheelchair in the hospital in Aix waiting for Laurent to come and take her home. Grace sat next to her flipping through a waiting room magazine.

"You know, I've forgotten almost all the French I ever knew," Grace said idly. "Trust me, all it takes is one year in

Indiana to erase any and all vestige of a foreign language from your mind."

"I think it has more to do with your mind than it does Indiana," Maggie said. "Have you even heard of Braxton-Hicks?"

"Of course, darling. Everyone's heard of it. Well, mostly just pregnant people, I guess."

"Well, how can you tell it apart from the real thing? Are you sure it's too late to catch Laurent? I hate for him to come all the way to Aix for nothing."

"It's not for nothing, darling. He's your husband. It's what husbands of pregnant women do."

"Yeah, I guess. Listen, Grace, speaking of that, I hope I don't need to tell you that this afternoon is not the kind of thing we share with Laurent, right? I mean, it's bad enough that I spent way more than I told him I would at that one shoe store, but being attacked by a maniac with a baseball bat...well, you know how Laurent is."

"Darling, you know that I am the *last* person to give marital advice."

"And I'm really grateful for that. It's just that I know you and Laurent have your little talks now and then so I'd appreciate it if you don't mention this."

"Well, you must know best as you are still at least presently married, and I am soon not to be."

"This thing between you and Win doesn't define you, Grace. You're not a failure. You're a million really good things."

"Thank you, darling. Now *that* is why I came to France." She reached out and took one of Maggie's hands. They held hands silently for a moment and then Maggie shifted uncomfortably in the wheelchair.

"So what am I to think about the fact that it's *Annette* who's Lily's heir? What a shocker."

"Especially for Michelle," Grace said, picking up another magazine. "It was almost worth your being assaulted to see the look on her face when she found out."

"You realize this pushes Annette up to pole position on my suspect list?"

"Because she has motive now?" Grace frowned. "I think she had plenty of motive for killing Jacques before this, just being the ex-wife of the slime bag. Besides, at the time she didn't know *she* would be next in line."

"Or did she? All I know is that when you add financial motive to personal animosity and throw in opportunity— you've got the ultimate prime suspect. *Julia* didn't stand to gain financially from Jacques's death."

"There's Laurent, darling," Grace said as she stood up and straightened her sweater over her slim hips. "Remember now to act grateful for the attention or trust me, the next four kids you're in labor with, he'll be texting you from *Le Canard*."

Maggie waved to Laurent as he approached from across the waiting room.

"You think I'm joking, darling?" Grace said under her breath with a wry smile.

"And you are sure you are alright, *chérie*?" Laurent asked, tucking the wool rug around Maggie's knees where she sat on the couch. Grace had opted to stay the night with Zou-zou over at Danielle and Jean-Luc's again, though Maggie was tempted to ask her not to. She knew Laurent was worried—especially with the false labor scaring everyone half to death. Historically, his worry and her secrets were not the best combination for a serene evening at home with just the two of them.

Laurent handed her a cup of tea and sat down in his easy chair opposite her. He sipped whiskey from a small glass. "You got another ticket."

"No way!" Maggie said, startled. "When?"

"It was on the car when we came out of the hospital."

"I didn't see it."

"I removed it before you could."

"What was the infraction?"

"Having a broken tail light."

"Are you serious? The entire windshield is bashed in! If I didn't know better, it would be almost funny."

"But you do and it's not."

"Unbelievable."

"I'll have to talk to him."

"Oh, Laurent, no. It'll die down, don't you think?"

He didn't answer, but regarded her closely as he finished his drink. She made a point of touching her stomach in case he needed reminding that she was vulnerable tonight, and to perhaps forestall any attempt on his part to confront her or start an argument.

In Maggie's experience, Laurent's worrying usually translated into an attempt to stop her from doing something she was doing and she knew tonight was no different. When she looked at him, she felt a rush of love and guilt. As big as he was, as capable as he always behaved, she knew he felt helpless to protect her—*especially* after today. And although he didn't know—couldn't possibly know—what had happened in Florrie's bar earlier, she also knew his senses were operating in overdrive. He knew *something* had happened. Something above and beyond the rush to the hospital for the false labor. Something that had likely *triggered* the false labor.

"Can we do an early night tonight?" she asked sweetly.

"Of course."

"I wish you wouldn't worry, Laurent. Everything's going to be fine. How's the grape processing going? Any sense of what kind of year it'll be for us?" She watched him struggle with himself for a moment. As focused as he was on getting to the bottom of her recent activities, he was also right in the midst of bringing this year's wine harvest to production and to market. She probably couldn't have asked him anything else that would distract him as well.

Except tonight.

"You were on your way back from Aix when the contractions started?"

*Like a dog with a bone.*

"That's right. I heard Grace tell you that already."

"*C'est ça.*" He put his glass down on the coffee table. "And Grace was driving?"

"Yep. As I've already said. Wasn't that lucky?"

"Much about this afternoon appears *lucky*," he said darkly.

"Okay, Laurent, you might as well come out with it, as difficult as I know it is for you *not* to beat around the bush."

"You are still investigating Jacques Tatois's murder."

"See? That wasn't hard, was it? Well, first of all, we never said I wouldn't. And second of all, I was out shopping with Grace today. As you know."

"And there was nothing about today that involved working on the murder case?"

"Again, I never said I wouldn't work on the case. Julia is after all still in jail."

"I want you to stop all inquiries until after the baby is born."

Maggie took in a sharp breath. The direct approach was new coming from Laurent. She couldn't remember a time when he actually asked her straight out for something. And because of that, she had the decidedly uncomfortable feeling that it wasn't really a request.

"I can't," she said. "You know I can't."

"You can and you will."

Maggie was stunned to hear the edge of steel in his voice. Gone was the phlegmatic and affable Laurent who worked behind the scenes to orchestrate his desires but never directly commanded. She wasn't sure how to respond to him like this.

"I…Laurent, you know Julia tried to kill herself two days ago."

"That is unfortunate but irrelevant," he said, his eyes hooded and cold. "*Not* until after the baby is born."

"Look, Laurent, I know you're worried. We're both stressed after what happened today. I'm reliably told that all new parents are…"

He stood up and approached her on the couch. She gasped as she felt his hands slip under her and lift her effortlessly into his arms. If he was trying to remind her of who was the more physically powerful, he had done it.

In spades.

Maggie allowed him to carry her up the stairs to their bedroom, where he deposited her on the bed and began silently undressing in the dimly lit room. She watched him for a moment and then got up to pull her nightgown from a dresser drawer. While no more words were spoken that night, Maggie had the inescapable—and unsettling—feeling that the argument of whether or not she would work on the case had somehow been completely and irrevocably resolved. At least in Laurent's mind.

The next morning, before either of them was fully awake, the quiet was assaulted by a tremendous banging on their front door and a police bullhorn instructing them to come out. Laurent was at the bedroom window overlooking the front door before Maggie had even pulled the duvet back.

"Who is it?" she asked, half wondering if this were just a terrible dream.

Laurent didn't look away from the scene below him. He opened the window to let in the onslaught of noise of what sounded to Maggie's ears like doors slamming on several police vans, and a team of men crunching through the gravel to their front door.

"Monsieur Dernier!" a familiar voice called from outside. "I have a warrant to search your house."

*Roger!*

"Please allow us entrance before my men break down your front door."

Laurent turned to grab a pair of trousers and, without a glance at Maggie still in bed, left the bedroom. She listened in numbed shock, her trembling fingers touching her parted lips, as his footsteps thundered down the stairs.

Susan Kiernan-Lewis

# Chapter Seventeen

By the time she made it downstairs, after hurriedly throwing on a corduroy jumper and cardigan, the search was in already in progress. Laurent leaned against the kitchen counter, his brow knitted as he read the warrant. Roger was directing his men—at least a half dozen of them—to ransack their living room, go through the drawers of the buffet in the dining room and fan out into the basement where Laurent kept his wine cellar. Two men were in the process of rolling up the living room rug when Maggie entered. She went straight to Roger.

"Are you crazy?"

He looked at her and she couldn't help but notice that his eyes went to her very pregnant belly first before they found their way to her face.

"I have a warrant, Madame," he said, his face devoid of emotion.

"On what possible grounds?" She saw Laurent toss the warrant down on the kitchen counter. "Is this about Annette? You know, I'm really starting to think the two of you have something going, Roger, because you're like her little lapdog the way you respond to every single complaint from her. Was it her? Did she make a complaint?"

She watched his mouth twist into a smile and at that moment she could have happily ripped his features from his face.

"Madame Tatois filed a complaint through proper channels that you accosted her daughter yesterday at Florian Tatois's establishment."

Out of the corner of her eye Maggie was aware of Laurent approaching. "She accosted *me!*" she said, and immediately wished she could bite the words back. Even from the corner of her field of vision, she could see Laurent stiffen.

"In any case," Roger said, gesturing to one of his men to go upstairs, "that is not why I am here."

Maggie heard a low growling sound and she whirled around to see a uniformed officer holding Petit-Four in one hand and trying to stuff her into a small dog carrier.

"What are you doing?" she shrieked and ran to him. She snatched Petit-Four from him and backed away, the dog nestled in her arms. "Roger, what is the meaning of this? I knew you would stoop to any level but trying to steal my *dog*?"

Roger reached over and plucked Petit-Four from her arms and held his arm out to prevent her from grabbing the animal back. "The dog is forensic evidence," he said, keeping an eye on Laurent, who was now standing very close to him.

"What are you talking about?" Maggie said. Just seeing Petit-Four squirming in Roger's grasp was enough to break her heart. *Dear God, he can't take my dog, can he?* "So now *I'm* a murder suspect? You really have lost your effing mind."

"Not at all, I assure you," Roger said as he handed the dog to the man with the dog carrier who was standing next to him. Maggie's eyes tracked her dog as it was pushed into the carrier and taken outside. A part of her wanted to look to Laurent to make him stop all this. Another part of her, realizing it was all her doing, didn't dare.

"You see, I remembered what you said about how Madame Patrick's apartment—the crime scene—was compromised. Do you remember when you came to my office to tell me that?"

Maggie forced herself not to look at Laurent. She didn't have to. She could tell what he was feeling by the way he stood —absolutely still—with his hands on his hips.

He was furious.

"And it occurred to me," Roger continued, "that you were right. And it was *you* who compromised it."

"You think *I* destroyed evidence of the mushrooms that Jules supposedly used to kill Jacques." Maggie's voice was breathless. She would *not* cry in front of him. She would get her little dog back *today*.

"Well, we didn't find any in her kitchen and he *did* die of mushroom poisoning."

"And *that* doesn't add up in your book to the possibility that you have the wrong person in jail for this crime?"

"No. It adds up to the possibility that you would do anything to help your friend. You forget, I know you, Madame Dernier. You are very passionate. You break the rules."

"Then why aren't you arresting me for accessory to murder?"

"I may yet. When we see what these samples reveal, I very well may."

"You are a total asshole, Roger. This has nothing to do with Julia Patrick and you know it."

"I would hate to put a pregnant woman behind bars, Madame. It's not a very nice place. Ask your friend Madame Patrick."

"Do your worst, you insufferable prick. If you were on the Atlanta police force, you wouldn't last ten—" Without warning, Laurent lifted Maggie off her feet and removed her to the dining room where he set her down solidly and stuck a very large warning finger in her face, which made her focus on his own face and its carefully controlled fury.

Without a word or a further glance in her direction, he closed the doors behind him as he left, leaving her alone. She could hear his low murmur through the closed doors as he spoke to Roger.

Maggie pulled out a dining room chair and sat heavily, realizing her knees were about to give way. The pounding of her heart blotted out the sounds of the police as they packed up their collection of rugs, pillows, hair, as well as what she would later discover was the full contents of their vegetable crisper

She knew Laurent was angry, but more than anything she was sorry to have disappointed him so badly. His wife was pregnant with his first child and all the joy of that was being strangled to death by Maggie's insistence on putting herself and the baby in precarious positions. And poor Laurent was powerless to do anything about it.

And then there was Roger. As much as she wanted to pound his taunting face into mush with her bare hands, she had to admit that she had personally given him every tool to hurt her—and Laurent—today. She desperately wanted to deflect the responsibility of Laurent's anger, but she knew she couldn't.

She stood up and went to the window to watch the procession of police vehicles as they backed up the long serpentine driveway. *They're leaving.* As Maggie watched them through the dining room window, it occurred to her that she had no concept of how long they had been there, or for that matter how long she had been in the dining room. No one had entered, and after the first few minutes of being able to hear Roger and Laurent talking underneath all the noise she realized she hadn't really heard any other sounds.

On the floor of the dining room under a chair lay one of Petit-Four's little chew toys. Maggie clapped a hand to her mouth to prevent the groan that she knew would precede hopeless tears if she didn't staunch them now. Petit was gone. But she would get her back! *Oh, how terrified she must be! I won't cry,* she thought. *I will not cry.*

A creak from the dining room door told her that Laurent had entered.

"They are gone," he said.

She took a long breath, resolving that she would take every angry word he had to give her and, because she knew how it would soften her chastisement, no matter *what* she would *not* cry. She turned to face him.

He stood in the doorway, his head cocked to one side and little Petit-Four in his arms.

Maggie burst into tears.

An hour later, Petit-Four in her lap and an untouched sandwich on a plate before her on the coffee table, Maggie and Laurent sat together on the couch and processed what had happened. She would never know how he got Roger to leave the little dog; she was just grateful that he had. Nearing losing her beloved pet helped her to understand how Laurent must feel when she foolishly endangered her and the baby's wellbeing.

"Again, Laurent, I am so sorry," she said, reaching out to touch Laurent's strong jaw. She could feel the stubble of his beard. He still hadn't shaved yet today. "I'm sorry I was so selfish. I can't believe I put you through all that."

"Bedard is like a man crazed."

"That's for sure."

"With a woman he cannot have."

"I didn't realize until it was too late that he was all…you know."

"*Oui*. But now you know. He is not playing around."

"Could he cause trouble for you?" Maggie knew Laurent's past as a *Côte d'Azur* conman had a habit of cropping up in some very undesirable ways.

Laurent snorted.

"But it's not good for *anyone* to have a policeman gunning for them," she said.

"It is for this reason that I will need to handle it once and for all."

*Shit.* Maggie seriously hoped this *once-and-for-all handling* didn't involve a face-to-face with Roger whereby the little slime-weasel would feel it necessary to mention that he and Maggie had kissed. *He will absolutely make it more than it was.* She was sure of that. But it didn't matter. Once she was forced to confirm that it *had* happened—*and* that she had never mentioned it to Laurent—it wouldn't matter if it had been an innocent peck on the cheek.

Which, of course, it hadn't been.

*So should I say something now?*

Laurent leaned over and kissed her. "I must meet with the co-op," he said. "You will be all right?"

"Of course. Grace is due home any minute."

"Are you going out?"

She shook her head and smiled sweetly at him, hoping she looked the very picture of the angelic, docile and non-troublesome wife. "Nope. Just a quiet afternoon playing with Zou-zou and talking with Grace. Maybe I'll make dinner."

Laurent's eyes widened in surprise. "That would be very nice," he said. "You'll have to do it without mushrooms, though. They took all of ours."

\* \* \* \*

Mathieu had nearly dozed off when he heard the police come up the stairs. He had been sitting in the dark for hours with the television off so he would know when they came. He wanted to be ready.

They were noisy in their arrogance, uncaring if they awoke the neighbors, if their cars blocked the street below, if their feet flattened the little gardens out front, so carefully protected by little wrought iron and mesh fences to keep out the rabbits and the squirrels——no match for the city's officers of the law.

He waited until he heard them pass his door and continue up to her apartment. He knew they wouldn't be long. He could tell there were two of them. They would make quick work of removing the police tape and taking down any surveillance equipment that was in place. Mathieu knew their coming meant things were moving along quickly now. She had either confessed or new evidence had been uncovered to ensure the State's case against her. Either way made no difference to him.

He leaned against his apartment door and waited until the sounds of the footsteps and the mindless laughter of the men had passed by his door again and disappeared into the street below. It was difficult working with no information to go on. He had been unable to have even one phone conversation with Julia to find out what they knew. What they still didn't know.

Perhaps, in the end, that had been best. Although he cared little for the thoughts or opinions of the pigs who had trampled her apartment and who held her from him, he had to admit it seduced him. And when it did, he weakened. When they finally knew that it was *he* who had killed the bastard, they would also know that he had let his love, his one heart of his heart, rot in their prison alone and tortured. They would all know he had allowed Julia to be punished for his crime.

Yes, in the end, everyone would know that.

Mathieu leaned his head against the doorjamb until the silence was complete. He took in a long breath and tried to remember how he had succeeded in not caring what they thought of him—what they would think of him when they knew. When he was ready, he unlocked his door and stepped out into the hallway with his suitcase.

* * *

"What happened to the living room rug?" Grace stood in the hallway with the toddler in her arms and Danielle's husband, Jean-Luc, who had driven her home, behind her.

Maggie roused herself from the remnant of the nap she had just enjoyed on the couch and went to greet them. "Oh, it's a long and painful story," she said, "that I'll tell you over dinner. Have a nice sleep-over, you two?"

Grace bounced Zou-zou on her hip. "Oh, we did, didn't we, lambkin? *Grand-mère* Danielle showed us how to make *gnocchi* and we made a big mess!"

Zou-zou giggled and then squirmed to be put down. Grace held onto her even tighter. "Oh, no you don't," she said. "We've got a date upstairs in Nap City."

"Nooooooo, *Maman!*" Zou-zou shrieked, trying even harder to break from Grace's embrace.

"Sorry, puddin,'" Grace said, heading for the stairs. "It's a law in the bible of Keeping Mama Sane that cannot be broken. Catch you later, darling," she said to Maggie as she climbed the stairs.

Maggie turned to Jean-Luc, who stood silently in the hallway. It was unusual for him to come into the house when Maggie was here. Now seeing him stand there, she felt a little guilty about that. Years ago she had reason not to trust Jean-Luc, but she had to admit he had redeemed himself many times since then.

Plus, he was very dear to Laurent—practically an honorary, beloved uncle if Laurent went in for that sort of sentimental thing, which Maggie wasn't at all sure he didn't. But he was also the newlywed husband of Danielle, who *was* beloved, no doubt about it. There had been many occasions when Maggie (not to mention Laurent) had scolded herself for not reaching out more to Jean-Luc. As a result, the man tended to hold back when she was around.

"Would you care for a drink of something, Jean-Luc?" Maggie came into the kitchen and smiled at him. Besides, it had occurred to her that nothing would garner her more redeemable points with Laurent than being sweet to Jean-Luc.

Clearly startled by the offer, Jean-Luc dragged his farmer's cap from his head and held it twisted in is dark, gnarled fingers. He cleared his throat and then nodded.

Maggie pointed to the barstool by the counter and went to get the jug of *pastis* that Laurent kept chilled in the fridge. She wasn't sure whether Jean-Luc drank it straight as so many of the old village grey beards did, or cut with water. She poured water into a pitcher and set it in front of him with the anise liqueur. She sat opposite him on a bar stool, taking a good two tries to get settled onto it. He watched her as he poured the water into his glass.

"You and Danielle are having fun with your little American granddaughter, huh?"

He looked at her with confusion.

"Zou-zou," Maggie clarified.

"Ahhhh!" His whole face brightened and Maggie realized that it wasn't just Danielle who was enjoying the foster grandparent role. Neither of them had children before they married each other and it was way too late for that now. They were clearly loving being partners in spoiling little Z.

"She is *merveilleuse!*" he said. "So smart, that one. I am teaching her to count."

"Oh, that's good," Maggie said. "You know, Jean-Luc, I was wondering if you had heard anything this year about the *Mistral Promis*?"

The words weren't out of her mouth before she saw the light die in his eyes and the wall slam back down between them.

*Whoa! What is all that about?*

"I understand they are not doing it this year," he said carefully, appearing to seriously study his drink glass.

"Oh? Is that because everyone and his brother lost so much last year?"

Jean-Luc didn't answer but Maggie thought she detected a slight shrug.

"Did everyone bet that day?"

Jean-Luc gave a grunt and, still looking only at his glass, said, "Everyone who had testicles."

"Did you lose much?" Maggie tried to sound sympathetic, but with Jean-Luc refusing to look at her, it was hard.

"I don't have much so it wasn't so bad."

"How about Laurent?"

She thought she saw the slightest of smiles edge on his lips. "You'll have to ask him."

Deciding to abandon that approach, Maggie hopped up to see if there were any fried plantains in the breadbox. Laurent made them with salt and garlic. She found a container of them and slid them onto a plate, which she brought back to the counter with a jar of pickles and a dish of tapenade.

"Can't drink on an empty stomach," she said cheerfully.

"It was a sure thing," Jean-Luc said, eyeing the tapenade. Laurent was famous for his tapenade.

She handed him a spreading knife. "Except that it wasn't. Yves Briande told me that Jacques Tatois lost everything that day."

Jean-Luc snorted in contempt. "The man was a fool." Maggie wondered briefly how Danielle was doing with her don't-talk-ill-of-the-dead philosophy with Jean-Luc.

He spread a huge dollop of tapenade on a plantain. "The surprise wasn't Jacques but his cousin Florrie."

"How so?"

Maggie watched Jean-Luc push the plantain into his mouth and hopped up to get a napkin. Or a mop.

"Up until then nobody knew Florrie had that kind of money."

"Florrie's rich?"

"Well, at least he was before the *Mistral Promis.*"

"I guess you could say that about a lot of people."

Jean-Luc finally looked at Maggie. And smiled. "That's true," he said.

\* \* \*

Roger had been careful not to choose the same table at *Le Canard* where he and Maggie had once met. He sat at the table furthest from the square and remembered that day two years ago. She had been wearing a sundress of some kind, her legs tan and shapely. He remembered the sight of her approaching the table, her hips swinging slightly as she walked.

He would have known her to be an American just by the way she walked, he mused. Not that French women weren't the sexiest most provocative creatures on the face of the earth, of course. But Maggie walked with confidence, almost…swagger. He used to tease her that she was his image of the female John Wayne. As he recalled, she wasn't at all offended by the comparison.

Winter was nearly here and the pale yellow leaves were stripped from the linden trees that hemmed the square of the little café. The proprietor had obviously swept up all evidence from the terrace that there had ever been a bright canopy of leaves protecting the outdoor patio. Roger saw that the plant pots sat dark and naked, awaiting spring's inspiration.

He had pulled Dernier's file, of course, years ago. When he first began to work with Maggie—and had begun to have feelings for her—he had studied the kind of man she had chosen. It didn't surprise him to know that she could be attracted to both the criminal and the cop. She was, after all, a complex, colorful woman. Unpredictable, indefinable. He had to admit, too, that his few run-ins with Dernier had been unsettling. For a *goniff*, he was surprisingly sure of himself. Roger assumed that was due to his size. Big men were used to looking down. They were used to being taken seriously. They were used to being unafraid.

Roger lit a cigarette and watched the opening of the café for Dernier's entrance. It occurred to him that he hadn't thought the situation out totally, so that when Dernier asked to meet he could only bluffly agree, as if he had every confidence in the outcome.

*Was the man here to assault him?* Surely Maggie had told him of their liaison two years ago? While in the end, Maggie had chosen to remain with Dernier, she had been torn, of that much Roger was convinced. It was, in fact, sometimes the only thing that kept him sane.

"Bedard."

Roger was jerked out of his memories by the shadow of the man himself, concomitant with the recognition that Dernier hadn't bothered to address him by his title, or even in a questioning manner. Immediately, Roger felt on a back foot. He blushed to further realize that he had to force himself not to stand when Dernier appeared. He grunted, not looking at him, and nodded to a chair. "Dernier," he said.

Dernier seated himself and a waiter immediately placed a drink in front of him. Roger cursed the wisdom of agreeing to meet on Dernier's home turf. He had the advantage in all things, it seemed. A drink was placed in front of Roger and he looked at Dernier in surprise. Dernier was holding his drink up as if to toast.

"To Maggie," he said, throwing the contents back in one gulp.

Roger felt an instant rush of kinship with the man that he couldn't help. Like a wasp drawn into a spider's web, he felt himself being pulled into a warm confederation: *the men who love Maggie Newberry.* He returned the gesture and drank his down.

Roger had expected Dernier, if not to punch him in the nose, then at least to ask how they might sort this out as civilized men. Clearly, that was not the route Dernier chose to take. He wasn't the kind of man who reacted to how someone *else* saw the world. He was the kind of man who had his own ideas about how things would be. Roger decided to sit back and get as comfortable as he could.

"What do you want?" Dernier asked him straight out.

Roger waited until the waiter had replenished their drinks before answering. He had already decided he wouldn't play games with Dernier. The man was a con artist. There was no ruse or gambit he hadn't seen or played a hundred times. That was his *milieu* and Roger wouldn't be so stupid as to attempt to enter into it with him.

"She is complicating my investigation," Roger said flatly. "I need her to stop talking to people. Keep her at home, can't you?" He had been planning that last line to be a little more damaging than it finally came out. He noticed with mounting frustration that Dernier appeared not to have even heard it.

*To assume that,* he reminded himself, *would be folly.*

"She is a pregnant woman ready to deliver her first child at any moment," Dernier said dismissively. "How much trouble can she be causing you?"

*So he wants to play it that way?*

"Perhaps you don't know your wife as well as I do," Roger said, sipping his drink and never taking his eyes off Dernier.

To his credit, the man laughed. "I doubt that," he said, belying his laugh. "Do you *know* what it is you want?"

*A man of few words.* He expected that. Experienced hustlers typically did way more thinking than talking. He would have to proceed with caution.

Before he could speak, Dernier added, "Besides my wife."

Roger spilled his drink on the table, but before he could wipe it up the waiter appeared from nowhere and attended it. Roger now had the unmistakable and vastly uncomfortable feeling that he was being watched—and not just by Dernier.

So there it was, out in the open. Perhaps, in the end, it was best this way. Roger actually felt a release of tension in his shoulders. This time, he got the glass to his lips without spilling it before speaking. "Your wife and I have a history."

"Not an important one. Except perhaps in your own mind."

"She kissed me."

"I heard it was the other way around, and that she rebuffed you."

Roger stared at Dernier. *So she had told him.* He knew his face was as readable to the con man as a child's primer. He realized he had been counting on Maggie keeping the kiss from her husband.

"I'm going to help us to come to an understanding," Dernier said, nodding at the waiter, who quickly brought over two menus. Dernier glanced at the menu and then looked at Roger. "She's mine," he said. "She'll always be mine."

Roger stared at him as if hypnotized, pulled into his magnetic orbit.

"But there may be a way for you to stay in her life." He waved a hand dismissively. "Not by stealing her dog or ticketing her car."

Roger felt the blush inflame his neck and face. To have his childish actions outlined so baldly made him wish he could deny them with any credibility. Acknowledging that was impossible only deepened his shame. *This is what comes from living alone. There's no one to point out to you when you're making a total and complete ass of yourself.*

"As it happens," Dernier said, "I know something that you would do well to know, too."

Roger cleared his throat and found it difficult to look at him. "What is that?" he asked, stubbing out the cigarette he had forgotten to smoke.

"I know that you and I are going to be friends, Bedard. What do you think of that, eh?"

Roger snapped his head up to look at Dernier to see that the man was absolutely sincere, his face open and amused at the apparent ludicrousness of the situation. Before Roger knew what he was doing, he was genuinely smiling back at him.

After a pleasant evening watching old Masterpiece Theatre reruns with Grace, Maggie felt more relaxed than she had in weeks, and certainly more relaxed than she had any right to imagine she would after a day which saw the invasion of her home, the near loss of her beloved *petit-ami*, and the stark realization that she and Laurent had probably taken a severe financial hit during the last year—meaning at the very least that Laurent was up to his old tricks of not sharing with her when there was something to worry about money-wise.

Even so, after Grace had gone up to bed and Laurent still wasn't home from whatever mysterious outing he was on, but which almost certainly included drinking vast amounts of wine or *pastis* and then winding his way home on the narrow and precarious back roads from the village, Maggie found herself too edgy to sleep. Envying the easy sleep that Grace always found—even in the midst of her trials—and Laurent, too, for that matter, Maggie put a small pan on the stove and filled it with milk.

Petit-Four followed her from couch to kitchen and back again as Maggie settled in with her warm cup of milk. It tasted terrible but was the best she could do this late in the pregnancy. *God! How much longer?* She rubbed her belly. *Hurry it up, Chico. Mummy has things to do and your papa won't be happy until he's the one carrying you around.*

As she sat in the comfort and warmth of her living room—even sans the wool area rug that Roger's thugs had taken—Maggie couldn't help but wonder what Julia was doing tonight. *Was she afraid? Was she able to sleep? Were people hurting her in there?*

She had to admit that her so-called investigation into Jacques's murder and her attempt to clear Julia was at a dead-end. Not only did Maggie have no idea who might have done it but Laurent had finally put his foot down and there would be no edging around *that* fact, no "reinterpreting" what he said in order to go her own way.

She had to face it: her involvement in helping Julia was finished at least until after the baby was born. And if what Grace said was true, even then.

A muffled sound from the small anteroom between the kitchen and the mudroom snagged her attention. Petit-Four lifted her head too and looked in that direction. Maggie frowned and put her cup down on the coffee table. She had put seed in the little lovebird's bowl last night, but in all the excitement hadn't checked on him since then. The least she could do for Julia at this point was take care of her little bird. She padded into the kitchen, picking up her vibrating cellphone as she went.

It was Laurent. "Hey, lover," she said. "On your way home?"

"*Oui.* You are still up?"

"I can't sleep."

"I have some news for you, *chérie,* and it's not good. Are you okay to hear it?"

Maggie stopped walking. "What is it? Is it Jules? Is she dead?"

"*Non, non, chérie.* She is fine. Will you wait to hear it from me in person?"

"No, tell me now, Laurent." *Whatever it is, at least she's alive.* She walked into the anteroom where the noise had come from.

"I'm sorry, *chérie*," he said. "The murder case *est fini.*"

"Finished? How is that poss—" Maggie stopped with her hand frozen on the wall switch as she snapped on the light in the anteroom.

"Julia confessed today," Laurent said.

Maggie heard him at the same time she saw the motionless little body of Julia's lovebird at the bottom of the brass cage.

Susan Kiernan-Lewis

# Chapter Eighteen

Laurent decided that telling Maggie over the phone last night had been one of the truly bad miscalculations of his life. Sometimes she acted so calm and composed that he forgot she was also a hormonal, pregnant woman prone to exaggeration and over simplification from years of too-stimulating American television. She had been nearly hysterical when he walked into his house, the dead bird in her lap, and more tears than he remembered seeing from her in the whole time that he'd known her.

He figured it had to be the pregnancy.

This morning he brought her a tray of tea and toast. Although he would never understand the American and English fascination with rough, scratchy toasted bread when *beignets* and *croissants* were available, he'd compromised by slicing and toasting *brioche*, buttering it and serving it with a little pot of fresh raspberry jam.

"Any chance you will stay in bed today?" he asked as he set the tray down on the bed.

"I'm not sick, Laurent," she said, eyeing the tray but making no move to reach for the teacup.

"*Je sais.*" *I know.* He stood next to the bed and placed a hand on her cheek. "I'm sorry, *chérie*," he said.

"I don't suppose it matters," she said. "The confession. The lovebird."

"Ah, Maggie." He lifted her chin in his fingers but she pulled away.

"I guess you're happy, though," she said. "There's definitely no murder case to distract me now."

"Okay," he said, moving to the door. "Grace is up when you want company. I'll be back around dinnertime."

"Sure," Maggie said, looking away as he left.

*No, whether he'd told her on the phone or told her in person would probably have made no real difference in the end. She will have to come to her own happy ending with it all in her own time. Or not.*

Maggie bit into the toast and watched Laurent through the bedroom window as he maneuvered their Renault down the driveway and disappeared around the stand of the tall hundred-year-old cypress trees that lined the opening to their property. She sighed. He was probably happy to escape, she thought, and she could hardly blame him.

Just thinking of that tiny, vulnerable little body at the bottom of the cage was enough to bring tears to her eyes. She sniffled and the sound brought Petit-Four out from under the covers where she'd been patiently waiting for Maggie to get up.

It was worse because the little bird was so beautiful, so colorful with its pale peach head and bright green and pink wings. It was hard to see something so gaily colored, just lying there. Dead things should be brown or grey, she thought inanely. They shouldn't be so beautiful even in death.

She sipped the tea and felt a wave of guilt at how she had treated Laurent. He always took such good care of her. He couldn't help that he didn't want her to get hurt or kidnapped or whatever crazy scenario he had dreamed up if she continued to try to help Julia.

*Julia.* Maggie felt the tears threatening again and she took a quick restorative sip of the tea and leaned back into her pillows. She heard Petit-Four sigh and relax when she did.

*So Julia had given up.* Maggie had been wrong not to press the issue with her after Julia had hung up on her that time. Why didn't she push it? Had Maggie's feelings been hurt? Maggie frowned and pulled the duvet back to swing her legs out of bed. *Well, it didn't matter now.* Nothing did. Julia was going to prison for a murder she did, or didn't commit, and Maggie was going to have this baby in any event. Preferably sooner rather than later.

She showered, dressed and carried her breakfast tray downstairs. It was a little past eleven but she wasn't surprised not to hear Zou-zou's high pitched laugher ringing through the house. Grace had obviously shifted the child to Danielle's house in order to give Maggie a quiet morning. Downstairs was silent except for the sound of Petit-Four's nails against the hardwood floors of the hallway.

Suddenly, the little dog barked and ran to the front door.

*What the hell, dog?* Maggie thought with annoyance, realizing how pleasant the silence had been up to now. She walked to the front door and pulled it open expecting to see nothing and was startled to see a large man in uniform with a huge roll of carpet over his shoulder.

"Special delivery for Madame Dernier," the young officer said, hesitating only long enough to nod a brief salute to her before pushing his way past her to the living room.

The lavender fields were not totally spent. Annette could see how they would have been glorious a few months earlier, but the late cold snap that had delayed the grape harvest this year had also extended the beautiful vistas of dramatic lavender just a little bit longer. The neat mounds of purple positioned against the golden autumn trees were as pretty as a tourist's postcard. She threw her cigarette out the car window, blowing smoke against the inside of the windshield.

"Can you smell the scent from here? It's faint, but it's there."

She sighed and turned to him in the passenger's seat. "I can't smell the fucking lavender, Florrie," she said.

"Well, it's a ways off," he said, fumbling for the crank on his door to lower the window a little more.

As sunny as the day looked, the Mistral had settled around the morning like a death shroud. It was cold and windy outside of the car.

"Roll up the window, for God's sake," she said. "I'm freezing."

"We could do this at my place," he said easily, cracking his knuckles and making her want to shoot him where he sat.

If she only had a gun.

"It's a lot warmer there. And I made a *ratatouille*."

"Are you insane? You are talking about *ratatouilles*? We are meeting here, Florrie, because of the disaster of our last meeting. You do remember that, do you not?"

He shrugged. "Now that everyone knows…"

"Everyone does not know! Nobody knows!" She fished another cigarette out of her purse and tapped its filter against the steering wheel. "I must have been mad to even think about doing this."

"You hated him more than anyone," Florrie said quietly. "It is fitting."

"Fitting," she spat. "Tell me again how it is to my benefit? Because you can trust me about this, widowhood suits me very well."

"You were no longer married to him, Annette," Florrie said.

"Whatever."

"I have, of course, a sizable fortune of my own to offer you."

"As sizable as Lily's?"

She noticed he shifted uncomfortably and that made her smile. Just a little.

"Perhaps not," he admitted. "But not inconsequential, I assure you. Let me ask you, is it true you had no idea that Lily intended for you to have it after Jacques?"

"You hate that, don't you?"

"Not at all. Lily knows I am comfortable. It makes sense that she would want to take care of ..." Florrie groped for words.

"The *widow* of her beloved nephew?" Annette said, grinning at him. She lit her cigarette and blew out a thin jet of smoke into the car's interior. Florrie cranked down his window again. "What do *you* think? Do *you* think I knew before he died that I was next in line?"

Florrie was watching her carefully. "I really don't know," he said. "Did you?"

Annette turned away to stare back out at the picture postcard view. Her smile grew as she thought of the money that would soon be hers. It grew as she imagined the home she would build. Finally. The home she had always dreamed of owning. The laugh was bubbling up inside her and she let it come. She heard herself cawing with mirth—a most unladylike sound—but it didn't matter. She was rich! And she didn't need Florrie's pathetic fortune or anyone else's patronage ever again. She could do what she wanted, when she wanted. As her laughter eased, she turned to see Florrie's face with its expression of horror and, yes, revulsion, and she didn't care. She didn't care! She was rich enough now that she need never care.

"Oh, yes," she said to him, blowing smoke between them, her lips stretched tightly over her teeth in a predatory grin. "I knew."

* * *

Maggie poured her tea and brought the mug with her into the living room to curl up with an afghan and Petit-Four on the couch. She usually loved to watch the weather from the French doors that opened off the terrace and gave a sweeping view of the vineyards. Today the vineyards look like naked crosses in a cemetery—one where massive casualties have resulted in a homogenous attempt to honor and remember everyone because there's too much death to do it one at a time. The rows of staked vines looked desiccated and creepy, the wooden structures holding only stripped black branches if anything at all.

The terrace, with its brittle canopy of yellow linden leaves, had enjoyed afternoon relief from the autumn sun all month. Now the leaves lay scattered on the stone tiles, not a single one left on the branches, allowing the sun drill relentlessly onto the patio.

Maggie sipped her tea and felt the weight of her failure. She touched her stomach as the baby moved restlessly inside her. *It's so unfair. This should be a time of amazing anticipation and excitement for me. And for Laurent.*

Her eyes strayed again to the ugly rows of stripped vines. The phone rang. She leaned across her dog to reach it on the side table.

"Hello?"

The voice that answered hesitated, and then was clipped and businesslike. "Hello, Maggie. Is your husband home?"

"Nope. Just me, Roger." Maggie put her hand on Petit-Four's head, feeling her silky curls between her fingers. "Why are you calling? Did you get a complaint about someone loosening the bolts on the wheelchairs down at the hospital? Are you calling to fine me for burning the soufflé this morning?"

"Look, Maggie…" There was a pause that Maggie didn't try to fill. "I'm sorry…about all that," he said.

Maggie didn't answer immediately. Finally, she said, "Your guy delivered our rugs and stuff back. Thank you."

"You're welcome. Look, I'm calling to say I got some information about Julia Patrick's case and I told Der—your husband, that I would keep him informed. I want you to know, Maggie, that I take no pleasure in telling you that Madame Patrick was arraigned this morning on the charge of first-degree murder…"

Maggie felt like she had been punched in the stomach.

"…and is being moved tomorrow to a more…secure facility."

*More secure. He's trying to make it sound like it's for her safety or something.*

"Anyway, if you want to see her, I can arrange that," he said. "But it will have to be tomorrow morning."

Maggie's eyes were swimming with tears. The one thing she thought never in a million years would happen, was happening. *Julia was going to prison.*

"Maggie? Will you come?"

"Yes," Maggie said, her weariness so bone deep she had to sit down on one of the barstools before she fell down. "Yes, I'll come."

\* \* \* \*

The streets in the old part of Aix were never more beautiful in Michelle's opinion than early in the morning. The tourists weren't up, the shops weren't open, so all the people with more money than need weren't lining up yet to buy more useless things than they could never use.

Had Michelle *ever* felt like she had enough?

Even when her parents were still together, there had been no money. She could remember them when they were together. She had been young, but not so young. There had been few treats, she remembered that. But there had been enough for her mother to dress and have her hair done. Yes, there had been enough for that.

Michelle sat on the park bench in *Parc Rambot*, a white paper bag of day-old rolls next to her. Two pigeons stared at her from the pavement in front of her. She'd made the mistake of throwing a piece of bread to them. Now, nothing short of death would release them from their focus on her as their benefactor. She thought of the chickens she had killed last month and smiled. She had hidden behind a farmer's truck to witness the bitch's reaction to the car's damage and the note. She hadn't been disappointed.

She reached into the paper bag and threw another piece of roll to the two pigeons, hitting one in the head. She watched them fight over it until several more birds appeared. She picked up the rock she had brought and waited until two were trying to peck the bread more than each other.

It was the so-called *lucky one* who would die, she decided. The one with the bread. The one with more than the others. She waited until the largest bird had taken possession of the bread and she fired the rock at it, hitting it full in the chest. She was rewarded by a terrified squawk and a cloud of feathers as it and the others flew away. She was sure she saw his wing at an unnatural angle. She saw the bread sitting on the pavement, and the blood on the pavement next to it, and she smiled.

The next time she would be smarter. As with the car, she would take her pleasure from afar. It wasn't quite as satisfying, but it was more certain. It didn't matter quite so much that she *saw* the bitch contorted on the ground in agony. It only mattered that it happened. That was the mature approach. The adult approach. But then, if her plan came off as she imagined

*—and it was so simple, how could it not?—*she felt sure she would be able to have both.

Grace tiptoed down the stairs, Zou-zou's stuffed bunny in her hand. She walked into the kitchen and opened the door to the *cave,* where she could hear someone, probably Laurent, moving boxes around. She shivered in the doorway of the basement stairs. It occurred to her that this was the first time she had been at this spot in Maggie and Laurent's house since Connor was murdered. In the basement. On Thanksgiving Day three years ago. A wave of sorrow and loss slammed into her and she grabbed the door jamb to keep herself from sagging to her knees.

*Dearest Connor. How I have missed you these last three years. And here is where you died. Full of life and piss and lies and so much laughter. And your life seeped out of you in the coldest part of a one hundred year old basement while I was drinking and eating turkey upstairs.* Grace took a long breath and hardened her thoughts. Connor was gone and Windsor was going and it didn't help anyone to dwell on it. She pushed away from the basement and the innocuous sounds of Laurent tinkering and working below.

She moved into the living room and sat down next to Maggie on the couch. "Don't you two ever watch television?" she asked as she nodded to the notebooks and mini tablets on Maggie's lap.

"We do," Maggie said absently. "We watch Netflix sometimes."

"You're kidding. You get Netflix?"

"Yeah, it came to France a few months back." Maggie pushed her notebooks away and arched her back trying to massage the base of her spine. "God, I'm in agony. I cannot remember the last time I slept through the night. Just to turn over requires being fully awake and practically getting out of bed to reposition. This part of the deal sucks." She looked out the French doors to the vineyard beyond. "Promise me it gets better when he's born."

"When he *or she* is born, you mean." Grace sat cross-legged behind Maggie on the couch and put her hands on her friend's shoulders and began to massage between her shoulder blades. Maggie groaned with pleasure.

"It gets better as far as being able to move around more easily," Grace said. "But it's worse as far as always being exhausted. Much worse. Plus there's the worry. Once the little dear's born, you will never again have a single worry-free moment until you drop down dead of old age."

"Don't sugarcoat it for me," Maggie mumbled.

Grace laughed. "It'll all work out, darling."

"Sure doesn't feel that way now."

"That's because this whole Julia business is complicating everything."

Maggie turned to face her. "I cannot believe she confessed. She did it to protect her boyfriend, I'm sure of it."

"Probably."

"I'm sure she's really discouraged. I was doing what I could but I got nowhere. It's been three weeks and she's still in jail. She obviously lost faith in anyone being able to help her."

"These things take time. Especially with your being on such a short leash. Half the people you needed to talk to you couldn't because of Laurent."

"Tell me about it."

"I know things look bleak at the moment. Trust me, nobody knows better than I do how one or two setbacks can color the whole picture."

"She's given up on me, Grace. She's given up on herself."

"Well, you can't give up, too, sweetie. Things have looked this black before."

"Have they, Grace? The police have a confession, plus incriminating forensic evidence. And I don't have anybody better than who they have in jail right now. If I were Jules, I'd be confessing too."

"Now you're just feeling sorry for yourself. You've got all the late trimester discomfort to deal with, not to mention hormones, but you need to snap out of it. For Julia's sake, if not for your own."

"This is so unlike you, Grace." Maggie turned her back again so Grace could resume massaging her shoulders. "But I like the new you," she moaned.

"Come on, sweetie, bounce some of your theories off me. I've been out of the game but I'm back now. What have you got?"

"Well..." Maggie rotated her neck and gave a deep sigh that Grace interpreted with satisfaction was from her ministrations. "I still like Mathieu for this. I'm sure he could have done it. He has no alibi but plenty of motive, and he's got the same access to the crime scene that Julia did. Plus, it explains why Julia would confess."

"Okay, that's good. So you think it's Mathieu."

"Well, except for the fact that Annette is still my number one suspect. Especially since we learned she inherits when Lily dies. *And* she has no convincing alibi for the time in question."

"What *is* her alibi?"

"Roger would never tell me, which makes it *really* unconvincing."

"Ohhhhh," Grace said knowingly.

Maggie turned to look at her. "What does *that* mean?"

"Roger wouldn't say because it involves someone in his organization higher up."

"What?"

"Sure. Annette is obviously boffing Roger's boss. Or someone like that. Could be a politician, but I'm betting it's someone in the police hierarchy. Are you and Roger back on better terms since Laurent and he talked?"

"Somewhat."

"If he won't tell you what her alibi is, it's because he can't."

"It *does* fit."

"Yes, but her being protected by someone high ranking in the police department is bad because it means her alibi is gold-plated."

"And that really sucks because everything else fits for her being the murderer. She loathed Jacques, and with him dead she stood to inherit Lily's estate. When you add motive with personal animosity and throw in opportunity you've got a prime suspect. I mean, Julia didn't stand to gain financially from Jacques's death like Annette did."

"Okay. So you've got Annette and possibly Mathieu. See? You do have some likely candidates for the murderer. Well done!"

"I guess so. But the fly in the soup is the question I keep asking myself about all this. *Why* is all the evidence laying at *Julia's* feet? *Why* does she look so guilty to everyone?"

"Um, because she's guilty?"

Maggie stopped and looked at Grace. "You think Julia is guilty?"

"I think it's possible."

Maggie looked pensively at her hands. "You don't know her like I do."

"No. I do know, however, that you've staked your claim on her as your new best friend. I can see why you wouldn't want to believe you're wrong about her."

The look on Maggie's face betrayed her feelings. Grace watched her face animate and flush with color.

"Facts, unpleasant as they may be, don't lie," Grace said.

"Except in this case," Maggie said heatedly, "all the so-called facts don't measure up to what I *know* about the person."

"Even people we know really well can be capable of doing terrible things. May I remind you of a dear sweet village baker who tried to kill both of us?"

"Yeah, okay, Grace. I get it. I'm not saying I know anything for sure. I'm saying, in spite of not knowing, I need to take my friend at her word or else friendship doesn't mean anything."

Grace looked serenely at Maggie before answering. "And isn't that exactly what I've been trying to tell you ever since I arrived, darling?"

Maggie stared at her with her mouth open and then slowly smiled. "Yeah, I guess you have." They were quiet for a moment, both lost in their own thoughts. "What's with the bunny?"

Grace picked up the stuffed animal and tossed it onto the coffee table. "Evidently its left eye is hanging by a thread. I've been informed it's a necessary repair."

"We don't have a seamstress in residence."

"I think I can manage it. Z isn't a stickler for even stitches."

Maggie reached over to squeeze her friend's hand. "Thanks, Grace. I feel a lot better."

"That's what I'm here for, darling. Now show me how to get Netflix working on the TV. I hear Laurent coming up the stairs and I'll bet he'd just love to get us each a nice glass of wine. Well, juice for you. And maybe you can get him to rub your feet."

"You're just full of great ideas tonight," Maggie said, snuggling deep into the couch.

That night, as Maggie was putting lotion on her elbows in bed, she turned to Laurent, who had already positioned a pillow over his head to block out the light.

"I've been meaning to ask you, what did you say to Roger?"

"Pshht, *rien*," he said. "The light, Maggie?"

"I don't think it was *rien*. I think it was the opposite of *rien*. He called to talk to you today and when you weren't here he *apologized* for harassing us."

Laurent grunted but she couldn't tell anything more from his reaction.

"You're an alchemist, Laurent," she said. "Do you know what that is?"

"Does it involve total darkness when I sleep?"

"I'm going to be expecting you to work your magic on the baby when he comes," she said snapping off the light. "A man who can make difficult people do his bidding is a valuable man to have." She snuggled down next to him and he pulled her in close to his chest. "And I am very glad to have him," she whispered into his neck before closing her eyes and succumbing to sleep.

Michelle looked up at the darkened bedroom window of the stone mansion. She wasn't expecting to see how large the house was. Her mother had only said it was old. Of course, she knew the bitch's husband was a wealthy *vigneron,* but to see the fields of stripped vines stretching for miles in every direction—even in the dim morning half-light—had been galling. Of course she was rich. As with the English whore, she had brought her money with her from America to live like royalty in the beautiful Provencal countryside.

It had been a long walk in the dark and the bitter cold to the *mas,* but her moment of triumph was at hand. An hour's bus ride from Aix in the middle of the night—with every form of vermin and degenerate riding with her, followed by a two-hour stumbling walk to reach the house. She knew there were wolves in this part of the country, she had heard them during her walk. But she had let her fear drive her steps, one after another, until she stood beneath the bitch's window.

*The arrogance! She felt she could sleep so soundly without even a dog to warn against attack. So comfortable and so sure of her safety that she couldn't be bothered to lock her doors.* But Michelle didn't need to get inside the castle to kill the bitch.

That was the beauty of the plan.

She had arrived early, just to be safe. She found a large yew tree near the entrance of the house that was crowded by dark bushes. She slipped inside the thick underbrush, feeling the long daggers of the branches cut her arms and neck but not caring. Her excitement kept her immune from the pain. When her mother had reported back about her visit to the *mas*, Michelle had demanded she tell her everything about what she had seen. She had been hungry to hear how rich the bitch was, but in the telling her mother had given her the most vital piece of her plan—the key, in fact, to Michelle's ultimate revenge.

*Maman had mentioned the empty milk bottles on the front steps.* She had told Michelle of the fact with disdain in her voice, but Michelle knew that disdain was driven by envy.

Only the rich had milk delivery in this day.

*How perfect that the very symbol of wealth—a blatant heralding of their superiority over others—would be the very thing that brought them down.* As Michelle took her seat in the bush, she could see a direct line to the front steps. She saw the three empty bottles that sat there. The longer she looked at them the angrier she became, and she had to force herself to remember that by this time tomorrow nobody would ever order milk delivery at this address ever again. The thought calmed her.

It wasn't long before she heard him. It seemed her ears picked up the sound from miles away, but that was probably because she imagined him in her mind driving closer, ever closer, in his delivery truck. When he finally turned down the long driveway in the dark wee hours, it was all she could do not to crow with delight and anticipation. She knew he would be too focused on his task to notice her, but even so she held her breath as the truck stopped in front of her, blocking her view. It took only seconds, but when the vehicle began to slowly back up the drive, restoring her line of sight, she saw the one thing she had been seeing in her dreams for weeks now.

Three full bottles of milk stood on the slate steps by the front door.

Hesitating only a moment to make sure no one in the house was yet awake, Michelle slipped from the bushes toward the front steps. She was proud as she approached the waiting bottles that her hands did not shake as she withdrew the plastic flask of bleach from her coat.

# Chapter Nineteen

Roger was on hand in person early the next morning to escort Maggie to the detention section of the *Palais de Justice*. He spoke very little, but was absolutely courteous as she followed him in single file down the corridor to the room where she would wait for Julia. In fact, the only real difference that Maggie could detect in his behavior from the man who had stomped into her house and attempted to take her dog was in the fact that he had begun calling her *Maggie* again.

After he instructed the police officer at the end of the hall to unlock the door to the meeting room, he turned to her. "Officer Picard will be down in twenty minutes to escort you out."

"Okay. Thanks."

He gave a curt nod and left her. When she had settled herself into one of the two metal chairs in the room, she willed herself to be calm and confident for Julia's sake.

*No matter what she looks like.*

In the end, she was wise to have prepped for the worst. When the door opened, Maggie hauled herself to her feet to greet her friend. Julia had lost weight, her hair was long, her tiny gold hoop earrings were gone, and her face was a roadmap of lines and sagging flesh.

Maggie went to her and the two women embraced. Julia's arms felt as frail as the bones of a chicken. Maggie had to stop herself from squeezing too hard. When she pulled away she saw dark bruises up and down Julia's arms.

"Thanks for seeing me, Julia."

As frail as her friend looked, Julia's voice was strong and level, and for that Maggie was hopeful.

"Look, I'm sorry about hanging up on you the other week."

"Do not apologize. I can't imagine what you're going through in here."

"Best not to try."

"I don't know what to say about...everything that's going on with you, Jules."

"Don't say anything. How's that? The suicide, the confession...how about we just stick to what friends do? I don't want to talk about that other shit."

"Okay." Maggie leaned over and picked up one of Julia's hands and held it in hers. Julia didn't respond, but she didn't resist either. "Can I ask you a few questions about that night with Jacques?"

Julia looked at Maggie as if she didn't have the energy to register incredulity. Her eyes were flat and nonexpressive. "If it makes you feel like you're doing something," she said. "Shoot."

Maggie fought against reacting to Julia's pessimism. She smiled encouragingly. "What did y'all talk about that night?"

"He asked me about my cookbook. He said he was coming into some money. He suggested we get back together."

"He said he was coming into some money? Did you tell the cops this?"

"Of course. My lawyer urged me to hold nothing back."

"Great lawyer. So was Jacques in a good mood at dinner?"

"I told you. He wasn't feeling well."

"That's right. You said he told you that even before he came over."

Julia didn't answer.

"You said he made you feel sorry for him," Maggie said.

"Did I?"

"Was there anything that happened during the actual evening that made you feel *less* sorry for him?"

Julia ran a hand through her hair, her face a mask of concentration as she tried to reconstruct the night in her mind.

"No, not really. I don't know what I was expecting but... he hadn't changed. He was still full of himself. He totally believed we were getting back together." She looked at Maggie. "He mentioned his daughter, Michelle."

"Mentioned how?"

"Said she was hounding him for money, which wasn't new, but that he would be able to be a little more generous with her soon."

"So he wasn't a total sod."

"No, he was. But you're right. It was a strange thing for him to say."

"Anything else?"

"Well, he talked about visiting his Aunt Lily on Sunday. There was a big Sunday lunch at her estate every week. He was always kind of derisive about going. About Florrie, too, whom he called the "good" nephew. Is any of this helpful?"

"I don't know yet. In the back of my mind I can't help but think the murder has to do somehow with the inheritance. And Lily."

Maggie watched Julia's shoulders sag inside her baggy prison jumper and she leaned out and touched her arm gently. "Julia, I know it's hell in here, but please don't give up."

"You don't know what it's like."

"That's true. But confessing to something you didn't do is not going to make things easier."

"It will just make them happen faster."

"The law and all its processes are going to happen at the pace they're going to happen. You can't speed that up. Besides, that's not why you confessed."

"No."

"It's because of Mathieu, isn't it? Because you're trying to protect him?"

"No!"

"Okay, but you know, Jules, if it *was* Mathieu, it's not very loving of *him* to let you take the fall for this."

"You're right," Julia said, crossing her arms across her chest. "Which is the best argument for why it couldn't be him."

"Well, then who?"

"I don't know. Why not Annette? Nobody hated Jacques more than she did."

"I thought of that. The problem is, Jacques was going to inherit money in a very few months and Annette would be able to sue him to get a good chunk of that."

"I thought you said Annette was the new heir?"

"She is, but she didn't know that at the time Jacques was killed. It wouldn't have made sense to kill him when he's about to inherit. Especially since the general assumption was that *Florrie* was next in line to inherit."

"Sometimes killing doesn't make sense. Sometimes it's about exterminating someone so vile that you can't stand the thought of him breathing the same air that you do."

"Whoa. Seriously, Julia. You and Annette are neck and neck for how much the two of you hated Jacques and I never really knew that before."

"I wouldn't be where I am if not for him," Julia said with weariness,

"That would only be true if *you* killed him, Julia. It's the person who did kill Jacques who's responsible for your being in here. Jacques is dead. He can't hurt you any more."

"God, you're naive, Maggie. Or maybe you've just never been hurt by anyone. You're lucky."

"Just a little bit longer, Jules."

Julia's face became more animated as a thought came to her. "Listen, can you get a message to Mathieu for me? They won't let me contact him."

Maggie frowned. "Laurent has forbidden me to see him. But I suppose I could get Laurent to come with me."

"I'd appreciate it, Maggie. Thank you."

"What's the message?"

"Just that I love him and I trust him and I beg him not to do anything rash."

"Rash, like what?"

"Just tell him, Maggie."

"Okay."

Grace sat at the *Café L'etoile Verte* opposite the police detention center and waited for Maggie to appear. What remained of the pale golden leaves of every plane tree that lined the street in front of the restaurant gave the appearance of a heavenly gateway——an avenue of ethereal light, especially when the early morning sun slowly illuminated the street. A Sunday morning, it was too early for any real shopping to help while away the time, and in Grace's experience, whenever she stayed still for longer than five minutes in public she was usually approached, whether physically or just with inquisitive, suggestive glances. In some ways, those were even more invasive. She brought her coffee cup to her lips and kept her gaze directed toward the front door. Even so, she could feel them watching her.

She'd been told before, countless times, of her physical likeness to the long-dead princess Grace of Monaco. *You'd think there would be at least two generations past those who wouldn't even remember who she was, let alone what she looked like.* But this was France, and worse, the south of France. Memories were long here, especially when they involved beautiful American actresses who claimed royal princes and thrones that should have gone to French natives.

Grace watched Maggie hesitate in the archway of the café terrace, scanning the outdoor tables looking for her. *Good Lord, she looked like she was about to drop that baby any minute now. No wonder she was miserable.* Grace lifted her hand to get Maggie's attention, and when she did she could see out of the corner of her eye that heads at every single table in her near vicinity turned toward her.

*Were they hoping to see what my husband looked like?* she thought with amusement. *Did any of them think they now stood a chance with me, seeing that my date was only a very pregnant woman, also clearly not French?*

"Hey, Grace, what are you having? I need to get off my feet. Oh, my God, that was intense." Grace watched Maggie turn to the waiter before she draped the shoulder strap of her handbag on the back of the chair. "*Café crème, s'il vous plait.*"

Grace smiled at her, wondering if she had any idea of the public theatre she was a part of. She was half tempted to turn to the surrounding tables—all men, of course—and ask if they could hear okay or should she and her friend amplify a little more for their comfort?

"How was she?" Grace asked.

"About what you'd expect. Not great. She asked me to give a message to Mathieu."

"Will Laurent allow you to do that?"

"I'll have to do it with him." Maggie smiled briefly at the waiter as he set her coffee cup down in front of her. "*Merci.* I've been dying for this," she said taking a quick sip of her coffee. "Sorry we didn't have time this morning for a cup at home."

"No problem, darling," Grace said. "My phone reception is spotty. Do you know if Laurent got Zou-zou up yet?"

"No, he had to go out but he said Jean-Luc came over to mind her. Danielle's at Lily's today. It sounds like it's a death watch or something."

"I hate to hear that. So it's Jean-Luc and Z today?"

"Oh, my God, Grace, he's crazy about that little girl! You have brought new life to his world. And Danielle's, of course."

"Glad to be of service. He must have come over awfully early on a Sunday morning."

"Yeah, he must have gotten there seconds after you and I left. Laurent said he heard him bringing the milk in."

"Zou-zou loves them both."

"Can't have too many people who love you," Maggie said. "Unless, of course, they're putting your photos in weird wallpaper collages in their back bedroom or something."

"Well put, darling. And speaking of that, did you run into Roger in there?"

"No, he doesn't work on Sundays unless there's a body that's been discovered, and even then, you know how lazy he is."

Grace laughed. "No, but I'm heartened to hear it sounds like he's settled down a bit."

"Yeah. I have no idea what Laurent told him but it seems to have worked."

"Laurent definitely has a way about him."

"That is true," Maggie said, rubbing her stomach.

"You feeling alright, darling?"

"I am just so ready to get out of this fat suit, I could scream. How about you?"

"I'm not the one about to go into labor any minute. Oh, there's my phone." Grace picked it up and looked at the screen. "The call failed," she said. "But it was from Danielle. Can we go some place in this adorably quaint and antiquated town where I can get a damn phone call?"

"You sure you're okay?"

Grace tossed her phone back in her purse and sighed. "I'm fine. I talked with Windsor last night and he's eager for me to come back with the baby."

"Come back...?"

"Not like that. He misses her. We've been gone a month."

"Are you afraid he won't let her come back with you?"

Grace hesitated and then shook her head. "No, not really." She shrugged. "It's Windsor."

"Yeah," Maggie said. "A good guy."

"Yes, yes, a good guy. Get the waiter's attention, will you, darling? I'm going to try my luck with better phone reception out under the plane trees." Grace stood up and looked around. Sure enough, three tables with one to two ogling Frenchmen per table grinned at her.

*Well, at least it looks like dating won't be a problem*, she thought with a sinking heart as she wound her way through the tables to the street in front of the café.

\* \* \* \*

If there were another way to do it, by God, he would have done it. How things had gotten so far down this path, he would never know. But now that he'd started, he knew he couldn't stop until it was finished.

He parked his car down an adjacent alley to the café. Because it was Sunday, it had been difficult to follow them without looking like theirs were the only two cars on the highway. But also because it was Sunday, there was no one to see him sitting now in the car, waiting, watching.

Dernier's wife went across the street to the jail and the other one—the beautiful one—walked into the café, clearly waiting for her friend to finish her errand. That meant he had time. Probably more than enough, but in the event that he was, once again, fatally wrong about that, he wiped the sweat from his palms and grabbed the ice pick out of the glove compartment. He hesitated just a moment to pray—for everyone's sake—that he would not be seen, and left the car.

# Chapter Twenty

Danielle smoothed the covers back over the withered hands. They were pale, but that was not surprising. Lily had never been one for the outdoors, for walks or gardening. Her hands, for as old as she was, still looked younger than Danielle's after sixty-five years of an active life under the Provencal sun.

"Are you the only one?"

Danielle was mildly startled by Lily's voice. Lily had been asleep, soundly, she was sure of it. But now she regarded her with an alert, cool gaze.

"The only one, *what*, my friend?" Danielle asked, settling down on the bed next to her.

"Here to watch me die."

"Don't say that. You're not dying today."

"You *are* the only one." Lily turned her face away and Danielle stood to pull the curtains back from the long window in the room. The early morning fog had burned off, leaving a crystal clear autumn day. *The kind of day that made you glad to be alive*, Danielle thought.

"The others will be coming, soon," Danielle said. "It's still early."

"Not for me," Lily said, looking out the window at the brilliant blue sky.

"Can I get you something? Are you thirsty?"

Lily turned her gaze back to Danielle. "We were never close. Why is it you are here when my family is not?"

"I was always sorry our friendship…faded. And then, when life intervened, I married. It became too difficult to have the time for other things."

"I heard about Eduard," Lily said. Danielle turned her head sharply to her. "Oh, yes. You didn't think I knew? You married badly, Danielle."

"The first time, yes."

"And I never married at all."

"We each made our choices." Danielle watched Lily carefully, wondering if the woman was fading into dementia at the end.

"You remember Bernard, of course?"

Danielle stared at her uncomprehending when an image of a boy, a handsome young boy with very black hair and the bluest snapping eyes, came roaring back into her memory.

*Bernard.*

"You remember him, don't you?"

Danielle had been in love with him. How could she have forgotten? She was so young, not even sixteen, but they had kissed in the washhouse. Her first kiss. As she sat by Lily's bedside, she remembered the relentless, impenetrable quiet of the thirteenth century stone house, the coldness and the dampness of the interior wilting her dress, her hair. And she remembered the boy who put his warm lips to hers and made her feel alive for the first time in her life.

And very nearly the last.

"I do," she whispered, seeing him in her mind—laughing, always laughing.

"He's a butcher in Dijon now. And fat."

Danielle brought her attention back to her friend.

"He was my first," Lily said. She laughed bitterly. "My only. I know you never knew that. You only knew when he stopped speaking to you at school."

Danielle's skin tingled. The memory of the nausea of the rejection came rushing back to her as she sat on Lily's bed—sixty-six years old, the bulk of her life behind her, her youth, her beauty, what there had been of it—and she was filled with an uncomfortable, unusual feeling spreading to the tips of her fingers.

Rage.

"You took him for yourself," Danielle said, her words stilted and blunt as she fought to quell the sensation of anger building in her chest.

"I *gave* him myself," Lily said, watching her intently. "You gave him kisses. Would you have done more?"

Danielle couldn't respond. She didn't know. *I was only fifteen...*

"Yes, I took him." Lily looked back out the window as if she were seeing the boy, herself. The handsome future butcher from Dijon with the laughing blue eyes and the shiny black hair. "And so we both lost him."

They sat quietly together, lost in their memories of their first love, and when their eyes finally met, full of all the sadness of lost opportunities and lost youth, Danielle realized she wasn't angry at all. She reached out and took Lily's pale, cold hand and held it in her warm one.

"I am virtually a vegetarian," she said, a smile forming on her lips as she watched Lily's startled face slowly form into a mute, gasping series of heaving laughter.

\* \* \* \*

Maggie struggled into the car seat and waited for Grace to start the car.

"Buckle up, darling," Grace said as she backed out of the tight parallel parking spot a block from the café.

"I can't," Maggie said. "I'm too fat."

"That's not true, dearest, and I won't get on the highway until you do."

Maggie groaned and pulled the strap across and under her belly. "I am so ready for this to be over," she said, squirming uncomfortably in the seat.

"I know," Grace said, taking the entrance ramp onto the D7.

"I don't remember you looking like this," Maggie said, eyeing her suspiciously. "In fact, I don't remember you looking any different when you were pregnant with Z than you do right now."

"I was, of course, gargantuan. You were just so self-absorbed you never noticed."

"Oh, funny. Thanks. I just think some people can carry it off with style, and other people just look like they're always searching for the nearest all-you-can-eat buffet."

"You do not look fat, Maggie. You look pregnant."

"Oh, quit trying to mollify me. And you know what the worst of it is? Laurent and I had *just* figured out how to be happy together, you know?"

Grace gave her a side glance.

"I mean, just when I stopped whining about being homesick and having nothing to do, we really came through the fire out onto the other side. And now this!" She gestured to her stomach. "What in the hell is *this* going to do to us?"

"Well, it's a little late to be thinking about that now." Grace said, smiling.

"I totally do not want anything to torpedo what we've got together," Maggie said, staring morosely out the car window at the brown and yellow landscape of the passing scenery.

"What makes you think it won't enhance it?"

"Okay, now I *know* you're mollifying me. Everyone says having kids makes marriage harder. And I have only recently figured out how to be happily married."

"There's more to it than that. Kids may add more stress to your relationship with Laurent, that's true."

"That's what I'm saying."

"But they also bring a whole lot more love and joy into your life as a couple."

"How does that fit with the first thing you said?"

"I don't know, darling, but it does. You just have to trust me on this. You and Laurent are fine now and you'll be fine after the little blighter is born."

"How about better than fine?"

"Don't push it. The most you can hope for is that it doesn't screw things up. Hoping for it to make your marriage better *is* crazy. You're not hoping to make things better with this baby?"

Maggie shook her head. "No, I can't imagine being happier with Laurent than I am. That's why..." she rubbed her stomach, "...as excited as I usually am about meeting this little fellow, I find myself fretting that he'll somehow hurt what I have with his daddy."

"I know very few things for absolutely certainty, darling," Grace said, putting on her sunglasses against the bright autumn day. "In fact, me less than most. But I am completely confidant in saying, knowing your man the way I do, that *that* will not happen."

"A part of me knows that," Maggie admitted. "I've never met anyone on this planet that I trust more than Laurent. How did I ever get so lucky that he could love me back?"

"I'm sure I have no idea. But speaking of how you were able to save your marriage by shaking off such nonessential worries like homesickness and not having a job to occupy your mind, any word from your editor?"

Maggie grimaced.

"She hasn't returned your emails?"

"No."

"Still think everything is okay because you have a contract?"

Maggie sighed. "I read the contract last night."

"In a rare moment of panicked insecurity?"

"Yeah. And it seems that by missing the deadline, I've already voided the contract."

"Oh, Maggie!"

"I know. I cannot believe how stupid I am. I can't believe I screwed this up."

"Darling, do you know *why*? I mean, I'm sure book contracts are very difficult to acquire, aren't they?"

"Oh, don't talk about it, Grace! It just makes me sick!"

"No, come on, now. You're a big girl. *Why* did you sabotage yourself like this? Especially after you just got through telling me that it was partly the book writing that kept you and Laurent together."

"Yeah, when you put it that way, I really sound self-destructive."

"Quit the negative self-talk and *tell* me what is going on with you. And thank you, by the way. I like to be reminded that I'm not the only basket case in this friendship."

"You're welcome. I'm pretty sure you can always count on me for that," Maggie said bitterly as she picked at the hem on her tunic. "I just freaked when I saw all the corrections that she wanted. It just…overwhelmed me. And then I started to think that maybe I shouldn't be doing this, you know? That maybe the editor was right."

"What do you mean *the editor was right*? They *bought* your book. They bought *two* future books from you. She wasn't setting you up to fail, Maggie! She was helping you get published."

"Don't you think I see that now? *Now,* when she's not taking my phone calls anymore? *Now,* when my contract is voided and my name is shit in the world of New York publishing?"

"All right, sweetie. I guess learning the lesson is what's important. At least someone liked your writing well enough to buy it."

"Yeah, now all I have to do is have lightning strike twice in the same place and not throw it away with both hands when it does."

Grace looked over at her friend and smiled sadly. "Something like that."

"Your phone's vibrating," Maggie said distractedly.

"Do you mind getting it, darling? I've got my hands full just figuring out the exit to St-Buvard."

"That's not for ages yet," Maggie said, as she punched on the phone.

"Hello? Oh, hey, Danielle. Everything okay?"

Grace frowned and glanced at Maggie questioningly. Maggie held up a finger to her while she listened on the phone.

"Okay, let me ask her," she said. "Danielle says Jean-Luc says that Zou-zou is getting hungry and does she take her bottle warm or chilled?"

Grace snorted and Maggie couldn't help but notice that she even did that adorably. "Tell her to tell him that it doesn't matter. I'm usually lucky to get the carton all the way out of the fridge before she's guzzling it down. Tell him not to bother heating it."

"Did you hear that, Danielle?" Maggie said.

In all his years, never would Jean-Luc have imagined he would some day be in the position he now found himself in. Contorted, on the floor, his rump high in the air with a squealing two-year old bouncing on his back, her little heels digging into his ribs, Jean-Luc had to admit he had never been happier.

His friends down at *Le Canard* would think he had lost his mind. A bachelor well into his sixties before he finally married, Jean-Luc had never known or expected the experience of fatherhood. He had long accepted that there would be no children to whom he might pass on what little wisdom he had, so the thought that the joys and pleasure of being a *grandfather* might yet lie in store for him had never occurred to him.

He gathered his giggling jockey up into his arms and gave her a wet kiss on her forehead. "Snack, Zou-zou?" he said. "Or read a book?"

"Snack! Snack! Snack!" the little girl sang, wrapping her chubby arms around his neck.

"I agree," he said. "I have already called *Grandmama* Danielle this morning to ask how Mademoiselle likes her milk. Milk is a good snack for Zou-zou, yes?"

Zou-zou began counting her fingers and singing as Jean-Luc carried her into the Dernier kitchen—a marvel of gleaming stainless steel, burnished hardwood and gleaming copper pots hanging from an overhead rack the size of a small Peugeot.

Jean-Luc was a farmer. His father had been a farmer. His brother, ah, well. Jean-Luc looked at the chubby baby in the crook of his arm, her fat little legs wrapped around his skinny hip as if it were she who orchestrated her perch and not he. Someday he would tell her about his brother. It was a fine story. A sad story, to be sure, but majestic in its sadness.

Young people today weren't interested in the war, at least not *that* war. They cared little about who fought, or who died, so that they might enjoy their iPods and video games. Zou-zou began to fuss and he bounced her on his hip to distract her. Someday, she would want to hear about *Grandpapa's* brother, the war hero. Someday, she would ask to hear the whole story again and again.

"*Mon lait*, Papa," she said to him. "*Zou-zou a faim!*"

"I know you are, cherub," Jean-Luc said holding her in one arm and her empty bottle in his free hand. "You will let Papa fix it for you, eh? *Oui?*"

"*Now*, Papa! *Zou-zou a faim now!*"

Jean-Luc loved that she was always hungry. He and Laurent had laughed about that. It meant that you could always make her happy just by feeding her. He set her on the floor and she instantly plopped down onto her bottom.

Nearly seventy years old and never blessed, until his precious Danielle, with a wife or children, no one was more astounded than Jean-Luc at the pull this little one had on his heart. When she looked at him with those saucer-big blue eyes, he was powerless to deny her anything. He chuckled, remembering his conversation with Danielle earlier that morning.

"Children won't thank you for giving them everything they want, Jean-Luc," she had admonished. "Children need boundaries, not endless chocolate *bon-bons*."

"Oh, yes, my dearest, like you do with her?"

He loved to tease her and they had laughed well at that. Zou-zou was their first, their only, grandbaby. And while it was true, she was not blood related to them, she was theirs, nonetheless.

His thoughts were interrupted by a piercing shriek from the floor.

"*Ma petite*," he exclaimed. "Papa is doing it as quickly as he can!"

But the baby wasn't having it. He watched in horror as she flung herself down face first and battered the gleaming hardwoods with her tiny fists and heels in a fury of impatience. "Zou-zou hungry noooooooooowwwwww!" she howled.

Jean-Luc twisted off the lid to her bottle and grabbed the fresh bottle of milk from the counter—he hadn't even had time to store it in the fridge this morning when she began demanding his attentions. He ripped off the silver foil and poised it over the mouth of her bottle, spilling it down the sides in his hurry.

"Coming, *ma petite*," he soothed, but he was drowned out by her urgent screams. His fingers trembled as he recapped her bottle, then turned to scoop her up into his arms, already enjoying the look on her face of anticipation of her desire fulfilled.

"You see, little one?" he said, handing her the bottle. "That didn't take long now, eh? Your Papa will always give his *cher grand bébé* what she wants."

"So where does this put us?" Grace asked. "You can't work on the case until after the baby is born and Julia is being moved, where did you say? A hundred miles away?"

Maggie sighed heavily. "Something like that. It feels like the end. Let me ask you: did you get the impression that Annette and Florrie were together?"

"You mean at the bar when she spilled the beans about her inheritance? Kind of."

"Think about it. She was carrying flowers and Florrie was all spruced up. Michelle said he was wearing a new shirt."

"Is that relevant?"

"I don't know. Why would Annette and Florrie get together? Maybe they were together all along?"

"You mean when she was married to Jacques?"

Maggie shook her head. "Again, I don't know how that's significant."

"Have you heard any more from Michelle?"

Maggie shook her head. "What a whack-job."

"Did you tell Roger about the attack?"

"No, because that would involve Laurent knowing and so far he still doesn't."

"How is that possible?"

"Well, there was just so much going on that he never asked, but, knowing Laurent, he probably knows all about it."

"Should you come clean in that case?"

"My policy is pretty much to tip-toe past the doghouse and let sleeping dogs have their afternoon naps."

"Probably wise."

"Oh!" Maggie said looking at her cellphone. "*Speaking* of the little devil..."

"Laurent is *anything* but little, darling."

"He just texted me! Oh, listen to this, Grace. He says to meet him at Florrie's bar. He's got some great news about the case. Finally! I knew he'd be able to get more out of Roger than I ever could."

"That's wonderful! Unless you're sure he's not having you go to Florrie's to confront you about the whole baseball bat incident."

"Not his style. Don't you see? Because I've agreed to stop the investigation, he's stepping up. Plus, now that things have eased up on the grape harvest and production for the year, he's got more time." Maggie noticed the battery level on her phone was low and so she turned it off and slipped it in her purse. "I'm just surprised to get a text from him. I didn't even know he knew how to do that."

"Well, he'll definitely need to know how once the little tyke comes along so he can communicate with him. I swear the only connection I've had with Taylor in two years has been by way of a phone screen."

"Okay, you need to turn around at the next exit. Drop me off at Florrie's and then just head on home to relieve Jean-Luc. I'll get a ride back with Laurent."

"Sounds like a plan."

"I'm dying to know what he found out."

Susan Kiernan-Lewis

# Chapter Twenty-One

Grace watched through her rear view mirror as Maggie went into the bar. It hadn't seemed to bother Maggie that Laurent's car was not yet in the parking lot—or that *no* car was. She was just excited about the prospect of Laurent finally joining her in her investigation, whereas mere minutes before the text she only wanted to get home so she could get in the tub. Grace left her as animated as she could remember seeing her since before they'd gotten the news of Julia's confession.

It was hard to imagine the kind of person Julia must be to elicit this kind of loyalty and fierce determination in Maggie. Grace admitted that a certain dark side of her personality wasn't at all disturbed by Julia being taken so forcibly from the playing field. She wasn't proud of that thought and she wouldn't dilute the ugliness of it by reminding herself that she, too, was going through a life crisis. *Just not one that involved doing serious prison time.*

No, she wished this Julia person well. She hoped she would soon be released, and while not looking forward to actually meeting her, she did feel sure she would be able to convincingly fake her happiness for Maggie's sake.

*Well, that sounded selfish,* she thought as she readjusted the rear view mirror and accelerated to merge with the flow of traffic on the Route d'Avignon. There still weren't many cars on the road—most self-respecting French men were already firmly ensconced at their big midday meal. When she needed to be alert was when they all decided to weave their way home, several bottles of good Cote du Rhone under their belts.

She glanced at the screen of her cellphone to see if she could get the GPS to work. She knew exactly where she was and how long it would take to get to *Domaine St-Buvard*—fifteen minutes at this speed—but she was wondering if there might possibly be a shortcut through a nearby village. She noticed she had no signal, no reception and she cursed these little backwater villages that wouldn't put a cell tower in.

That was one of the things that Windsor liked best about living in France, she realized. And how bizarre was that, when he made his living—his fortune as it turned out—on the whole electronic software business. It occurred to her that unlike most of his contemporaries, Windsor still wore a wristwatch. She had an image of him checking it—usually to stall for time when he was trying to get his thoughts together. It was so much a part of him, her image of him, that she was shocked to realize she hadn't really noticed before.

*You don't really know what you've got 'til it's gone.*

Would they still be separating if they'd stayed in France? Would there have been some little short-skirted French cognate to Miss Leeza? Was it all Grace's fault or had there been a problem before they moved home? Before Zou-zou was born.

*Before Zou-zou was conceived.*

She pulled off onto the exit to the village of St-Buvard and the car hiccoughed harshly and seemed to momentarily miss a gear shift. As she drove onto the lonely two-lane road with towering plane trees on both sides that led into the village, she thought of Connor again. Of how he had made her laugh, how he made her feel—as if there were no rules or at least nobody to care if there were. Suddenly, the road in front of her seemed to vibrate in her vision as she realized with astonishment that it wasn't the fact that Windsor had insisted, in the end, about finding out who Zou-zou's father really was. That wasn't it at all.

It was because by doing so he'd put to death—forever and ever amen—any remnant hope she had of thinking there was still a piece of Connor left to her.

The car gave a violent lurch and Grace found herself punched against the strains of her seatbelt. *What the hell?* She twisted the wheel to pull the slowing car onto the verge, praying there was no self-locking mechanism when power was lost. It hadn't even occurred to her to look at the petrol gauge. Laurent was meticulous about making sure the car was filled. But now, as she sat on the side of the road in the disabled car, she could see the petrol needle on the gauge sitting on empty. When she rolled down the window to get some air before she thought about her next step—which she was pretty sure was going to be *literally*—she smelled the gas.

\* \* \*

On Danielle's tenth trip to the window in an hour, she made up her mind to lie. It wasn't something that came easily to her—especially to *plan* to do it—but she was resolved nonetheless.

The sun was dropping and she could see the rain clouds bunching up over the tree line. She had a windshield wiper on her car that didn't work properly and now it appeared she would drive home in the rain. A stab of shame erupted in her chest. *Lily* would not have to deal with any such inconveniences, she thought.

Ever again.

"They're here," Danielle said brightly. "They're here, Lily. I see them. They're just parking. I told you they would come." She hesitated at the window then scolded herself for delaying. *If I am not here to give comfort, then why am I here?*

She went back to Lily's bedside. The room was almost larger than her and Jean-Luc's entire house. She could see that it had once been lush with stylish furnishings, but it was shabby now, as if the inhabitant couldn't be bothered to keep it all up, or keep it clean.

It had taken her by surprise, the fact that Lily lived with the worn carpets and the broken furniture, the clutter and the dust and the dirt. *Where was her immense wealth? Was she like a character from a George Eliot novel? Rich, but so miserly that she lived as meanly as the poorest of her tenants?*

Danielle took herself in hand and shook the thoughts from her mind. Lily Tatois—for all they shared a first love—was never someone she knew well, or was now ever likely to. How she lived and why she lived that way would remain a mystery to her now.

Reseating herself at Lily's bedside, she could see it wouldn't be long now.

"Did you hear me, Lily?" she whispered. "They're here. They're coming."

"I heard you," Lily rasped slowly, each word an effort. "Is…is Jacques here?"

Danielle hesitated. "Jacques is gone, Lily. But the others…"

"I loved him," Lily said painfully. "Best."

"I know."

"He didn't deserve it."

"Just rest now, Lily," Danielle said, although she wasn't sure why. Resting wouldn't help anyone at this point. Lily's next rest would be forever.

"Tell Florrie I'm sorry."

"You'll tell him yourself. He's downstairs right now."

"Tell him."

"I will, Lily."

Not knowing whether she should or what the old woman would prefer, Danielle took Lily's hand gently in hers and squeezed it lightly. When she looked into her eyes to see if she had more to say, she could see that she had gone.

\* \* \*

A sudden panic seized Grace and she disconnected her seatbelt and bolted from the car. Not knowing exactly why the gasoline smell scared her, Grace stood staring at the car from the middle of the road, from where she could easily see the puddle of petrol dripping steadily out from underneath the car.

All she could think was, *Michelle wanted to kill Maggie, and somebody had tampered with Maggie's car.* A vision of car bombs—probably the result of watching way too many television police dramas—kept her from going near the car. Unable to reason herself out of her fear, she turned and walked away from the car—the keys still in the ignition—to begin her long walk to *Domaine St-Buvard.*

The sun was starting to drop in the sky and the wind was starting to rise. The village of St-Buvard was arguably closer— by at least a mile—but that required confidence that Grace did not have that she could get help there, or a ride.

After a few minutes, she turned to look back at the car, now far in the distance and looking positively malevolent hunched on the shoulder of the paved road. Laurent and Maggie will drive this way on their way home, she thought. They'll see the car and wonder what in the world had happened. Should she have left a note on the windshield? *Car ran out of gas. Think it's probably rigged to explode.*

She turned back in the direction of *Domaine St-Buvard,* wishing she had a collar to pull up against the chill. She knew she was almost definitely being ridiculous and the sweater would have made a big difference. Well, they could laugh at her all they wanted. She wasn't taking any chances these days.

* * * *

The door was unlocked but there was obviously nobody here. Maggie sat at one of the little café tables in Florrie's bar and wondered if the place was empty because it wasn't open on Sunday? That was possible. Many of these little country places didn't open on Sunday, she reasoned. She found it hard to believe this place had enough business opening on the rest of the days of the week to survive. But then, she'd been told Florrie had money.

The initial excitement at hearing that Laurent had news, combined with the fact that he wanted to work with her to solve the case, had worn off. As Maggie sat in the uncomfortable wooden chair in the deserted café, she wished he could have told her his "wonderful" news at home, maybe while she was in the bathtub. She massaged the small of her back and felt a shooting sciatic pain needle into her hip. She shifted to assuage it but it hung on. Now that she thought of it, it was damn strange for Laurent to ask to meet her here. *Had he ever asked to meet her someplace ever? Anywhere?* A sick feeling tingled in her stomach and she tried to push the feeling away.

Maybe it was the bar. This is where that psycho tried to kill her. Maybe this was her favorite place to murder people. Maybe *she* had somehow gotten a hold of Laurent's phone.

Maggie stood up and walked to the bar. If she couldn't find a glass of water to help with the burning sensation that had just erupted in her esophagus, perhaps she could find a nice butcher knife to defend herself with since the silence and the incongruity of the message had begun to weigh on her.

And the result was a steadily increasing uneasiness.

Before she looked for a glass, she dug out her cellphone. There were no recent calls and she could see her battery was about to die. She opened a cabinet and pulled out a glass, filled it with water and stood behind the bar, drinking and trying to think.

*It's Michelle, isn't it? She's coming for me and I have played right into her hands.*

Maggie put the glass down. *Which is so weird, because although I definitely think she's crazy, I hadn't pegged her for Jacques's murder.* That was when it occurred to Maggie that the two did not at all need to go hand-in-hand. She heard a muted pinging sound and glanced at her phone to see that she had received another text message, this time from Roger. The light on her phone began to blink quickly and she guessed she had time to read the text, but not enough to make a phone call. It didn't matter. Surely the bar had a phone. She clicked on Roger's name. *Just keeping you in the loop. Annette Tatois was murdered this afternoon at 1500 hrs.*

Maggie stared at the words until the phone died in her hand and went black. Still staring at the blank screen, her stomach cramping hard as she registered just how bad her situation was, she realized with a sudden shudder that it wasn't Michelle who lured her to the bar.

It was at that moment that she heard him walking toward her from the back room of the bar.

Susan Kiernan-Lewis

# Chapter Twenty-Two

Florrie looked at her with hooded eyes, his expression blank. As she watched him walk toward her, Maggie couldn't believe it hadn't seriously occurred to her that it had to be him. It was so clear now. Florrie, who inherited third behind everyone else. Florrie, the good one. Florrie, the one nobody respected.

Or noticed.

"Madame Dernier," he said in a flat voice, "what a surprise to see you."

He walked closer and Maggie felt the muscles in her shoulders tense. The bar counter was to her back and she pushed into it. She cleared her throat and willed the voice that came out to sound normal.

"Oh, hey," she said, her hand going involuntarily, protectively, to her pregnant abdomen. A searing pain emanated from deep inside and she grimaced as Florrie stood next to her. She was close enough to smell the garlic and the wine he'd had for lunch.

"I'm afraid the bar is closed Sundays," he said. "No one else will be coming today."

"I'm just waiting for Laurent," Maggie said cheerfully, watching Florrie's face as he studied her. Why had she dismissed him so soon? Because he hadn't threatened her?

Because he had a full head of nice hair and didn't wear a ring in his lip?

"I got a text message from Laurent saying to meet him here," she said, trying to sound upbeat. Trying not to sound like she knew he was a killer.

"Oh, of course. What am I thinking?" Florrie said, licking his lips and staring dully into Maggie's eyes. "Laurent *was* here but he had to leave. He asked me to tell you he couldn't wait. A round goose chasing for nothing, eh?"

"Wild."

"*Comment?*"

"It's…it's a *wild* goose chase. Yeah, never mind. Wow. It's just that that's so unlike Laurent, you know?" *Should she have said that? Did it matter?* Florrie had lured her here for a reason. The tips of her fingers began to tingle in an uncomfortable way.

*For a reason.*

Florrie shrugged, but there was nothing insouciant or casual about his face. In fact, Maggie couldn't help but see that he looked as if he were rehearsing something he was about to do.

Something terrible.

"If you can wait a moment," he said, "I will be happy to take you home."

"That'd be great. Thanks, Florrie." *So he wants me in the car.* Maggie could hear the rain coming down against the front windows of the little bar and the light outside seemed to noticeably dim.

Just then the phone rang and Maggie jumped. It was a landline sitting just under the counter. Her fingers itched to snatch it up and blurt out that she was being held by a homicidal maniac, but she still hoped it could all be reasoned out—*as long as Florrie doesn't know that I know.* Maggie stepped aside to allow him access to the phone.

He hesitated.

"Aren't you going to answer that?"

"People know we're closed on Sunday."

"It could be about your aunt. I understand she's fading fast."

He looked at her, startled, and then snatched up the phone receiver. "*Allo?*" he said breathlessly.

Maggie could hear Danielle's high-pitched voice on the other line and it was all she could do not to scream, *Send help!* Over the phone line and through the muddied vowels of the southern country dialect, Maggie was just able to make out the conversation.

"Florrie? I am Danielle Pernon, a friend of your aunt's. I am so sorry to have to tell you this but your aunt has passed this afternoon."

Maggie watched Florrie lick his lips again. If she had been expecting sorrow or remorse or any other human emotion connected to the death of a loved one, she was disappointed.

"What time?" he blurted out.

"Excuse me?"

"What time did she die? Exactly."

There was a pause on the other line as Danielle attempted to understand this most unlikely response.

"The doctor isn't here yet to pronounce time of death officially," she said.

"Yes, *officially*! So she isn't dead until he arrives to *officially* pronounce her dead."

*Holy crap. Florrie was counting on Lily outliving Annette so he would be the one who inherits, not Michelle.* Maggie glanced at the door to the bar and saw the rain coming down in sheets.

"I know I don't know you very well, Monsieur Tatois," Danielle said icily on the other line, "but can I ask why, after all those years of attentive care to your aunt, you did not come to her *this* Sunday of all days? She asked for you repeatedly."

Maggie grabbed the back of one of the café chairs as the first solid contraction hit her full force and without warning. She gasped with the impact of the pain and Florrie turned to watch her. He hung up the phone without answering Danielle.

"You are alright, Madame?"

*This. Is. A. Nightmare.* Maggie thought as the agonizing spasm slowly receded, allowing her to get her breath back again. She looked at Florrie and knew the only possible way out of all of this was to make him believe that she didn't know, that she didn't suspect. It was all she had.

She debated asking him to call an ambulance, but if he hesitated the game was up. Because what possible reason could he have for not? Other than the one that would surely leave her very dead. The only safe alternative she had was to stall for time by allowing him to drive her—as seemed to be his plan—and then just hope for the best.

"You know? I think I'm not really all right, Florrie," Maggie said, easing into a chair. "I think I may actually be in labor at the moment. So, if instead of running me home you could drop me off at the nearest emergency room, that would really be awesome."

"Labor?" Florrie frowned and gawked at her enlarged form as if he hadn't noticed before.

Should she ask about the phone call? Should she ask about his aunt? Maybe she could tap into some reservoir of grief or human feeling—surely he had some, he'd been a dutiful loving nephew for decades before he decided to become a cold blooded mercenary killer. Maggie remembered stories of kidnapped victims who claimed that attempts to humanize or personalize themselves with their captors worked well in getting them, if not to outright release them, then to at least delay in killing them. *And when you're being held captive by someone who wants to kill you, delays are what it's all about.*

Another agonizing stitch began working its way up her diaphragm and she tensed in anticipation.

*That is, unless you're about to have a baby, in which case delays don't exist.* Maggie squeezed her eyes shut and let a low moan escape at the same time she deposited a small puddle of water beneath her chair. She looked at Florrie in mounting horror. It was do or die time now. There would be no turning back.

Her water had just broken.

\* \* \*

Grace glanced at her watch. She had been walking nearly an hour, but guessed she was still only a couple of miles closer to home. And warmth. She had been afraid to pull her cardigan from the backseat of the Renault. She knew it was probably silly. Hell, she had been afraid to get her cellphone or her purse out of the car.

Maggie and Laurent's *mas* was still a good three miles away, at least. At least the sun was still up to counter the chill that pierced her as she walked away from the car on the deserted road. *Was it an accident? Was it deliberate? How would Laurent retrieve the vehicle?* He and Maggie only had the one car. Was she being paranoid? *Probably.*

She rubbed the goose bumps from her arms and quickened her pace, hoping the exercise would help to warm her. She found herself wondering what car Laurent was using today since she had the Renault?

When she got to *Domaine St-Buvard*, she intended to walk in the front door, kiss her baby, and go straight upstairs for the most heavenly, hottest and intensely luxurious bubble bath of her life. *Surely, dear sweet Jean-Luc could watch Zou-zou for another hour after she got home?*

She felt the first cold drops of rain on the back of her neck.

\* \* \*

Maggie clutched the arms of the wooden chair and pushed herself to her feet. She looked at Florrie, who was staring at the puddle beneath her chair with disgust.

Maggie's mind raced. Grace had dropped her off nearly thirty minutes ago. Domaine St-Buvard was thirty minutes from the bar. *That meant Grace was home by now. If, please God, Laurent was also home, they would know something was wrong.* That meant she had to hang on—and *not get in that car,* where Florrie could take her to God knows where—for the thirty minutes it would take for Laurent to get back to the bar.

*Correction. The way Laurent drives, I just need to hang on fifteen minutes.*

"I have to use the facilities," Maggie said, holding her purse to her chest and eyeing the path past Florrie to the toilets.

"Clearly, Madame," Florrie said, his face twisted in a grimace of distaste.

*Thank God for common courtesies,* Maggie thought as she edged past Florrie. Even in the middle of a planned murder, it seems most civilized people will make allowances for a call of nature. She began walking down the hall, registering the increased level of discomfort in her stomach as she did. With the buffering amniotic sac gone, she felt her bones grinding against each other as she moved. She put a hand out to touch the narrow wall in the hallway for support, her eyes going inadvertently to the hole Michelle had put in it last week.

"Do not be long," Florrie warned from the head of the hallway.

"I won't," Maggie said, hearing her voice shake. She reached the bathroom and stumbled inside, feeling the harbinger of another pain beginning to creep up on her. She shut the door. Above the sink was a mullioned window that opened outward. Maggie twisted it open and looked out.

The rain was still coming down hard. There was only scrub and bushes in the back. And one lone sedan parked on the grass. There were no houses or comforting lights to indicate there would be anyone to hear her screams. Escape through the window was unthinkable. She couldn't fit through it at her present size. And there was nowhere to run to even if she could.

*Her only hope was to stay in here as long as she could to give Laurent time to get here. Surely, Grace was home by now? It was pouring rain. Laurent wouldn't be in the fields in this kind of weather. Surely, he would be home.*

No matter what, Maggie knew she couldn't let Florrie get her in his car.

"Madame?" Florrie's voice was loud and Maggie jumped. He must be right on the other side of the door.

"Yes?" she said, her breath coming in short pants as her fear and the pain of the next contraction began to bear down on her. "Just a m-m-moment!" She felt the cold smooth curve of the sink behind her as she instinctively backed into the furthest point in the small room. What time was it? How much longer would she need to stall before help came?

*Oh, please let help be coming.*

At the moment the contraction reached its peak and Maggie sank to her knees to endure it, she heard the crash of splintering wood and, out of the corner of her eye, saw Florrie's form fill the doorway. A piece of wood had shot under the hem of her long tunic as she knelt on the filthy floor. When she felt the pain receding, she steadied herself against the sink and looked up to see Florrie rolling up his sleeves.

"I'm afraid these old doors sometimes stick," he said dully as he approached.

Susan Kiernan-Lewis

# Chapter Twenty-Three

The driveway that led to Maggie and Laurent's home on the far side of the village of St-Buvard was long and twisting. Grace stumbled down the length of it, encouraged by the imposing beckoning closeness of the tall *mas* itself, cold and wet, her heels stinging with broken blisters, and desperate to go to the bathroom.

She thought of how they would all laugh at this night—after she'd showered and been bolstered by a nice gin and tonic. During half of her walk in the rain she had expected Maggie and Laurent to appear behind her on their way home.

It hadn't occurred to her that she would walk the whole rest of the way in the pouring rain. She saw that the terrace light was on and that surprised her, because as dark as the weather had made the sky, she thought it was still just late afternoon.

She came to the front door and realized she had left the door keys on the ring that was still attached to the abandoned Renault. She grabbed the heavy brass doorknocker with fingers so numb and cold she could barely use them and banged three sharp whacks on the front door. She ran her hands up her bare arms and waited, relieved to hear footsteps coming across the foyer to let her in. A feeling of foreboding needled into her mood as it occurred to her that the footsteps sounded too heavy to be those of the wiry little Frenchman, Jean-Luc.

The door swung open to reveal Laurent standing there in the doorway looking at her with surprise. Grace stared at him. She was having trouble putting her thoughts together, but seeing Laurent on the other side of this door was wrong.

Very wrong.

Laurent seemed to put it together within seconds of seeing her standing there, wet, shaking and alone on his doorstep. The faint smile he'd opened the door with dissolved instantly. "What happened? Where is Maggie?"

"What…what are you doing here?" she asked. "You're supposed to be meeting Maggie at…you know, the bar at…" Grace shook her head.

*What was Laurent doing home?*

Laurent was by her side in a flash, his large warm hand on her arm. "Where is Maggie, Grace?" A thunderclap underscored his words and she jumped and looked frantically toward the inside of the house.

"She got a text from you saying to meet her at…at that guy's bar. Florrie's."

He looked out into the storm. "A text?" She could see he wanted to move, to *go*.

"On your phone," Grace said, now violently shivering on the doorstep. "D-d-didn't you send her a text? It said *Meet me at Florrie's. I have great news.* I left her there. It's…more than ninety minutes ago now."

He stepped out into the rain and then turned back to her. "Where is the car?"

"It…it ran out of gas on the other side of St-Buvard."

"Ran out of gas?"

"Out of petrol. Yes. I left it on the side of the road. I walked here to…Laurent, you didn't send the message?"

She could see his mind was whirling as he processed what he was hearing. "I lost my phone," he said. "I sent no message."

"Laurent, she's in trouble," Grace said, feeling the panic rising up inside her throat. She stepped into the foyer and saw Jean-Luc standing there. She nodded at him and then looked around him for the child.

Jean-Luc interpreted her look and answered quickly. "She is asleep," he said. "Don't worry. She is dead to the world."

Laurent stepped back into the house and went to the telephone. He picked up the receiver and put it back down. "The phone's out," he said and held his hand out to Grace. "Your phone, Grace."

"I...I left it in the car," she said wishing she had gotten blown up rather than have to tell Laurent that.

He turned to Jean-Luc. "Is Danielle home yet with your car?"

Jean-Luc shrugged helplessly. "She hasn't called in a couple of hours. I didn't know the phone was out. She might be." He pulled out his house keys and handed them to Laurent who took them and plunged into the night without another word.

Grace stood in the foyer shivering and dripping onto the slick hall tiles.

Jean-Luc stood in the open doorway and then closed it against the night. He turned to Grace and gestured awkwardly to the stairs. "If you want to take a bath," he said. "I'll keep an ear out for the child."

\* \* \* \*

Florrie held Maggie's elbow with one hand and an umbrella with the other as he helped her into the passenger's side of his Peugeot sedan. The hand on her arm was as fierce and pinching as a manacle. The pains had started coming stronger and more often now that her water had broken, and Maggie's mind raced trying to alternately think of what happened next in this stage of the labor and delivery and how in the world she was going to get away from the man who wanted to kill her.

Clearly, by removing her, Florrie must have hopes of keeping his bar clean. Maggie knew it was always tricky cleaning up after a murder, and although she wasn't absolutely positive of the criminal evidence advances in backwater France, she had to assume they at least had access to Luminal and other basic forensic investigating tools. She decided to look at it as a good sign. It meant he still had something to lose. It meant he intended to try to continue to live in the community after everything he'd done. Maybe it meant he wasn't going to kill her.

"I'm sorry you had to be involved in all this," Florrie said as he started the car and backed it out of the parking lot.

*Do not let him confess to you while you're helpless and two centimeters dilated,* Maggie thought feverishly. *He'll have no reason not to kill you.*

"Oh, not at all," she said. "You know, I'm only trying to help my friend, Julia. Well, you know Julia, of course, through Jacques, and…" The pain heralded its advent with a slow but sinister preview and Maggie found herself clutching the car door handle trying to push against it in any effective way she could.

"Another pain?" he sounded almost cheerful, certainly unconcerned. *Not a good sign.* "No, I guess I was apologizing about today," he said. "I hate all of this and I do feel like you are an innocent party to a certain extent."

*Do not let him reveal anything incriminating!*

"Please!" she gasped, wiping the sweat off her forehead from the last contraction. "Think nothing of it. Laurent is always saying I poke my nose in where it doesn't belong."

*Perhaps reminding him of Laurent will shame him into not doing what ever it is he's thinking about doing?*

"I just wanted to say I'm sorry," Florrie said.

A part of her wanted to ask him *for what?* to stop this agonizing game of cat and cockroach. But she didn't dare.

"Not at all," Maggie said. "I'm just grateful that you were here to help me today. Laurent will be so grateful, too. We're both just so—"

"Annette said you knew. About me."

*No! No! No! Nooooooooo.....*

"I have no idea what you're talk—"

"I don't think she really knew herself until the end, but I'm sure she probably suspected."

The next pain hit Maggie without warning and she allowed the scream to escape and career off the interior of the little car without attempting to temper it. *What is this kind of pain that's so unholy that you can scream your damn head off and not even care?*

She could hear from somewhere in the background recesses of her mind that Florrie was still talking. Incredibly, he seemed to be trying to talk *over* Maggie's moans and intermittent shrieks. Was it possible he was so focused on his own trauma that he was unaware of her writhing agony in the seat next to him?

"It wasn't a crime of passion," he was saying, staring thoughtfully at the road in front of him through the windshield. "That's what gets me. Most people can forgive that. But I'm not like that. It's hard for me to get worked up." He laughed. "A part of me envied Michelle for her ability to feel so strongly." He shook his head. "Crazy bitch."

Maggie was so relieved from the respite from the last contraction that, while she registered that Florrie was confessing to her, a part of her just didn't care any more.

\* \* \*

Grace picked up the phone again.

"Is it working?" Jean-Luc asked from the kitchen. He poured a glass of wine.

She shook her head, then walked over to the kitchen counter and took the glass he held out to her. She noticed a stark discoloration on the beautiful granite counter top behind him and wondered idly when that had happened. "It's unusual for Zou-zou to sleep so long," she said. "Or so soundly. We usually have to tiptoe around when she's taking her nap."

He shrugged and glanced at the clock on the wall. "I should go now," he said. "If Danielle is home, Laurent will have her car. Or at least her cellphone."

"And if she isn't home?"

"Our phone lines are newer than the ones at *Domaine St-Buvard.*

"I thought it was the storm that caused the lines to go out?"

Maddeningly, he shrugged again. "Laurent should be able to call from there."

"Who will he call?" Grace said, sitting down on the couch. She had taken Jean-Luc up on his offer to watch for the baby to wake while she showered and dressed in dry clothes. Now that she was dry and had a glass of wine and a piece of Laurent's quiche in here, she was ready to start worrying again. She stood up and glanced toward the stairs.

"How long has she been asleep?" she asked.

He shrugged again, that quintessential movement of every Frenchman since the beginning of time, Grace thought with building irritation.

"How long is that, Jean-Luc?" She could see he didn't look comfortable answering and that prompted an unexpected rush of concern in her. "What is it you aren't telling me?" she asked. Perhaps it was the nascent terror building over Maggie's situation—*Where was she? Who texted her? Why hadn't she called? Who disabled the car* —but Grace realized that she found Jean-Luc's obvious attempts to dissemble a billboard invitation to totally lose her shit.

"Jean-Luc!" she screamed. "*Why* is Zou-zou sleeping so much? What's wrong with her?" She was up the stairs before she even thought to put her drink down first and spilled most of its contents down her forearm and the front of her dry cotton sweater. Jean-Luc was behind her on the stairs and the two of them burst into Zou-zou's room, knocking a lamp over in the process and breaking a small picture frame that had been hung too close to the light switch.

The child lay immobile and oblivious to the noise.

"Zou-zou! Zou-zou!" Grace cried, reaching into the bed and pulling the dead weight of the baby into her arms. She turned to Jean-Luc, her face a mask of terror and disbelief. "What's the matter with her?"

"It's nothing, Madame!" Jean-Luc said, starting between the two in horror and biting his lip. Grace could see he was blinking rapidly and rubbing his face with a trembling tic. "There was a problem…"

"What kind of problem?" Grace roared. "Zou-zou, baby, Zou-zou, sweetheart, wake up now, lambie, wake up, honey."

"She…I…she was so hungry and she cried so pitifully that I could not send her to bed hungry," Jean-Luc said, his face full of misery and shame.

"What did you do?" Grace shrieked, clutching her unresponsive child.

"The milk was bad!" Jean-Luc said. "I had to give her something so I gave her a glass of Laurent's *chocolat liqueur*. She was starving!"

Grace looked at Jean-Luc and then Zou-zou, who was beginning to rouse herself.

"Laurent's *chocolat liqueur*," she said. "That's like ninety proof or something, isn't it?"

"I cut it with water," Jean-Luc said, "but I couldn't give her *just* water and there was nothing else. She cried so bitterly, Madame."

Grace sagged onto a chair at the foot of the bed, little Zou-zou yawning and stretching in her lap. "So, the little sot's drunk?"

"Not at all, Madame!" Jean-Luc said indignantly. "She is just...very relaxed."

"*Maman?*" Zou-zou looked up at Grace and grinned. "Zou-zou wants Oncle Laurent's chocolate milk!"

Grace felt the hysterical laughter welling up inside her, and when Zou-zou turned to Jean-Luc and held out her arms to him, she released her daughter to the adoring *grandpère* who had just coordinated her first bender and sat in the chair, laughing and crying into her hands.

\* \* \* \*

"I killed Jacques," Florrie said. "And then I was forced to kill Annette, too. But of course, you knew that, didn't you?" He looked at Maggie and smiled as if he'd just asked her for her assessment of his latest soup special at the bar.

"Well," Maggie said, the exhaustion of dealing with and waiting for each contraction sapping her strength to the point where she knew she didn't have the energy to open her own door, let alone rescue herself, "all I can say is it must be a boatload of money for you to go through all this."

Florrie slapped the steering wheel with his hand, but when Maggie looked at him she saw that he was laughing. "That's the absurdity of it, don't you see? It *isn't* a boatload at all. It's the *opposite* of a boatload." He shook his head but continued to grin as if the joke was just *too* good.

Maggie stared at him for a moment before it hit her. "Lily was broke."

"*C'est ca.*"

"And you were handling her money."

He wasn't laughing now. In fact, his face took on a fierce intensity as if he had had this argument in the mirror many times over. "There was this amazing opportunity last year. It was virtually a guarantee."

*The Mistral Promise.*

"I would have been rich." He shook his head as if he still couldn't believe that it didn't turn out like that. "I borrowed the money from Lily's estate. I fully intended to return it when I won. No one would ever know. When I lost, I thought, no problem, I have plenty of time to replace it before anyone discovers it."

"And then you learned that she was going to die sooner rather than later."

"Not only that, I discovered that I was *not* the one to inherit. The theft would be discovered in a matter of weeks. Can you imagine anyone in the world *more* likely to prosecute me for embezzlement than Jacques? I would go to jail!"

"After all you'd done for Lily, you must have been bitter."

"Let's just say I won't mourn her. I wasted enough time on her while she lived."

Maggie thought it had been several minutes since her last contraction. She wondered if labor had stopped. *Is that possible? Maybe it was another false labor?* But her water broke. To answer the question once and for all, she was seized by the beginning build of another monstrous spasm. She grabbed the door handle and bit her lip as the pain charged her.

When it was over, she felt like she was seeing her situation with a startling clarity that had eluded her before, had eluded her, in fact, for the last three months of her pregnancy. It was clear to her now: *Talking* was not going to save her from this madman—as reasonable and measured as he sounded. If she and her baby were going to survive this terrible day, Maggie was going to have to actually *escape*.

"So that's why it was important for Lily to die *after* Annette," she said. "So that Michelle won't inherit."

"Yes, but in the end it doesn't really matter. I'd hope we could all go back to the way we were but I can see now we can't. With me in exile it will all default to Michelle."

"Who'll inherit a big pile of nothing."

"At least she can't sue me. I'll be unreachable by then."

"Why...why did you come after *me*?"

"I told you. Annette told me that you knew that I'd killed Jacques. Frankly, she and Michelle had become pretty obsessed with you."

*Annette must have just been talking out of her ass to try to delay the inevitable.*

*I know how she feels.*

"I needed to explain to you what really happened. Then, once I'm gone, you're welcome to tell the police everything you know." Florrie said, looking over at her. If the cold, forced smile he gave her was supposed to be reassuring, it failed. "I was impressed, you know. Even Annette didn't guess until the end."

*Neither did I,* Maggie admitted. "And by *the end*, you mean..."

"I gave her every opportunity to share the wealth with me."

"The nonexistent wealth."

"Yes, well Annette didn't know that."

"You asked her to marry you so she couldn't testify against you?"

*"C'est ca."*

"I'm pretty sure that wouldn't have stopped her."

"All the more reason why she had to die. Frankly, I'd originally hoped they would pin Jacques's murder on her. She was with him that night, too."

"The night he died? Well, they wouldn't do that because she had a special connection inside the police force."

"What? Annette was sleeping with someone on the police force? Why doesn't that surprise me?"

"The *head* of the police, yes." *She was totally blowing smoke right now but until she came up with a plan, she would need to keep him talking.* "Why else do you think she was never considered a serious suspect in his murder?"

"I wondered about that."

"So you framed Julia for it."

He shrugged again. "It was easy because of her obsession with mushrooms, and besides, she's English. What did Jacques want with an Englishwoman? He certainly couldn't *marry* her."

"Oh, right. That would've totally tainted the gene pool. Are we stopping?"

*Not good.*

Maggie put her hands on the dashboard to prevent herself from sliding forward as Florrie steered the car off the road. The light was dying now. Maggie could see by the dashboard clock that it was 5:45 p.m. She should have realized that they were not heading in the direction of Aix and the hospital. She'd been so busy alternately screaming in agony and chatting with a killer that she'd hadn't noticed.

It was a dark stretch of road, and as Maggie sat there with Florrie and the pings and clunks of the dying engine sounding in the quiet, she realized that there were no other cars on the road. The bushes and trees on the opposite side of the road grew tall and dense and blocked out what light there had been from the waning day. There were a few scrub bushes on the side of the road where the car was stopped, but no trees.

They were poised at the lip of a cliff.

Susan Kiernan-Lewis

# Chapter Twenty-Four

Laurent arrived at the Pernon home gasping and out of breath. A mile by road, he had vaulted over dry stone walls and cut between the vines in the vineyard to make it to the front steps in under ten minutes. The house was dark, so there was only the hope now that the phone worked.

He entered, absently greeted the two Pyrenean Shepherds that Jean-Luc doted on like children, and pushed his way to the comfortable French country kitchen. He snatched up the phone hanging on the wall and immediately got a dial tone.

As he was racing over to the house, he had put together in his mind as many scenarios as he could process, discarding them one after the other as they refused to fit the puzzle. There was no sense in trying to recreate when he last had his phone or where he might have left it. He hadn't seen it in days.

*Someone* had texted Maggie three hours earlier using his phone and lured her to Florrie's bar. *Why there? It was remote and often empty, but there could be no guarantee of privacy. Someone* had disabled the Renault in order to ensure that Grace was taken out of the picture.

The stretch of road that she traveled was notorious for no cellular service. *Even if she had tried to use her phone she would not have been able to alert anyone in time to prevent...*

Laurent dialed the number and waited impatiently for the other line to pick up.

*Maggie was alone at Florrie's bar. If it was the crazy woman who tried to attack her with the cricket bat last week, perhaps today she had graduated to a knife or a gun.* He glanced at his watch. It was a quarter to six. *She wouldn't need a two-hour window to kill Maggie.*

*But that was what she had.*

*"Allo?"*

Laurent spoke in brief, abrupt Parisian French. He tended to alter his speech for the general comfort of the prickly natives from this region, but today he had no patience or time for such courtesies.

*"I'm sorry, but due to the Aix-en-Provence Policemen's Ball tonight, there is only a skeleton staff of officers on patrol this evening and all complaints must be triaged. A tourist's complaint—I assume, Monsieur that you are from Paris? —of a wife lost in a bar would be relatively low on the priority list even with a full staff of—"*

Laurent slammed the phone down and dug out the business card from the front pocket of his jeans. Quickly he punched in the number and stood by the kitchen window watching as the light faded and the rain came down.

The call went straight to voice mail.

He left an abrupt message, hung up then turned to jerk open the front door. He plunged into the sheet of rain pouring off the roof eaves and ran up the long dark driveway toward the main road and the village, sheltered from the worst of the storm by the tunnel of hovering trees.

\* \* \*

When she emerged naked and dripping from the shower and snapped her fingers at him to get his attention, Roger had just picked up his phone to check to see if he'd gotten any messages. It had been four hours since Annette Tatois's body had been found. He'd agreed to let that moron, Manet, handle it *for the experience*—plus Roger's attendance at the ball was mandatory—but he would need to stay on top of it.

"A towel, *chérie?*" he said as he stood up, mesmerized by her confidence and audacity as she stood before him dripping water on the carpet.

"Later," she said, crooking a finger at him and smiling lasciviously.

Roger dropped the phone on the bed and began unbuttoning his dress shirt.

*After all, the ball isn't for another hour and Manet can probably handle a lot more than I give him credit for.*

\* \* \*

"Something appears to be wrong with the car," Florrie said, sitting in his seat and staring straight ahead. He turned to look at her and shrugged. "It just stalled."

"You know, Florrie…" Maggie tried to keep her voice as casual and nonthreatening as possible. "I have to tell you that when my friend gets home, Laurent will know that the text was fake."

He shrugged. "Haven't you wondered why no one has called before now?"

Maggie was *not* going to tell him it was because her phone was dead.

"I punctured the gas tank of your car," he said, matter of factly. "At this moment your friend is either on the side of the road somewhere in the pouring rain—I must apologize for the poor cellular reception in this part of the country—or she's lost control of her vehicle on the D7 and is in the city morgue. In any case, she won't be bringing help. Your husband is *not* worried *or* waiting for you to return, as he has no reason to believe anything is amiss."

Maggie felt her chest hitch painfully. She pulled at the collar of her tunic as if that might help her breathe easier. She felt the perspiration pop up across her forehead.

*Not coming? Was it possible that nobody was coming?*

Her stomach lurched in nausea and she felt her hands start to shake as she watched as Florrie twist in his seat and pull a backpack from the back, and then jam the car keys into his jacket pocket. *Something was about to happen. Something bad.*

"Surely you don't think you can get away with killing two people," she said, hearing the fear and desperation in her voice. *Or three or four...?* Maggie didn't know if he was going to strangle her in the car or leave her to deliver her own child before she died of massive blood loss, but either way the prospect wasn't good.

"I told you, I just need to delay things long enough to slip away. There's a steamer leaving Marseille tonight. I'll be in Oujda before the cops even think to look for me."

"Morocco doesn't have a reciprocal arrangement with France?"

"Let's just say I'll be able to live out my life there in comfort and anonymity."

"Look, if you're looking for a head start, I can promise not to speak to the police until you're well and truly gone. Trust me, I have many hours ahead of me where I'll be sufficiently distracted by other things." She put both hands on her stomach.

He hesitated. "I'm sorry if I gave you the impression that I would hurt you," he said. "I'm not a killer, you know."

*Of course not! Psycho!*

"Of course not," she said. "Can you get me to the emergency room in Aix?"

"I would, but the car is broken down."

"Oh, right." Maggie began to feel the beginnings of the next powerful contraction.

"Do you have a cell phone?" he asked gently.

"I—I do, but it's…it's dead."

"May I see it?"

She handed it to him so he could confirm it was useless.

"Too bad," he said. "I was going to take it and call an ambulance for you."

"Don't you have a phone?"

*How about Laurent's phone? Don't you still have that, you disgusting rodent?*

"Oh, sure!" he said, patting a pocket that didn't have a bulge large enough to conceal a cellphone. "So that's what I'll do. I'll call as soon as I'm down the road a ways. The reception here is very bad. Well, Madame, I am sorry again, for everything that's happened, but I wish you and Laurent and the little one every possible health and happiness.

*Unbelievable!*

"Yeah, okay, thanks," Maggie said as she felt the next contraction gaining ground on her. "Can I just ask you, before you go…?" She held her breath—like that was going to be any good in mitigating the tsunami of pain bearing down on her.

"Of course. Anything."

"How did…how did you kill Jacques?" Maggie knew she wouldn't be lucid to hear the answer. Her mind had gone somewhere safe while her body worked to destroy her from the inside out. But the words rang in the car even so. They embedded themselves in the very vinyl and plastic and metal of the car's interior—her own private torture chamber. And somehow, she heard.

"We met for drinks every Saturday," he said pleasantly, as if remembering a happier time. "For the six weeks before he died, I coated his glass with ground dust from the *agaricus* mushrooms that I acquired online.

"Jacques sickened immediately, but took six weeks to actually die. The police never looked at my computer. They never examined my glassware. In fact, if not for you, Madame

—a little terrier with a bone!—I think I could have called this the perfect crime."

As Maggie pawed at the dashboard to try to get back her equilibrium, Florrie opened his car door and heaved out his backpack. "I can see you're busy trying to get this baby born," he said jovially, "so I'll leave you to it and make that phone call. Good luck!"

He exited the car and slammed the door.

It wasn't until after Maggie fought her way through another mammoth contraction that left her sweating and weak that she felt the car moving.

# Chapter Twenty-Five

Maggie twisted to look through the back window to see Florrie, his face straining purple with exertion, as he heaved his body against the back end of the car. She whirled around to the gearshift to see it had been put into neutral.

The car made another lurch forward and Maggie screamed as she saw the ground disappear in front of the car hood and felt the vehicle fall into a dramatic slant forward as if falling into a ditch, slamming her against the dashboard. She thought she could actually hear Florrie grunting with effort as the car's nose dropped steeply, its front tires spinning free and revealing nothing but sky and encroaching darkness before her.

She grappled frantically for the car door but it was locked. She fumbled for the auto lock on the handle but it wasn't there. She couldn't help turning again to look at Florrie, whose only focus appeared to be pushing as if his life depended on it.

She saw a glimpse of satisfaction cross his features as he gave a loud expulsion and heaved against the car. Maggie screamed, and for one mad moment had a memory of her first roller coaster ride where she was suspended high above a theme park only to drop in a blinding squeal to the next death-defying peak.

She watched as if in slow-motion as the front of the car teetered precariously over the lip of the canyon before, with a final push from behind, it tipped head-down and fell.

The jolt as the car snagged on the sapling that stalled the car's descent sent Maggie slamming into the windshield. Terrified that her weight would help send the car over the edge, she scrambled to the backseat, where she could see the top of the small tree sag from view as the weight of the car crushed it into submission.

Maggie's face was only a couple feet from Florrie's—red with frustration and consuming intensity—as he labored in his final deadly assault to push the car over the edge.

As the pain of a contraction tore through her, leaving her legs and belly an amorphous ball of indefinable agony, Maggie's hand hit the console between the two front seats and her fingers found the auto-lock. She wrenched the back door open just as the car launched from its temporary landing pad into the air on its final descent into the cavernous and rocky bottom below.

Maggie watched the ground rush by her and under her as she jumped from the moving car, the grass and gravel and dirt running by as she hit the ground shoulder first and then she rolled and rolled. When she finally stopped, she was on her back, halfway down the ditch and just before the sharpest drop off. She lay still for a moment, the air still full of the echo of the sound of the car as it crashed to earth, a mechanical cacophony of crushed metal and rock.

She lay and listened to the noises ebb away in the air, and in her mind. Her ankle hurt. Her shoulder was on fire. She lifted her hands to her face and looked at them. Her knuckles were bloody and raw. She touched a tentative finger to her forehead and winced. Blood trickled down her arm from her face where she had smacked into the windshield.

She was afraid to move. Afraid he would see. If she lay perfectly still, he would assume she had gone down with the car and he would leave.

*Wouldn't he?*

She lay unmoving in the dirt, watching the light leach from the sky as darkness crept in and she was thankful for that. She held her breath to listen and that was when she heard the footsteps. Tentative, searching, furtive. Not a normal walking pace, but hesitant and disturbed. They were coming from just above where she lay and they were climbing down.

Toward her.

And then she felt the next one beginning to build. It started deep inside her core and quickly emanated out to touch every part of her with its grinding, relentless fury. She waited as it built and built inside her until the pain was her whole world and nothing—not cliffs or homicidal maniacs or giving birth alone in the dark—existed anywhere. Only the pain. She grabbed fistfuls of grass with both hands and let out a long and ragged groan of hopeless hurt.

As the contraction ebbed, she was showered with a spray of dirt and rock as he jumped down next to her, landing nearly on top of her. She felt him grab her by the shoulders and she knew she had gone as far as she could go.

She had let them all down. The little one who wouldn't be born, Laurent who had begged her to stop, Grace and Julia who she had failed in every way a friend can. And, of course, herself. She squeezed her eyes closed and tried to retreat back into that other world. The world of pain. The world of Only One Thing.

Harsh hands reached her, digging into her arms with hurtful urgency.

Roger sat on the edge of the bed listening to the voice mail. He was dressed and out the door before Dernier's message had finished.

And it was a short message.

"Roger? Where are you going? What about the ball?" His girlfriend chased after him into the hallway, her dress half on, her shoes in her hand, her mouth open.

"Take a taxi," he shouted over his shoulder as he ran down the stairwell to the parking garage. He punched in the phone number that showed on his phone as belonging to Danielle Pernon. A woman answered on the first ring.

*"Allo?"*

"I'm looking for Laurent Dernier," Roger said as he jumped in his car and slammed it into reverse, still holding his phone to his ear.

"He has my cell phone," the woman said and quickly gave him the number. He hung up and punched it in. *Should he head toward St-Buvard? The Aix Hospital?*

"Bedard?" Dernier picked up immediately.

"Yes, it's me. Where is she? Where are you?"

"I've just left Tatois's bar outside Lignane. She's not there. I'm on the D7 about thirty minutes from Aix. Where are you?"

"I'm just pulling onto the D7 out of the city. I'm thirty minutes from Lignane."

*"Merde."*

"How long has he had her?"

"Over two hours."

*"Merde."*

Later, Maggie would say it was like being roused from a waking nightmare by an archangel who descended upon her in glory with the muffled sounds of fireworks shooting off behind his bald head.

"Madame?"

She opened her eyes to see the darkened, hulking form of Sasquatch, his shiny head and tattoos gleaming in the dusk, leaning over her and peering into her face.

*Mathieu.*

"Can you stand?" Mathieu said, looking her over for any wounds. "Can you walk?"

"I need help," she croaked. "Hospital. Get me to the hospital."

"Are you out here alone? Did your car just go over the cliff?"

He pulled her to her feet. She cried out when she put weight on her ankle, so he held her up against him. As the next contraction took hold of her, Maggie didn't care if he flung her out over the cliff after the car. Her body stiffened as it railed though her. She threw back her head and screamed until it was over and she was left sobbing in exhaustion. When she could— and before the next monster contraction could sneak up on her —she opened her eyes to look at her savior.

"I'm sorry," she said. "I thought you were the bad guy. I'm sorry."

"I confessed!" Mathieu said, hoisting her arm over his as he fought to climb the steep incline with her at his side. "I went to the police and I told them that *I* killed the bastard. They sent me away. Said I was crazy."

"The police know nothing about true love."

Mathieu looked at her with confusion. "*Comment?*"

"Never mind. Look, he's around here someplace. Keep your eyes open. Before I forget or the next contraction drives me insane, I've got a message for you from Julia."

"*C'est vrai?* What is it?" He stopped climbing and stared at her.

Maggie started to laugh and hoped very much she wasn't getting hysterical. Mathieu must have been thinking the same thing because he was frowning now.

"She loves you…and she…oh, I can't remember the rest. And it doesn't matter. She'll be able to tell you herself now."

"Because she'll be free, yes?"

Maggie screamed and clutched his arm, barely registering the wince on his face as she fought the contraction. "Holy shit! That hurts," she said when it began to fade. "Yes," she said, closing her eyes and falling into the bliss of the temporary relief from pain. "Yes, she'll be free. And if you and I somehow live through this night, won't that be a great day?"

"Why would we not live?" Mathieu frowned in confusion.

"I guess it's just me that feels like I'm dying. Forget I said that."

"You are simply having the baby, Madame. *C'est tout.*"

"Remind me to kill you when I'm feeling better," Maggie said. "Dear God! Are we not there yet? Where in the blue blazes hell did you park your effing car? Are you some kind of *outdoor* freak? Where is the goddam car!?"

"I am sorry! I parked it at a distance to encourage more walking when I'm—"

"Stop talking! Shut up with the mindless, endless talking! Dear Lord, how does Julia put up with your constant, ceaseless yammering?"

"I haven't said but two—"

Maggie screamed and clutched him and realized that he had stopped walking, frozen still until her pain subsided. She sagged against him, exhausted. Once they were on flat ground, he put his arm under her legs and hoisted her gently into his arms. She groaned.

"If you *were* the murderer," she said, her eyes closed, "that would come in very handy right now because I really want to die. Please. Kill me now."

At her words, Maggie felt Mathieu come to an abrupt stop. "Noooooo! Why are you stopping? For the love of God, what now?" When she opened her eyes, she saw the reason he had stopped.

Unless it was the best dream she had ever imagined, she saw the wondrous sight of Laurent coming straight at her at a dead run. She could see the car behind him, the driver's side door still open to suggest that he had bolted from a car that was not completely stopped twenty yards in front of them. She could also see Roger coming from around the side of another car with his firearm pointed directly at Mathieu's chest.

*Oh, shit,* Maggie thought with irritation, her thrill at seeing Laurent tempered by the possibility that she was going to get shot before she could deliver the baby. Laurent reached them, whereupon Mathieu promptly handed her off to him and put his hands behind his head. Laurent knelt with her in his arms.

"Laurent, thank God you're here," she gasped into his sweater, smelling the wonderfully familiar scent of lemons and *anise* and Laurent, himself. "It was *Florrie,* Laurent! Florrie killed Jacques—"

"*Ensuite, mon amour,*" Laurent said. His hands were even bigger than Mathieu's and Maggie could feel them moving up and down her back, her legs, and her arms checking her for damage as he held her in his arms on one knee. "*Est-ce que tu es bien?*"

"No, I'm *not* all right, Laurent! I've never been more not all right in my—" While she didn't scream, the picture of agony searing across her face must have delivered the message better than words ever could. Laurent was on his feet with her in his arms. She could tell they were moving, that Laurent was walking fast, his long strides covering the distance quickly, and she said a prayer of thanks he hadn't decided to jog with her bouncing in his arms. Out of the corner of her eye she could see Roger and Mathieu trotting alongside them with nobody holding anybody at gunpoint.

*Oh, good,* she thought on the verge of hysteria. *Everyone's friends now.*

"Laurent," she said, panting in anticipation of the next contraction that she could feel coming.

"*Oui, ma chère?*"

"Promise me I'm not going to deliver this baby on the side of the road."

"*Jamais*, Maggie. *Je te le promets,*" he said.

*Never. I promise.*

# Chapter Twenty-Six

Ten fingers, ten toes. One adorable button nose, a set of already inquisitive blue eyes and a head full of dark hair. Jean-Michael Dernier lay nestled in his mother's arms and Maggie could not stop looking at him.

"He really is the most amazingly gorgeous baby in the world," Maggie murmured to Grace, who stood next to her hospital bed the morning after young Jean-Michael was born.

"That's not typically the sort of thing you say to someone who also has children," Grace said, tweaking the baby's fat little cheek. "But in this case you may just be right. We need to get him straightaway into baby modeling."

"Laurent would never allow it."

"I know, darling. It's a joke. You don't want to share this little angel with the world just yet."

After a hectic nick-of-time and very noisy entrance into the hospital yesterday evening featuring a full police escort and a frantic like-she'd-never-seen-him-before Frenchman rushing in with her in his arms, young Jean-Michael decided to slow his entrance into the world by some ten hours. Now, exhausted and filled with joy and wonderment, Maggie watched her precious bundle and found it hard to believe that the two of them had been joined together for nine months—and already a whole of adventure.

Laurent waited until Grace arrived before going off in search of a "proper lunch" for "*ma femme.*" Maggie couldn't help but grin as she watched him kiss the baby for the hundredth time, then her, and then Grace before heading out the door. She could hear him greeting people—probably total strangers—outside the room as he made his way down the hall.

Her husband was a happy, happy man.

"You doing okay?" Grace asked her as she gently picked up the baby in her arms. "Oh, my God, he is so tiny!" she said without waiting for an answer. "I'm not used to babies not weighing a ton. Oh, I love this stage! He smells so heavenly. Well done, darling. Laurent is over the moon."

Maggie watched her friend holding her son in her arms and swaying and rocking with him and she said, "Grace, can you forgive me for not supporting you during this whole separation thing? I know I acted like I was the first woman on earth to give birth."

Grace snorted. "Forget it, darling. You had a horse in the race. I understand perfectly. I would've felt the same way." She hesitated for a moment. "Believe me I *wanted* to make it work."

"I know you did," Maggie said, gazing at her baby's sleeping face as Grace settled him back in her arms. "But now what? What will you do?"

"I have no idea. Windsor is up for the idea of possibly trying again, but I don't think we need to put the kids through that. He says that Leeza is an absolute horse-whisperer with Taylor. Of course, he *would* say that. But maybe he's right. God knows anyone would be a better mother to her than me."

"That's not true, Grace."

"Well, true or not, I'm happy to have someone else come into her life who might help her. Even if it is my husband's girlfriend."

"I can't believe I'm hearing those words come out of your mouth."

"You and me both."

"I hope you know you're welcome to stay at *Domaine St-Buvard* as long as you want. We have plenty of room."

"Thank you, darling. Laurent's already offered and we'll probably take you up on it. At least for a little bit. Then we'll need to start over, just the two of us."

"Taylor will stay with Windsor?"

"Oh, yes, I think so. For now anyway."

"I'm just so sorry not to have been there for you, Grace."

"Darling, you were, though! In your own Maggie-like way, you helped me to clarify my feelings. What good is hearing *poor Grace* when what I really needed was perspective? Which you gave me."

"How in the world?"

"When I first got here I was hurt over Win having a girlfriend—and that wasn't the real problem at all! If you'd mollycoddled me, I would've let myself see *Win* as the villain instead of stepping up. You made me see how truly awful it all was, letting down the girls and everything. And *that* helped me see, eventually, that in spite of how bad it was, leaving was still the right thing to do."

An hour later, Laurent still hadn't returned and Maggie had dozed off. Grace sat next to the bassinet in the room with her hand touching the little fellow's blanket. Maggie woke up and smiled at the two of them. Before she could speak, there was a tentative tap at the door, and when it pushed open Julia and Mathieu stood in the opening.

"Julia!" she cried. "You're here!"

Julia entered, looking first to Maggie and then to Grace and then back at Maggie. She was wearing jeans and a cashmere pullover. Her hair looked wet, as if she'd just stepped from the shower. Her damp grey and brown curls wobbled against her forehead as she nodded and smiled shyly. "They released me last night," she said. "On my own reconnaissance or whatever it is. It's not official yet but it will be. I'm free."

"Good Lord, who is this fine piece of work?" Grace said to the hulking Mathieu, who looked to Maggie as if he'd also had a shower since she saw him last. His piercings and tats were even more noticeable in the glaring hospital light.

"Oh, Jules, this is Grace," Maggie said, "my best friend. You've heard me talk of her? Grace, this is Julia and her Mathieu, my guardian angel."

"I've heard so much about you," Grace said, extending her hand to Julia and then Mathieu. "But I believe the person you really came here to see is now receiving." She stepped out of the way to reveal the bassinet with its just-waking contents.

"Oh, Maggie, he's gorgeous!" Julia said going over to the baby bed. "He looks just like Laurent!"

"Good thing," Grace said, sotto voce.

"Shut up, Grace."

"I cannot believe how you did all this *and* had a baby too."

"It was nothing." Maggie scooted up to a sitting position in her bed, wincing slightly. "Roger released you?"

"In person, last night. Sorry I didn't come over straightaway." She looked adoringly up at Mathieu who was returning the gaze. "I heard you were otherwise engaged and I was, too."

"I'm just glad it's all over," Maggie said. She laughed and nodded toward the bassinet. "*All* of it. Can you bring him to me, Grace?"

Grace bundled up the baby, unable to take her eyes off his face. "He is going to keep you and Laurent hopping. I can tell."

"Laurent's already thinking of what duties he can assign him in the vineyard," Maggie said, holding her arms out for him. When Grace placed the baby in her arms, she turned back to Julia and Mathieu. "I wanted to tell you, Mathieu, that I'm so sorry I yelled at you yesterday."

*"Pas du tout."*

"No, you were a total prince and I was awful to you. If it weren't for you…what were you doing out there, anyway?"

He shrugged. "Looking for mushrooms."

"God, Julia, you guys really are two peas in a pod, aren't you?"

"Yeah, we are. Maggie, thank you." Julia approached the bed and reached out to touch Maggie's hand. "You didn't give up on me. And I'm sorry I made it so difficult."

"I don't think I really did anything," Maggie said. "Just made everyone's lives miserable."

"As per usual," Grace said with a smile.

"It was your relentlessness, in the end, that moved the boulder," Roger said as he walked through the door. He went to Julia and held out his hand. *"Je suis desolée,"* he said. "Again, please forgive my error."

Julia shook his hand and then hurriedly retreated back to Mathieu, where she wrapped her hands around his arm. She turned to Maggie. "I'll be by when you and the little sausage are home, okay?"

"Yeah, that'll be good. Bring Mushroom Boy with you. I seriously owe him one."

*"Ciao,"* Mathieu said, lighting up the room with the first smile Maggie had ever seen him give.

When they left, Roger came over to Maggie and peered into the blankets of the newest Dernier. "So," he said. "A boy."

"Yep."

"Good job."

"I'm pretty sure that part was out of my hands."

"Your husband must be very proud."

"Yeah, he's decided to keep me a little longer."

"I will never understand your sense of humor."

"I know."

"Do you two want to be alone?

"Knock it off, Grace. You've met *Inspecteur* Bedard, haven't you?"

"Years ago," Grace said, holding out her hand. "I had forgotten how positively dishy he was. Oops, did I say that out loud?"

Roger stared at Grace with his mouth agape and Maggie burst out laughing.

"Go easy on him, Grace," she said. "He's easily confused."

Roger cleared his throat and turned his attention back to Maggie, giving Grace one more curious look. "Do you want to talk of shopping?"

"Okay, I'm almost positive you mean talk shop, and hell yes, I do. What have you got?"

Roger crossed his arms against his chest. "Well, first of all, we found Florian Tatois."

"You did? How far did he get? Did you get him on that steamer out of Marseilles I told you about? Has he formally confessed?"

"He did not get very far at all."

"It's been twelve hours! I could *walk* to Marseilles in twelve hours!"

"We had an all points bulletin out on him, as you know, but when we went to process the crime scene at the crash site…"

"Oh, God."

"…we found him pinned beneath the wreckage."

Maggie chewed her bottom lip and watched Roger's face. She looked down on the cherubic face of her little son and the tension in her brow relaxed. "How did that happen, do you think?" she asked quietly.

"Well, clearly, he got himself caught on the tractor hitch on the back of the car." Roger shrugged.

"Is he alive?" Maggie asked.

"Somewhat."

"I love the French," she said to Grace. She turned back to Roger. "So, no confession."

"No. But it doesn't matter. As you saw, Madame Patrick goes free and there are no other suspects. His confession to you fits the facts of the case."

"How is it you think *I* solved this case? I was clueless until the murderer was sharpening his butcher knife over me."

"It's just as I said. Your relentless probing unsettled everyone, most particularly the murderer. Even with a suspect in police custody he didn't feel comfortable. It is one of your great gifts, Maggie. The ability to badger people into doing crazy things."

"Aw, you old flatterer," Maggie said.

"But not far wrong," Grace said.

"I forgot you were still here, Grace."

"And you said yourself," Roger continued, "that when you saw my text that Annette had been murdered you knew immediately the killer must be Florian Tatois."

"Sure."

Roger shrugged. "I did not make that immediate connection, you see."

"That's because *you* weren't working the whole inheritance angle like I was. Once you focus on that, it's obvious."

"That's just the point. I should have been working *all* the angles."

"Yeah, but I had a motive, Roger. I was trying to prove my friend innocent."

"I too have a motive, Maggie, although I can understand why you might not realize it. I am supposed to be trying to get the actual perpetrator of the crime."

Maggie shifted the soft, small weight of her little lad in her arms and folded back his blanket to better see his face.

"How did it go down with Annette?" she asked quietly.

"Are you sure you want to hear it? Today?"

"I'd just as soon hear it and then never have to hear any of it ever again."

Roger sighed. "She was strangled in her apartment. The forensic evidence, I'm sure, will confirm the confession Tatois made to you."

"And she died immediately?"

Roger frowned. "Of course. Why do you ask?"

"It's just that Florrie hoped Lily would hang on longer than she did. If her designated heir died *before* her…"

"Oh, I see what you mean. I do not know who inherits now. It won't be Michelle through Annette—since Annette died first—unless Michelle is Lily's third choice beneficiary."

"I don't suppose it matters. There's no money to inherit anyway," Maggie said. "Was Annette's boyfriend all strung out, I guess?"

"Her boyfriend?"

"You don't have to be coy, Roger. We figured out that Annette was boffing someone in the police department."

"I have no idea what you're talking about."

"Okay, have it your way."

The door from the hallway pushed open and Laurent entered the room carrying a large grocery bag, his brown hair long and ruffled around his face. It must be windy outside, Maggie thought with a smile when she saw him. He and Roger shook hands.

"Handsome boy you got there," Roger said to him.

Laurent accepted his congratulations, then gave Maggie a quick kiss and murmured something to the baby in French before setting out the food on Maggie's bedside tray.

Grace peered into the bag. "Ohhh, *religieuse au chocolat*!" she said. "Laurent where *ever* did you get them at this hour?" Grace pulled out a large chocolate éclair from its paper sheathe. "You know your wife's passions, that's for sure."

"Laurent's a magician," Maggie said. She looked up from gazing at her baby's face, a smile on her lips, and locked eyes with Roger. The moment was quick and then gone. Roger clapped his hands in a gesture that heralded he was about to leave.

"Oh, won't you stay for some *boulette d'Avesnes*?" Grace said, still rifling through the grocery bag. "I can't imagine you'll ever see such a thing in a *hospital* again."

"No, no," he said. "I too have a young one who awaits me at home. I just wanted to say, before we wrap this up, formally, that I am sorry, Maggie for not working more closely with you on this."

"That's okay, Roger."

"No, no it really isn't. Nobody knows better than I that, at the very least, if you'd had my help, we would've solved this murder much faster, and without your nearly having to have your baby in a ditch beside the road."

"Or in the smoking hulk of a car at the bottom of a cliff," Grace said under her breath.

"Anyway, I want you to know, and this I swear to you— next time we will work together." He glanced at Laurent, who paused in his unpacking but whose expression was unreadable. "If your husband approves, of course."

"Oh, of course," Grace said.

"Shut up, Grace," Maggie said. "And thank you, Roger. I look forward to that."

"Oh, one more thing," Roger said as he was leaving. "I arrested Michelle Tatois this morning."

"You're kidding. What for?"

"You go on, *Inspecteur.*" Grace said to him, smiling sweetly. "I'll fill her in on the details. But thank you for your prompt attention to that."

Roger nodded to Laurent and then Maggie, and finally to Grace, where the corner of his smile tweaked noticeably higher, and then left.

"What details?"

"A little matter of an attempted poisoning with the idiot girl's fingerprints all over the milk bottles *and* your doorknobs *and* mailbox and God knows what else."

"Poisoning? When?"

"Well, I'm not sure when she did it," Grace said, "but yesterday Jean-Luc said the milk smelled bad and I found bleach stains on the counter where he'd spilled it trying to get it into Zou-zou's bottle."

Maggie whistled and the baby instantly screwed up his face and let out an annoyed whimper. She jostled him to settle him down again.

"So it looks as if the whole troublesome Tatois clan is either dead or in jail," Grace said.

"Or on life support," Maggie said.

"I think Roger has a point, though." Grace said, "You do have a gift for unsettling people, darling."

"Bedard said that?" Laurent said.

"He did. Would you agree, dearest?" Maggie said, smiling up at Laurent as he leaned over her.

"*Absolument.*" He kissed her soundly.

After their picnic supper, Grace left with the car to go back to *Domaine St-Buvard* where Danielle and Jean-Luc waited with Zou-zou, and Laurent settled into an armchair next to the bed with his son in his arms.

"He looks like you," Maggie said.

"*Non*, he looks like his beautiful *Maman.*"

"Well, he's ours and that's all that matters. I'm so happy, Laurent."

"*Et moi, aussi, chérie*," he said. "Oh! I pulled your email messages from your laptop at home."

"Anything interesting?"

He pulled a folded piece of paper out of his back pocket and handed it to her. "Your editor apologizes for not getting back to you. She was having emergency appendix surgery."

Maggie read the printed email in amazement, her mouth open. She looked at Laurent, who was totally focused on his child, and then back at the paper. "I'm going to have it all," she said. "I'm really going to have it all."

"*Bien sûr, chérie*," Laurent said, looking up at her with a smile. "Haven't I been telling you that all along?"

Maggie smiled at him, watching him hold their son, her heart so full of joy she fought back tears. After a moment, she said, "But what you haven't told me yet is how you ended up coming to my rescue driving Jean-Luc's car."

"I met Danielle on the road coming back from Lily's."

"You were on foot?"

Laurent shrugged, his concentration on his son. Maggie watched him pick up the baby's tiny hand and kiss his fingers.

"How did you know how to find me?"

"I went to Florrie's bar first. Some kids on bicycles said they saw a man and a fat lady get in a car going south toward the D7."

"Thanks for that. So you headed toward Aix?"

"*Oui.* When I got to the curve above Pontès, I just followed the fireball off the first exit. It was like a beacon leading me to you, *ma chère*. Always I am seeing explosions and destruction in your path. It is like the little crumbs of Hansel and Gretel."

"Very funny. But that cliff is a good thirty minutes from Florrie's bar. How did you get there in *ten*?"

"I drove very fast."

"I can't believe how everything turned out," Maggie said, her eyes filling again.

Laurent looked up and smiled at her. "*Je sais.*"

"And thank you for working things out with Roger. It's helpful to have a friend on the police force. Even if he is terrible at his job."

"*Oui.* But he is moving ever steadily up the ladder. Someday he will be *Commissariat de Police*…as long as you are doing his work for him, of course." Laurent stood up and settled the sleeping baby back in his bassinet.

"This is the last time, Laurent. I promise. Never again."

"Shhh, Maggie," Laurent said with a wry grin. He leaned over her and tilted her face toward his to kiss her. "Let us not begin young Jean-Michael's life by having him hear his *Maman* tell outrageous lies to his *Papa*, eh?"

# ABOUT THE AUTHOR

Susan Kiernan-Lewis lives in Nocatee, Florida and writes about Europe, mysteries and romance. Like many authors, Susan depends on the reviews and word of mouth referrals of her readers. If you enjoyed *Murder in Aix*, please consider leaving a review saying so on Amazon.com, Barnesandnoble.com or Goodreads.com.

Check out Susan's website at susankiernanlewis.com and feel free to contact her at sanmarcopress@me.com.

Susan Kiernan-Lewis

Printed in Great Britain
by Amazon.co.uk, Ltd.,
Marston Gate.